"It's not *that* col

Max swam to her, dove under the surface, grabbed her ankles and jerked. With a "Whoop!" she lost her balance and fell backward. He walked his hands up her body, until she lay cradled in his arms.

She laughed up at him, water sparkling on her skin. As she sobered, her whiskey eyes grew dark. He bent to taste the water and sunlight on her lips. No reason to rush. They had all afternoon.

She asked, "Are you cold?"

He growled out, "Not with you in my arms, Darlin'." He lowered his head once more. She wrapped her arms around his neck.

God, I don't know what I did to deserve a woman like this, but I promise to do more of it in the future.

ACCLAIM FOR The Sweet Spot

"4½ stars! A sensitive, honest look at a family destroyed by loss...Drake's characters are so real, so like us, that you will look at your own life and count your treasures."
—*RT Book Reviews*

"The busy plot and large cast keep things moving along and lovers of Western settings will enjoy debut author Drake's detailed descriptions of bull riding and cattle ranching."
—*Publishers Weekly*

"Poignant, heart-wrenching, hopeful, and definitely not your typical 'saving the family ranch' romance. This realistic contemporary zeroes in on issues of trust, communication, healing, and forgiveness; a cut above the rest."
—*Library Journal* (starred review)

"A moving tale about love, forgiveness, and finding your way out of the darkness of your grief. I look forward to reading more of Ms. Drake's books."
—SeducedByaBook.com

Nothing
Sweeter

Also by Laura Drake

The Sweet Spot

Nothing Sweeter

Laura Drake

FOREVER

NEW YORK   BOSTON

Copyright © 2014 by Laura Drake

Excerpt from *Sweet on You* copyright © 2014 by Laura Drake

Forever
Hachette Book Group
237 Park Avenue
New York, NY 10017
www.HachetteBookGroup.com
www.twitter.com/foreverromance

Printed in the United States of America

OPM

First mass market edition: January 2014
10 9 8 7 6 5 4 3 2 1

Forever is an imprint of Grand Central Publishing.
The Forever name and logo are trademarks of Hachette Book Group, Inc.

The Hachette Speakers Bureau provides a wide range of authors for speaking events. To find out more, go to www.hachettespeakersbureau.com or call (866) 376-6591.

The publisher is not responsible for websites (or their content) that are not owned by the publisher.

*To the two constant men in
my life—Gary and Al—
the stars I steer by*

Acknowledgments

I'm so grateful to my sisters, Fae Rowen, Jenny Hansen, and Sharla Rae, who wouldn't let me start in the wrong place. To Tessa Dare, Susan Squires, Jacqueline Diamond, Charlotte Carter, and all the wonderful published authors at the Orange County Chapter of Romance Writers of America (OCCRWA) who give their time and patience to reach a hand back. Thanks to Donna Hopson, my lay-editor.

To the amazing Margie Lawson—thanks for the masters immersion class, the sparkle factor, and the friendship.

Thanks to Nalini Akolekar of Spencerhill Associates for taking a chance, and to my ever-patient editor, Latoya Smith.

Thanks to the bull-riding insiders who helped a city girl get it right: Clint Wade of Exclusive Genetics, for his time and knowledge of bull husbandry, and Cindy Rosser, who gave me insight into the life of a stock contractor. To Jay McNeilly of the Orange County Sheriff Department for insight into prison life, and John Girard for the great cop stories!

And to Jane and Kayla, the founding members of the Laura Drake fan club – before there was reason for one.

Nothing Sweeter

CHAPTER 1

Her "new" life was going be so much better than the last one. Aubrey Madison would make sure of that.

She savored the sight of a solitary saguaro standing sentinel on the flat Arizona landscape. She savored the red-tipped ocotillo branches that waved in the stiff breeze of the Jeep's passing. She even savored the chilled air that swirled in, raising the hair on her body in an exquisite shiver.

God, it's good to be out of prison.

Her face felt odd. Until she realized she was smiling.

Glancing at the gas gauge, she vowed to stop soon, only long enough to get gas and use the restroom. She had to keep putting on distance.

What if it's not possible to outrun your own conscience?

The pull of the road in front of her was as strong as the push from the vision in the rearview mirror.

A weather-beaten Sinclair sign in the distance made up her mind. She took the exit leading to a deserted corrugated building that might have once been painted white.

Pulling to the pump, she killed the ignition and sat a moment, listening to the *tick, tick, tick* of the cooling engine and the wind keening through the power lines. She stepped out, closing her denim jacket against the wind's probing fingers.

A bell over the station door jangled as she opened it, and a black-haired Native-American teen glanced up from behind the register.

Aubrey pulled bills from the pocket of her jeans. "I need to fill it up. Where's the restroom?"

His expression didn't change as his stare crawled over her throat. She fisted her hands to keep them still. When he finally pointed to a dark corner, she almost ran to it.

After solving the most urgent matter, she washed her hands. Her gaze locked on the black-flecked mirror. The ropy scar twisted from behind her ear to the bow of her collarbone, looking like something out of a slasher movie. Shiny. Raw. Angry. She jerked her gaze away, turned the water on full force in the sink, and tried once again to wash away the shame.

In her mind, she saw the sign she'd woken up to in the prison infirmary, hanging on the wall across from her bed.

If you're going through hell, keep going. Winston Churchill

In spite of her mantra, the walls closed in, as they always did. Yanking the door open, she fought to keep from running until she was outdoors, the wind kicking around her once more.

She reached for the gas nozzle, the tightness in her chest easing. When the Feds released her from eight months of perdition, her mother begged her to stay in Phoenix. But Aubrey couldn't get a deep breath there. The suburban ranch house crowded her with memories and worried eyes. This morning she'd packed and escaped.

Holding the lever in chilled hands, waiting for the tank to fill, she turned her back to the wind. *Alone.* She pulled the luxury of the empty landscape into her solitary-starved soul and lifted her face to the sun's tentative warmth, smiling once more. Nothing was sweeter than freedom.

Max Jameson twisted the cowboy hat in his hands and lowered his eyes to the body in the gray satin-lined casket. His father's broad shoulders brushed silk on both sides. His face looked unfamiliar, mostly because it was relaxed. But there was no mistaking the strong jaw and high cheekbones. Max saw them in the mirror every morning.

Just like you to duck out when the going gets tough, old man. His mouth twisted as his father's familiar chuckle echoed in Max's mind. *Leave me holding a sack of rattlesnakes. Lotta help you are.*

No response, which, on several levels, was probably a good thing.

Max scanned the empty viewing room. He dreaded the remainder of the day: the funeral, the cemetery, the reception at the ranch. *"Your dad is reunited with your mother after thirty-five years."* The thought of solicitous friends spouting platitudes was enough to make him bolt for the barn, saddle his horse, and get the hell out of his own life.

He surveyed his father's waxen features. *Yeah, and don't tell me you wouldn't do the same, you old boot.*

"Maxie?"

The singsong cadence in that single word snatched him back to when the man in the casket was a mountain, and a little kid with worshipful eyes dogged Max's footsteps. Only one person on earth dared to call him that.

Strap yourself in, Daddy. It's gonna get bumpy. He turned to face Wyatt.

His younger brother stopped a few steps short of the casket, his gaze dropping to his father. A worried frown marred the angelic face from Max's childhood. Wyatt looked familiar, but different, too. Soft cheeks had hardened to a man's, and his golden locks were gone, shorn short.

Well, the prodigal son returns. No points for bravery maybe, but—

"Did he suffer, Max?" Wyatt's voice wavered, his gaze locked on his father's face.

"Nope. One minute he's pounding in a post for the new fence line. The next, he's on the ground. Gone."

Wyatt's head snapped up, his eyes wide. "Jesus, Max. Do you have to be so cold-blooded?"

So much for the new and improved Max he'd committed to becoming just this morning while lying in bed, probing the scabbed-over edges of the hole in his life. "Kinder and gentler" melted before the blowtorch that was his life lately. "Just telling you what happened. Sugarcoating won't make it any prettier."

A hurting smile twisted Wyatt's mouth. "You sound like him."

Max knew he hadn't meant the words as a compliment. "Let's grab a cup of coffee before the vultures show up." He settled his Sunday Stetson on his head. "You and

I have a bucket of trouble, little brother. And trouble don't wait."

Three weeks later

Crisp, alpine air trumped the heat of the sun. Aubrey steered the top-down Jeep with her knee and swiped wind-whipped hair out of her mouth. The snow-capped Rockies whispered of winter, but brave weeds flowered at the side of the highway. With no set destination the past three weeks, the road had pulled her north. She'd slept in generic hotels and eaten at mom-and-pop diners. The familiar stiffness in her core leached out in the sameness of the days and the anonymity of her role as generic traveler.

A cautious optimism replaced it, along with a niggling of road weariness. When had she last felt excited about the future? College?

A quick look in the rearview mirror told her that her scrunchie had failed. Curly chestnut hair floated around her pale, too-thin face. That and the oversized cheap sunglasses made her look like a So-Cal heiress just out of rehab.

Except for the scar, of course.

She pulled the Dodgers cap from behind the seat and snugged it over the riot to solve two problems—she didn't need more freckles added to her collection.

A city limits sign announced her approach to Steamboat Springs. Her empty stomach growled demands.

Old-fashioned brick-fronted buildings lined the typical Western main street, foreground to a striking snow-capped mountain backdrop. She snagged a parking spot in front of a trendy bar and grill and climbed from the car, her joints creaking.

Noticing a stand of free local papers on the sidewalk, she grabbed one. She tugged open the heavy wooden door of the restaurant to lunch babble and a welcome blast of warm air. High ceilings and a long old-fashioned mahogany bar with a brass foot rail dominated the room. Midafternoon diners occupied the soda fountain–style chairs set around small wooden tables. The smell of onions and grilling beef told her she'd gotten lucky.

She chose a tall seat at the empty bar. The bartender appeared from a back room, a moonlighting college student, unless she missed her guess. "Sorry, ma'am. Didn't realize you'd come in. What can I get you?" He wiped his hands on a damp bar rag.

Ugh. My first "ma'am." Aubrey smoothed her hands over her waist to be sure middle-age spread hadn't begun since she'd gotten dressed that morning. *Everybody looks old to a baby like that.*

She ordered, then opened the newspaper. Designed as bait for cruising tourists, she'd found these local Realtor rags a good source for a quick area overview of the local geography, economy, and demographics.

An earsplitting shriek raised the hair on Aubrey's neck and arms. Her muscles jerked taut and she froze, head scrunched into her shoulders. The scream trailed off to a happy laugh. She spun in her seat.

A young couple sat at a small round table, attention focused on the baby in a high chair between them. The little boy was rapt, watching a small stuffed elephant his father held, his Cupid's-bow mouth open in anticipation. The man shook the toy and the ears flopped. He swooped down and burrowed it into his son's neck. The baby threw his head back and shrieked again, the pitch rising to dog-whistle range before trailing off in a delighted giggle.

Aubrey felt her mouth stretch in a dumb grin. The peals of laughter were more than carefree; they were total ignorance of care. How long had it been since she'd heard happiness like that? Heard it, hell, had she ever *felt* it? Nobody knew how to party like a baby.

The mother glanced at Aubrey before putting her hand on her husband's arm. "I'm sorry. We forget that what we think is cute can be irritating to others."

A band loosened in Aubrey's chest, releasing a small moth flutter of happiness. "Anyone that finds a baby laugh irritating is dead inside." She smiled at the mother. "Thank you for sharing your joy."

Lighter, she turned back to her research. Turning the page to a marketplace section, she read of lost dogs, goats for sale, litters of kittens, and a burro free to a good home. Aubrey noticed quite a few ranches for sale. She turned to the brief help-wanted section.

WANTED: FULL TIME STABLEHAND.

ROOM & BOARD INCLUDED. APPLY TO HIGH HEATHER RANCH.

That might be worth looking into. It would be fun to work with horses again. And God knows her new life could use some fun.

The band around her chest ratcheted as the craving for open air danced along her nerves. *I've got to find a way to stop this running.* She glanced out the window to where her Jeep waited, imagining spending the rest of her life as a ghost, driving across the country, never leaving a shadow of an impression on the places she left. Almost as if she never existed at all. A goose-on-a-grave shiver started between her shoulder blades and shot through her body.

Could she stop? Aubrey did a gut check, but her gut just repeated the demand for food. It didn't really matter if she could—she had to.

If I don't stop now, I never will.

She glanced at her faded UCLA T-shirt and sweatpants. Not quite interview couture. The college kid returned with a still-sizzling chunk of beef smothered in cheese. "Here you go ma'am. Anything else I can get you?"

"This looks great, thanks." Her mouth watered. "Can you tell me—is there a Western-wear store in town?" The kid filled her in as she reveled in her food, taking large bites of yet another meal that didn't come from a prison kitchen.

At the Western Emporium a half hour later, Aubrey stood before a mirror, a shirt in either hand, considering. She'd found the perfect pair of skinny jeans, and the paddock-style lace-up boots she'd tried on went well with them. Good for work, but stylish too.

The tailored shirt on the right was dressy, polished black cotton with pearl snap buttons and white embroidered roses on the yoke. The one in her left was blue windowpane plaid, more a workday shirt. If the High Heather was a dressage barn, she'd know what to buy, but from the merchandise here, odds were against that.

She'd already decided to buy them both, but which one for an interview? The business rule in her previous life dictated dressing one notch above the position. A booster of adrenaline dumped into her bloodstream. This interview would set a whole tone for her new life. In the past week, the shining promise of the open road had soured.

It now felt tainted, dark, and off somehow, like a whiff of carrion.

She *had* to get this job.

She changed into the fancy shirt and after a glance-in-the-mirror reminder, selected a package of bandanas on her way to the counter. She handed over her credit card and watched as the clerk ran it through the old-fashioned imprint machine.

She scribbled, *Aubrey Mad—*

Crap. Her fingers spasmed. Heat shot up her neck, making the scar throb. She scratched out her last name and wrote "Tanner" over the bad beginning, then pushed the receipt across the counter. Banks never looked at those things anyway.

CHAPTER 2

Max leaned on the pitchfork and wiped sweat out of his eye with his sleeve. He pushed his straw Stetson back, looking at the mess in the barn breezeway. He'd flipped Wyatt over the day's jobs, and Wyatt laughed when he chose the books, thinking Max had lost.

Shoveling shit is less depressing than wallowing in red ink all afternoon.

The past two hours he'd worked his way down the corridor, throwing soiled bedding from stalls into the aisle and laying new straw. Now he just had to bring the Bobcat around and push everything out the door. The ripe miasma of hot manure hung like a fog in the air. This job was *not* his career plan. He couldn't wait to hire somebody to take over.

"Hello?"

When he looked up, the brightness of the barnyard almost blinded him, but there was no mistaking the sleek feminine line of those long legs.

"Can you tell me where I can find your manager?"

He had to give her credit. Though she avoided the

reeking mess in the aisle, she neither minced steps nor held her nose, glancing into each stall she passed.

Creamy skin and high cheekbones spoke of good bloodlines. Curly hair the color of a chestnut's mane floated around her shoulders. Damn, red hair wasn't a dominant gene. So why did it keep cropping up in his life?

Sweet Jesus. He winced. When he realized he was staring at the angry scar on her graceful neck—and noticed that she noticed—he moved on to the fancy Saturday-night-go-to-town shirt. He propped the pitchfork against the stall door and wiped his hands on the seat of his jeans.

"You found the manager. Are you here about boarding your horse?"

"No, sorry." She pulled a folded newspaper from her back pocket. "I read you were looking for a groom," she said in a perky interview voice.

In that getup? He gestured to the corridor. "As you can see, we need one."

She put out a slim hand. "Aubrey Tanner."

"Max Jameson." Taking her hand, he let his eyes roam from the shiny new boots on up. "It's not a job you'll want." *This is a waste of time, but I need a break.* The scent of fresh lemon drifted to him. *And she smells a damn sight better than manure.* Besides, he could use this as practice for that kinder-and-gentler thing. "Sorry. Strike that. Let's go sit." He turned and led the way to the doorway in the center of the building.

They had to cross the tack room to get to the office. Dusty saddles straddled sawhorses, and more lay sprawled on the dirty tile floor. A few bridles hung from pegs, but he didn't even want to know what was in the pile in the corner, a snake's nest of dirty leather.

The office wasn't much better. He lifted a stack of battered *Western Horseman* magazines from the folding chair beside the WWII-era metal desk. He gestured for her to have a seat and then walked behind it.

"Our last groom ran out on us. Literally." The torn leather chair let out an alarming squeal when he dropped his butt in it.

She perched at the edge of the metal chair. "I worked as a groom at an English riding stable on the outskirts of Phoenix for four years."

"This is a working cattle ranch as well as a boarding barn. Our groom fills in as a cowhand during branding, castrating, and such. It's not a job for a woman." *Especially another good-looking redhead. The last one about did me in.*

She leaned forward, her back fence-pole straight. "I can handle myself around animals, and I'm stronger than I look."

His interest caught on the frayed-wire undertone of desperation in her voice. Why so twitchy and nervous for a job as a stable hand? While she recited her skills, he studied her. Those smooth hands weren't kin to manual labor. Her delivery was straightforward, yet she was clearly hiding something. She dressed like a rich client, yet she wanted a groom's position. The red hair reminded him of Jo, but nothing else did. A trickle of interest seeped into a tiny crack in his wall of chronic vexation.

She finished and sat looking at him, chin thrust forward.

"Okay." He lifted himself from the rickety chair. "Let's see what you can do."

Her brows scrunched. "Okay." She stretched the word like warm taffy.

• • •

Wyatt stepped from the back door of the house and took a deep breath. "Thank God that's over." Maybe Max had won the better chore after all. His wrestling match with the bottom line yielded worse results than Wyatt had feared. If something didn't change soon, making the payroll would be a stretch by summer's end.

He rolled his shoulders. A ride would serve two purposes. He could finish checking the herd and clear the smell of failure out of his sinuses. *If Max is napping instead of cleaning the stable, he's vulture bait.*

Walking to the barn, Wyatt noticed a mud-spattered red Jeep parked in the deserted dooryard. Monday afternoons were quiet. Most boarders worked days, and the crew had left before dawn to work fence. He stepped into the gloom of the barn and stood a moment to allow his eyes to adjust. His brother was nowhere in sight, but Max's black-and-white paint stallion, Trouble, stood cross tied in the aisle.

He raised his voice. "Max, why didn't you clean this mess before you got Trouble out?" He walked the aisle, watching where he put his feet. "Why *is* he out, anyway?"

A woman stepped from the tack room, a battered forward-seat saddle over her arm. She crossed to the stallion and tossed the saddle over its back.

Max barreled from a stall farther down the aisle. "What in holy hell!" Trouble sidestepped and reared, dumping the saddle in a pile of fresh droppings. Max ran up. Trouble danced, head thrown up, eyes rolling. Catching the horse's halter, the woman rubbed his forelock, speaking in undertones until he calmed.

"What possessed you to put English tack on my horse,

woman?" Max said in the Donald Trump "you're fired" voice that had scared off the last groom.

She flushed. "I don't know how to tie the girth on a Western saddle. I worked at an English show barn and—"

"Wyatt, meet Aubrey Tanner. She's applying as a stable hand."

Wyatt hadn't thought the woman could blush deeper, but Max's tone did it.

He took pity. "Ms. Tanner, please excuse my brother. Our father passed away not long ago, and Max has been out of sorts. Would you mind giving us a moment? If you'll just wait by the paddock, I'll be out in a few minutes."

Staring daggers at Max, she turned and stalked away.

She was barely out of earshot when Max started in. "Wyatt, this ranch needs new fences, repairs, more boarders. It makes no sense to hire some city cupcake who doesn't know how to tack a horse. God, she looks like a Friday-night buckle bunny!"

"Listen, Max, you pigheaded idiot." Wyatt held a finger inches from his older brother's nose. "One. You're the jerk who chased off the last stable hand." Max tried to interrupt, but Wyatt was only getting started.

He put up a second finger. "Two. No one in town wants to work for you. That ad has run all week and we haven't had one applicant. And after going over the numbers this afternoon, we don't have any time to waste."

"Hell, Wyatt—"

"Third. If you'd pull your head out of your behind, you'd see that this girl knows what she's doing." He gestured to the stallion. "Look at your horse." Trouble's coat gleamed, and even his hooves had a shiny coat of black polish. "I can't believe you gave her a stallion to work on.

You know as well as I that your cowhands wouldn't have succeeded in getting him in the crosstie, much less picking up his hooves. But she did. At least until you came out here bellowing."

Max sputtered. "I—"

"Just shut up and think a minute. If we open as a guest ranch, you can't see the advantage of having a female employee? Especially one who looks like that? She could do a commercial as the 'girl next door.' It won't hurt to have a view of more than the mountains for the male guests, you know."

Max glared. "I haven't agreed to your hair-ball dude-ranch idea. Dad's having a heart attack in heaven, and you damn well know it."

"Hey, if you've got a better idea for putting this ranch in the black, throw it out, bro." He stood tall, crossed his arms, and stared his brother down. "Okay, Max. If you don't want her, you go tell her. You're the one who interviewed her."

Trouble put his nose on Max's shoulder and blew a warm breath in his ear. "Don't you start on me too. You're a guy. Guys don't get pedicures. You oughta be ashamed." He walked the aisle, but hesitated in the shadow of the barn door.

The woman stood at the paddock gate, frowning out at the sage-covered plain he felt sure she didn't see. Resting a manure-encrusted shiny new boot on the bottom rail, she afforded him a great view of a slim backside in the snug, store-creased jeans. That damned wavy auburn hair lifted in the breeze. Bad enough he had to accept Jo— *his* Jo—married and settled with Trey Colburn. Could he stand walking around corners every day, having that red hair give him a cattle prod shot below the gut?

Yet as much as he hated it, Wyatt might have a point. If they were forced to turn the place into a "yuppie ranch" to keep the land, a female employee would be an asset.

As she turned her face, the wind blew her hair back. He recognized the "I will" set to her jaw. Maybe she had the stubbornness to survive out here.

He snorted. *Yeah, right.* Everything about her screamed "city." He expected she'd scoot at the first cold snap. This land didn't suffer fools, in spite of his brother's plans.

Well, there's enough starch in those new clothes. Let's see if there's any in what's inside 'em.

Aubrey crossed her arms, chest tight, anger hissing through her. Wyatt seemed nice, but his brother was a cowboy Cro-Magnon. Even his father's death was no excuse for total lack of professionalism or the manners of a baboon. She'd give Wyatt the courtesy of a goodbye, but then she was in the wind. Jackson Hole came next on her list, and she'd always wanted to see Wyoming.

"You have a résumé?"

At the sound of the gruff voice, she turned to face the jerk, happy to vent some belated comebacks. "To clean stalls? You've got to be joking. I don't need your job, Dude." She scanned the dilapidated buildings. "Besides, anyone can see this place is running like a well-oiled machine."

He grinned and tucked his hands in his back pockets. "Well. There's a little roar in the mouse after all."

The abrupt mood shift caught Aubrey flat-footed, as did the transformation the smile made to his stony features. Animal attraction hit her like a slap. She took a step back, snapped her mouth closed, and narrowed her eyes. With that lanky build and rugged good looks, he probably charmed the hell out of country girls. She continued the stare down, which was more like a stare up, as he was at least six inches taller.

"Look, I'm sorry. Wyatt has a point. Maybe my father's death affected me more than I realized."

She wasn't buying his line or the ingratiating look. He had no way of knowing that she'd learned about manipulation at the feet of the master, her scum-sucking former boss, Vic. More than once she'd seen him charm a ticked-off customer into apologizing for being rude. She ignored the stab of regret for her lost career and focused on the current irritant. "You used to sell used cars, didn't you?"

Wyatt walked up, relaxed and smiling. "Believe it or not, he's sincere. I've known him all his life. Trust me on this."

She glanced between the two men. It was hard to believe they were related. Wyatt was tall and fine boned, with blond hair, fair skin, and features blurred by softness in his cheeks and mouth. Max was the darkness to his light, with sable hair, brown eyes, and cheekbones as strong as the mountains that rimmed the horizon.

His gaze settled on her face, his intent focus warming it like the heat from the sun. She crossed her arms over her chest to cover her body's involuntary reaction. The guy fairly exuded testosterone—heady stuff to a girl who'd been locked up with women for a year. "Apology accepted. But be advised, my horseshit detector is set to high."

"Fair enough. I'll stop shoveling it." With a last lingering look and a potent smile, Max turned and sauntered into the barn.

Aubrey glanced to Wyatt, unsure of her footing again. The guy didn't even say goodbye.

"He's crude, but he does have some well-hidden charm." Wyatt gave her a salesman-on-commission smile. "Want a cup of coffee? I'd like to talk to you about our plans. That is, if Max hasn't scared you off."

"He hasn't," she said with a quick glance to the barn.

Wyatt led the way toward a long, weathered building. Aubrey followed him across the dirt yard. No longer preoccupied with the stress of the interview, she studied her surroundings. High Heather Ranch was settled on the plain ten miles from town. She'd seen only one other ranch on the way out. Something seemed wrong until she recognized the silence. No traffic rumbled on a two-lane blacktop. All she heard was the soughing of wind and the cry of a hawk riding thermals overhead. The smell of sweet grass came on the wind, the scent of wildness and high, empty places. It whispered past her ear. *A place to heal.*

She glanced past the imposing fieldstone and timber main house to a knoll behind it, where two white grave markers explained the small wrought-iron enclosure. The mounded brown scar in the emerald carpet declared the family's recent loss.

Wyatt's long stride had left her behind, and she trotted to catch up.

CHAPTER 3

Wyatt gestured for the "groom" to sit at one of the tables, then crossed the scuffed tile floor to an industrial coffeemaker on the counter. *Max is right about one thing. This woman fits in here about as much as I do.* He glanced to the hideous scar that the scarf at her neck didn't quite hide. "We have ten hands at present. There used to be more." He reached for the plain white stoneware mugs on the shelf. "How do you take your coffee?"

"Black, thanks."

He carried the steaming cups to the long table and sat on the picnic-style bench across from her. "So, why did you leave your last job?"

Her mouth twisted as if she'd smelled something nasty. Her eyes flicked around the room. "Bad breakup. I needed a change."

He started to ask another question, but she broke in.

"I worked at English riding stable in Arizona for four years. I can give you the phone number of the owner for a reference if you'd like." She set down her mug with a *clunk.* "I can get a horse show ready in two and a half hours, including braiding mane and tail. A Western stable can't be that much different. I can learn what I need to know in no time."

"You don't want to tell me about yourself?"

Her shoulders flinched before she straightened. "Sure. I'm a hard worker, and I'll give you an honest day's work for your wage." She lifted the mug again and took a sip. "How did the ranch get a pretty name like High Heather?"

He'd allow the subject change. For now. "My great-grandfather, Jock Jameson, was a prizefighter. Family legend has it that he left Boston one night after making a bundle throwing a fight. In any case, he had the cash to buy land when he arrived." He took a sip of coffee and licked his lips. "He said the blooming sage reminded him of Scotland, so he named it High Heather. It seems he had a bit of a soft spot, in spite of his violent career." He straightened and looked her in the eye. "Before I waste your time, you need to know that this job pays minimum wage. Room and board is included. You get one full day off a week, or two afternoons, if you'd rather."

"That's fine."

He waited, but that was all she had to say on the subject. "All right, then. Before you make up your mind, let me take you on a tour of the place." He stood. "It'll be easier to show you than to explain." She stood, and at her nod he led the way to the dooryard. *Hiring her would solve the groom problem.* He wished he could rub out the small kernel of homesickness in his chest. *And the quicker I get this place settled, the quicker I can get home to Boston.* The kernel opened to a pit of loneliness. *And to Juan.*

"We hope to open as a guest ranch." He gestured to the

cluster of buildings that made up the ranch headquarters: the rambling fieldstone and timber main house, barns, corrals, and several buildings adjacent to the dining hall. "You can see there is a lot of work to be done."

She scanned the yard. "If you don't mind my saying so, your brother doesn't seem as enthusiastic as you are about the project."

He snorted. "Max is not a fan of change. He expected to live his life as a cattleman, as our father did." He looked past the buildings at the scrub-filled grassland that stretched for miles. "But the demographics of the area have changed. The ski slopes brought wealthy tourists, who bought vacation homes. They've driven up the price of land, which jacked up the property taxes. Add to that the falling price of beef. Many ranchers are selling out, making more land open for development. It's a vicious circle." He turned to face her. "If you want the job, it's yours."

"But your brother—"

"Is an idiot and he's short a groom. Don't let him scare you off."

Aubrey smiled and extended her hand. "I'll take a chance on you, if you'll do the same."

Max needs someone to shake him out of his cave. I know him—he wouldn't have reacted so rudely if this woman hadn't threatened to get under his skin. This could be interesting. They shook on it. "You're certainly not going to fit in at the bunkhouse. We'll put you up in a bedroom at the main house. Follow me." He started off.

"I don't think so." Her voice was quiet and slow, but hard as frozen concrete.

He stopped and turned. "Pardon?"

When her face flamed, the ugly scar stood out in bold

relief. Her hands dove in her pockets, and she stuck out her chin. "I'll just bunk in the barn."

He frowned at her, head cocked. "Where? In a sleeping bag in the hayloft?"

"If you used to have a bigger crew, you've got to have an extra cot around here somewhere."

Her panicked demeanor reminded him of a cornered animal.

"I can sleep in the office. I'll clean it up, and with a stout lock, I'll be fine."

Her pleading look twisted Wyatt's gut. She wasn't going to budge. "All right, if that's what you want." He stood a moment, thinking. "There's a restroom in the dining hall, but you'll have to use the house to shower. Tia Nita is almost always there. She's our cook, housekeeper, and the boss most of the time. I'll take you up to the house later and introduce you."

"Sounds like a plan. Is it okay if I go unpack now?"

Wyatt nodded and watched her walk to the Jeep. He had more questions than answers, but at least he and Max wouldn't have to flip for *that* job anymore.

Her nose tickled. Aubrey grabbed a rag from her back pocket to cover an explosive sneeze. The past two hours spent cleaning had paid off. The office was now dust, cobweb, and vermin-free. She looked down. The same couldn't be said for her. Good thing she'd changed the fancy interview outfit for a T-shirt and worn jeans.

Sun streamed through the now-sparkling window set high in the wall, lighting a snowstorm of dust motes on its way across the floor to hit her favorite watercolor on the opposite wall. Under the window sat a narrow iron-framed cot that had been delivered by two shy, brown-skinned cowboys. She'd made it up with a Navajo blanket she'd found in a corner. The men had also carted off an ancient footlocker, trash, and other flotsam of her afternoon's labor.

At the head of the bed, an ancient gooseneck lamp and her laptop were all that remained on the battered desk. She'd almost left the computer in her mother's garage, but at the last minute gave in to the siren call of her old life.

Aubrey fisted her hands in the small of her back and groaned. *This room must have been a dump for every marginally useful piece of junk from the last twenty years.* Kneeling, she gathered a change of clothes from the suitcase she'd stowed under the cot. She had to find a bathroom—*soon*.

Trotting to the main house, she ignored the men who dismounted shaggy cow ponies outside the corral. When no one answered her knock, she cupped her hand around her eyes, and putting her nose against the screen, she peered into the shadowed kitchen. Manners might dictate she wait, but her bladder commanded otherwise, so she opened the door and rushed in.

"Hello?" Her voice echoed back. Thinking it would be less rude to wander in without invitation than to pee on the floor, she barreled through the door to the entrance hall.

"Ooof." Head turned, glancing through doorways, she collided with a solid chest. Bouncing off, she smacked into a hall table, dislodging a china pitcher. Max grabbed her upper arm to steady her, then caught the vase with his other hand.

He dropped her arm and replaced the pitcher, glaring at her all the while. "Who let you in?"

She rubbed her stinging hip as she clutched her change of clothes to her chest.

"I'll explain everything. But first, for the love of God, where is the bathroom?"

He stepped aside and pointed to a door down the hall. She ran, hearing what might have been a muffled chuckle as she closed the door.

An hour later, Max knocked on the doorframe of what she already thought of as her room.

"Dinner is ready in fifteen min—wow." He looked around the room, his glance stopping at the cot. "Who's going to sleep here?"

Aubrey finished capturing her damp hair in a ponytail, adjusted the bandana at her neck, and turned from the tiny mirror she'd hung next to the door. "I am."

The lines of his face morphed into the familiar stony mask. "We'll see about that." As his chest expanded, his gaze combed the room. "It smells like a damn beauty parlor in here."

"Glade PlugIns." She flounced by him. "The staple of any woman's emergency kit."

Outside, the sun hunkered at the horizon, washing the yard in soft gold. Several cow ponies stood drowsing in the corral. Aubrey walked a few steps ahead of Max, hoping to avoid an argument over her sleeping arrangements.

Laughter drifted from the open door of the dining hall, but everyone froze as they stepped inside. Her pulse sped up. Silence fell, and she paused, not sure what to say or do.

Before she could bolt, Max stepped alongside her. "Men, this is Bree, our new groom."

"My name isn't..." She'd always insisted people use

her given name. It was hard enough to be taken seriously as a businesswoman when you looked as wholesome as Sally Field. A flash of pain speared her gut. That world was gone. She'd dusted off her birth certificate to borrow her absent father's surname, so why not a nickname? "Never mind."

Max introduced her to each cowboy as they lounged, waiting to be called to dinner. Luis, Armando, Manny, Pedro. She worried about matching faces with names. All were tanned and tough-looking, wearing ranch uniforms of worn jeans, boots, and cotton shirts. They appeared of Latino or Indian descent and avoided her eye. She spotted Wyatt waving from across the room. Odd, but next to the real thing, Wyatt seemed a pale, city version of a cowboy. With his refined good looks and blond hair, he shone like gold among quartz.

She trailed Max to the kitchen, where a doughy Hispanic woman worked at a feverish pace, cutting tomatoes, flipping tortillas in a pan, and shredding cheese almost simultaneously.

Max came up from behind to lift the stout woman off her feet, hugging her tightly. Aubrey stood stunned. It was as if a roaring grizzly had suddenly turned playful. "And this is Juanita Peña, the real boss around here."

"Maxie! You put me down." He kissed her ear before complying. She swatted his arm with a wooden spoon.

He turned to Aubrey, playfulness gone so fast she felt delusional. "Tia Nita, this is Bree. She'll be working for us."

The round woman stared up in surprise. "Good to meet you, Miss Bree. *Mi hijo*, you take her to sit down. Dinner is ready in a few minutes."

"Let me help you." Aubrey reached for the cheese grater, but Max grabbed her forearm, tugging her away.

"She won't let anyone help." He led her from the kitchen to a table where Wyatt sat drinking iced tea.

Wyatt patted the bench next to him, inviting her to sit. "We've all tried to make Tia slow down, but she's more stubborn than Max, if that's possible."

Max scowled. "You just think that because I don't agree with you. If I'm stubborn, what does that make you, I wonder?" He rounded the end of the table to lower himself to the bench opposite them.

"It makes me correct."

Max ignored his brother's smug smile, put his elbows on the table and leaned in. "Wyatt, you should see the barn office. You won't recognize it." He arched a dark brow at Aubrey.

"That reminds me." Wyatt dug in the pocket of his jeans to retrieve a key, which he handed to Aubrey. "Not that you'd have any problems, but I'm sure you'll sleep better knowing you're locked in."

A rush of freedom blew through her like a strong breeze. Her fingers closed around the key. Not long ago, that scrap of metal represented power. Power she did not possess.

"She is *not* bunking in the stable." Max's face darkened. "It's not safe. Or appropriate." He glanced around the room. "She's a beautiful woman, and town's a long way off."

Ignoring heat that was probably a blush, Aubrey snatched the gingham napkin beside her plate and shook it open with an irritated snap. "I happen to be present and am capable of answering for myself. I hardly think my staying in the house with two single men would be seen as appropriate either."

Max sputtered, "Tia Nita is nearby. You'd be safe."

She glanced at the tawny skin at the top of his chest, exposed by his denim shirt. Lust filled her bloodstream and carried over to her nerve endings. *Maybe, but I'm not sure you would be.* "Thanks, but I'll be fine in the barn." Her voice sounded harsh to her own ears, but no one was going to dictate where she slept. Ever again.

"Three mules in one harness. It will not be boring here, I think." Tia Nita stood at the table's edge, her arms laden with steaming plates. The two men jumped up to take them from her.

"*Venido!* Or I'll throw it to the chickens!" she called to the cowboys, then shuffled back to the kitchen. The men bolted to the tables, elbowing one another for a seat. They hurried to pass bowls and dig in to heaping plates.

Max passed a plate of enchiladas to Aubrey. The corner of his mouth kicked up when her stomach growled. *First I almost wet my pants in front of him, and now...* She took a healthy portion. Others passed her plates of refried beans and Spanish rice.

At her first bite of enchilada, she closed her eyes to savor the rich, tangy flavor. Spices, pork, and smoky cheese blended into a flavor all its own. She made a contented sound deep in her throat and opened her eyes to Max's frown. His gaze lingered on her lips.

Compared to where she'd been the last eight months, this guy was as scary as a kid dressed up for Halloween. She smiled at him. "That is heaven."

"Tia Nita is the best cook in the county," Wyatt said,

scooping food onto his plate. "Wait till you taste her pie. It's better than sex."

Max let out a derisive snort and forked a third of an enchilada into his mouth.

The diners seemed relaxed with each other, and as the brothers discussed ranch business, Aubrey listened. She learned the reason she hadn't seen many cattle. The largest herd summered on the slopes of the mountains, to be brought closer in the fall, near the hay they'd need to survive the brutal Colorado winter storms.

Hoping for another serving of rice, she looked up to see that nothing remained but sauce-smeared platters. If she'd been alone, she'd have licked her plate clean. Seeing Max's smile, she knew he'd read her thoughts. *He must think I was raised by wolves.* She smiled across the table at him. Let him think that. It would lead him further from the truth. Her past was something she'd worked hard to leave behind far west of here. She was now Bree Tanner. And Bree Tanner could be whoever she decided she'd be.

After carrying their dishes to the serving counter and picking up a slice of cake for dessert, the ranch hands gravitated to the television. The brothers remained at the table with Aubrey, chatting.

Now that her belly was full and the tension of the day gone, she felt herself fading. *Jeez, you'd think I'd never done a day's work. I didn't even put in eight hours today.* She stretched. "If you gentlemen will excuse me, I'm hitting the sack. My day starts early tomorrow." As she rose to drag herself to the door, muscles that hadn't worked in years protested.

Save a lone floodlight on the barn, darkness reigned. She glanced up, and the huge dark sky opened to swallow her. The Milky Way spread across the great expanse, a creamy river flowing away from her. Individual stars were cold chips of ice, the mountains only a black outline at the horizon. Dizzy, she swayed on her feet, her stomach dropping in an overwhelming wave of awareness at her own insignificance.

"By night an atheist half believes in a God." At the deep voice, she spun to see Max's silhouette outlined against the light spilling from the mess hall windows. Broad shoulders, tapering to a narrow waist. A silhouette she knew she'd see burned on the back of her eyelids tonight, in the dark. He stepped off the porch. "Edward Young said that." He touched her elbow. She jerked away, hugging herself. She was unused to touch. Not gentle ones, anyway.

He hesitated, and she sensed his scrutiny in the dark. "I'll see you get to your temporary quarters safely."

As they walked, his scent came to her, the warm essence of leather and *man*. She breathed him in like a rare perfume. Male vibrations pulsed from him, touching her skin, raising the hair on her arms. She mentally shook herself. *It must be the dark. Senses are heightened in the absence of light.*

It had been a long time—a really long time, since a man showed concern for her safety. She'd never equated chivalry with sexy, but out here, under the stars, it turned her downright sinful.

He stopped a few paces short of the door, and as she opened it, she felt his gaze like a warm touch on the back of her neck.

"Sleep well. Busy day tomorrow." His voice rumbled softly from the dark, like the comforting sound of far-off thunder on a warm summer night.

He was still there, unmoving, when she closed the door.

A few minutes later, locked in and tucked under the covers, Aubrey tried to relax into exhaustion. Instead, her mind started the movie that ran whenever she wasn't distracted. Different scenes, but always the same horror story: Federal agents barging into her office, cuffing her and leading her through a crowd of gaping employees.

But that, as it turned out, had been the good part.

She rolled over, groping for the bottle of Tagamet she'd stashed under the bed. After taking a swig, she plumped the pillow and flopped on her other side, the gritty taste only part of what made her lips curl from her teeth.

Life here seemed simple and quiet. It might be a good place to rest for a while. As she took a deep breath, the heady scent of warm horseflesh opened the door to happy memories and a wave of burgeoning homesickness—not for another place, but for another time.

Her mom had worked long hours. Aubrey was left to her own devices, which suited her fine. A typical horse-crazy kid, she rode her bike to a boarding stable every day after school. She wore the owners down until, at fifteen, they hired her on as a groom. She'd have worked for free just to be near horses, but jumped at the owner's offer to exchange free riding lessons for her labor. They were days filled with sunshine, fresh air, and freedom.

Maybe at High Heather she could heal. She smiled into the dark. The Jamesons. She'd never seen two brothers so different—in looks and temperament. Wyatt reminded her of a teddy bear. Max, a grizzly. One that just woke from hibernation. Still, she couldn't deny that his rugged, Marlboro Man looks had caught her attention. And he *had* been sweet to Tia Nita, at least.

She yawned, exhaustion lulling her tired brain at last. Who cared? She'd lose herself in physical labor and horses. They'd been the anchors that had gotten her through puberty. Maybe they'd help her sort out the mess she'd made of her life.

If not, there was always the road, and Jackson Hole.

CHAPTER 4

Aubrey awoke with a panicked start, holding her breath until a hoof kick on a stall door reminded her where she was. She glanced to the travel alarm on the desk—four a.m. Groaning, she flopped back on the pillow.

Dreaming of her job at Other Coast Trends had left a sheen of sweat on her skin and a greasy film of guilt in her mouth. She'd known it was her responsibility as controller to report the customs violations she'd discovered. But good jobs didn't grow on So-Cal palm trees, and the high-profile position was a great start to launch her career. And Aubrey knew Vic. He'd have done everything in his power to ruin her if she'd ratted him out. Of course, as it turned out, she'd been ruined anyway.

To him, blind loyalty was more important than morality. How twisted is that? Vic was also a good judge of character—or lack of it. He must have realized that she wouldn't go very far down that crooked road, so he'd hired a CFO who would. At that point, Aubrey became expendable. He'd taken a chance, though, that she'd retaliate and call Customs.

Yeah, but I didn't. Apparently he knew me better than I did. How can you trust yourself after you make a decision that cataclysmically stupid?

Her stomach burned. Rather than delve any deeper into that sludge pit of remorse, she threw back the covers and put her feet on the icy concrete floor. The barn air was chill, but thanks to a space heater, bearable. She jerked on jeans, a turtleneck sweater, warm socks, and her sheepskin-lined denim jacket. The morning would be cold until the sun came up.

Minutes later, from where she stood at the lip of the barn door, Aubrey recognized the shifting shapes of the cow ponies, just darker shadows against the backdrop of night. Figuring that would be as good a place to start as any, she grabbed a box of brushes and flipped the switch on a floodlight that spotlighted the dooryard.

The ponies slept standing in the corral, their breath clouding the still air and forming frosty icicles on their whiskers. Aubrey started with a shaggy dun, brushing and warming as she leaned in to penetrate the heavy winter coat. The broomtail grunted in pleasure. She inhaled the mixture of frigid air and warm horse. A bubble of happiness built in her chest, rising to explode in her brain.

She worked her way through the string, and the ponies crowded her, curious, each wanting to be next. She spoke to them in a low voice of silly endearments, enjoying both the solitude and the camaraderie.

Time passed quickly in that peaceful place. Giving the last pony a final swipe, she let the brush fall to her side and massaged her biceps. It was going to take a few days to build up the grooming muscle. She glanced up to the welcome light of the dining hall, shining warm and yellow on the brightening yard. The aroma of fresh-brewed coffee drifted to her.

After dropping the brush box in the barn, she strode to the weathered building and shivered, imagining warmth enveloping her. Stepping onto the porch, angry male voices brought her up short. She hesitated, reluctant to have anything shatter the fragile calm of her morning. All she wanted was coffee.

"I heard in town yesterday that Trey Colburn married Jo Clark last fall." The morning paper rustled as Wyatt turned the page. They'd been the first to arrive at the mess hall. "Didn't you tell me on the phone once that you and she were dating?"

Max shot a look over the edge of his coffee cup. "We were."

"So, what happened?" Wyatt scanned the page, then turned it.

Something in Wyatt's uninformed nonchalance loosened the tight wad of words in Max's throat. He barked them out. "Goddamn Colburn came back to town and sidled up to Jo, with his baby face, smooth ways, and family money." He lifted his cup, but the slug of coffee he took had turned bitter. He forced himself to swallow it.

"I'm sorry, Max." Wyatt looked up. "I'm surprised. I remember Jo being such a sweet girl."

"She is. It wasn't her fault. It's that weasel Colburn." He said the name like it was Osama bin Laden. He scanned the walls, the ceiling, looked out the window, but the silence pulled him back to his brother's puppy-dog eyes. "Okay, so maybe some of it was me." He clunked the cup on the table. Coffee sloshed out. "Shit, you know me, Wyatt. I don't go around calf-eyed, spouting poetry at a woman."

Wyatt studied the paper, but his eyes didn't move across the page. "No, no one could accuse you of that."

So I have more in common with Dad than just his looks. But why do people have to run around talking, spewing their feelings all the time? And if he were the type who did, would Jo be asleep in his bed at the main house right now, instead of in another man's, a few short miles down the road? "I'd planned to marry that girl," he almost whispered. The sadness he heard in those words burned almost as much as Wyatt's pitying look.

"If you never told her how you felt, how could she have known that?"

"I don't want to talk about it, Wyatt." He needed to change the subject and fast. Living in the past never did anyone any good.

Max took a sip from his mug, trying to find the right words. "Wyatt, I know the ranch is half yours. I'm good with that. But let's be realistic. At some point, you're going to go back to your boyfriend and your fairy tale life, and I'll be the one left to deal with whatever we decide."

Wyatt leaned in, his face red. "Damn it, Max, you're just like Dad."

"That's bullshit." He snapped out. "If I were just like the old man, you wouldn't have come home. And you damn well know it." He forced a deep breath and got control of himself. "Wyatt, this isn't about Dad. It's not even about you. It's about me. Humor me for a minute, will you?" *Walk gentle. Your future depends on this.*

"I've thought about your dude-ranch idea. Let's ignore

the fact that the repairs would cost more than we have in the bank. The bottom line is that I can't live with it. I'm not willing to sell off any land for yuppie vacation retreats, so why would I run a ranch to cater to them? To give them a 'real Western experience,' whatever the hell that is. Can you see me doing that?"

Max looked across the table to the face he'd missed and been glad to be quit of all these years. He had always loved his little brother. How could he not root for the little underdog of the Jameson household? But Wyatt's sexual orientation raised close-to-the-bone questions for Max. Questions he found easier to ignore than deal with. That philosophy had worked for years—as long as Wyatt was two thousand miles away. Lately, though, not so much. Max shifted in his chair.

Looking into his empty coffee cup, the tense lines on Wyatt's face relaxed.

"I guess not." He leaned forward, over his coffee mug, and looked straight into his brother's eyes. "I know you don't want to consider this, but what if we sold out? We could split the money, and you could get a good job as a ranch foreman somewhere. Think about it, Max. You'd still have the parts of the job you like, but none of the headaches of ownership."

Max's deepest fear, spoken out loud, hung in the air over the table. He smothered it with his bellow. "Jesus, how many shades of stupid are there?"

Wyatt flinched.

Max forced his voice lower. The anger made it come out in a hiss. "I make a pittance as a lackey for some rich dude? I still have all the problems without the pride of ownership?"

Wyatt raised his head. His entreating expression

reminded Max of that little kid, expecting his big brother to make everything right. "So what are we going to do, Maxie?"

Max's hands tightened on the edge of the table. Building frustration and a haunting sense of failure made him want to throw something. "I don't *know*, Wyatt," he ground out, staring at his fingers, willing them to relax. "I've looked into alternatives. Kobe beef looked good, but then the economy tanked. People aren't willing to spend the money for it, and the price has fallen to where it isn't profitable either."

Wyatt toyed with his coffee cup. "Then it looks like we're back to selling some of the land. I don't want to do it either, but we have to be realistic."

The dark clouds of foreboding he'd been turning his back on could no longer be ignored. The too much coffee he'd drunk burned in his stomach.

His brother continued. "I know Colburn has already put in an offer. Wouldn't it be better if we sell some land and at least have cash to run the rest?" Wyatt's look speared him. "I know it would stick in your gut to sell to him, after Jo. But if we don't, we're going to lose everything. Every day that goes by—"

Max exploded to his feet, his chair hitting the floor with a clatter. "*Goddammit,* Wyatt, don't you think I know that?" He strode to the wooden door and yanked it open, slamming the screen door against the wall as he barreled through. Sensing movement, he turned his head to see the city girl lurking against the wall, a startled deer-in-the-headlights look to her huge brown eyes. The high color in her cheeks told him she'd been standing in the cold for some time, spying, no doubt.

"This day just keeps getting better and better." He snorted in disgust and kept walking.

After sharing a quiet breakfast with Wyatt, Bree followed him to the barn for a rundown of her job duties.

"We don't expect you to groom the working ponies. The cowboys do that."

She waited in the doorway. "Oh, that's okay. I'm awake early anyway, and we all enjoyed it."

Wyatt walked past her, leading the way down the aisle. "I'll explain the routine to you." As he turned, she almost walked into him. "And don't let me forget to show you how to cinch a Western saddle." The corner of his mouth lifted, and Aubrey smiled back.

Wyatt introduced her to her charges and the details of their care. Various breeds occupied the twenty stalls: Arabs, Thoroughbred crosses, a Tennessee Walker, and most prevalent, the quarter horse, king of the West. By the time they'd worked their way back to the tack room, Aubrey had relaxed. Wyatt knelt at the door to her room, pulling a screwdriver and a small paper bag from his back pocket.

"What are you doing?"

"I'm installing a dead bolt and a slide lock."

She crossed her arms and leaned against the doorframe. "Oh, thanks. That's thoughtful of you."

As he looked up, she was struck again by his golden handsomeness. "Don't thank me. This is Max's idea. It's his concession to allow you to sleep out here. It's more to make him feel better than out of necessity." He must have seen her stiffen because he said, "Look, Bree, you'll find it's best to choose your battles with Max."

"Is that how you've gotten along with him all these years?"

"No." He bent to his task and screwed the plate in with more force than necessary. "This is my first trip home since I left when I was seventeen."

"Can you tell me something? Does Max have a problem with mankind in general, or is it just me?"

Wyatt smiled up at her. "Both, I think." His smile slipped. "You may want to give Max a bit of a break. He's taken a lot of hits lately." His gaze sharpened on her face. "One of the hits had auburn hair. Just like yours."

"Oh." The revelation hit her brain like a punch. She, of all people, could understand loss of a dream.

Wyatt looked back to the doorframe. "Don't feel bad. There was no way you could know."

She hesitated to bring up the next subject, but she didn't want to put it off. Besides, she'd already put one foot in her mouth—God knew, it was big enough for two. "I overheard you and Max in the mess hall this morning."

Wyatt's neck turned red and the screwdriver slipped off the screw head.

"This must be a stressful time for you." His head came up. She touched his shoulder. "I just wanted you to know that I'm here, if you ever want to talk."

"Hello the barn!" A female voice drifted down the breezeway, announcing the first boarder of the day. "Anybody here?"

"Well, that's my cue." Aubrey glanced into the tiny mirror and slapped on a baseball cap instead of trying to tame her unruly mane.

Wyatt stood and slipped the screwdriver into his back pocket. "That's Sue Phelps. Her horse is Winter Park, the big Appaloosa. You'll do fine, Bree. This will all be routine in no time."

She took a deep breath and got to work.

The days of her new life flew by, filled with simple tasks: grooming, feeding, and getting acquainted with the horses. Aubrey enjoyed their individual personalities, even Trouble, Max's bad boy. She saw through his testosterone-fueled fractiousness. All he needed was more exercise and something to distract him.

If only his owner were so simple. The brothers seemed busy as well, appearing at mealtime to bolt food, then disappear back into the house. Their overheard conversations were all business, but she sensed a fragile truce between them.

Bree finished picking out the hooves of a mixed-breed bay belonging to an executive in town before picking up his empty water bucket.

"Where *is* everyone?" A shrill voice shattered the late-morning quiet.

Bree stepped out of the box stall and slid the door closed. A raven-haired woman in tight jodhpurs strode the aisle, a riding crop slapping lustrous knee-high riding boots with every step. Her white blouse exposed a generous swell of creamy cleavage. A man in a business suit trailed in her wake, fingers tapping an iPhone, one eye downcast, wary of the shine on his Toschi loafers.

"Why isn't my horse saddled?" The woman stopped and looked down her imperious nose at Bree. "And who are you?"

Well, la-di-da. "I'm Bree, the new groom. Can I help you?"

"Jesus, this place changes grooms like I change lipstick." She looked Bree over from top to bottom. "And now I've got to break in another one."

Bree recognized the aggressive glint in her eye from her shark swim at Other Coast Trends.

"This is Tuesday." The woman lifted her arm, glancing at a glinting Rolex on her slim wrist. "It is ten thirty. In the future, I expect my horse groomed, saddled, and waiting. This day, this time, every week. Understand?"

The businessman raised his head, as if sensing chum in the water.

Aubrey pasted a helpful smile on her face. "Yes, ma'am, perfectly clear. Might I inquire as to your horse's name?"

"Jolie Danse, the registered Thoroughbred in the end stall." She turned to the man, Bree dismissed. "He'd better not be the mess he was last week, or I swear I'm finding another barn. I don't care if the Jamesons *do* need the money."

What a bitch. Bree turned on her heel, not sure if she was angry for herself or the brothers. And what kind of man would put up with that for more than two minutes?

She slung the stall door open and caught the halter of the rangy gray gelding who high-stepped in anticipation. After cross tying him in the aisle, she tacked him with the expensive bridle and English saddle that hung outside the stall. The woman sashayed over, and Bree caught the assessing look out of the corner of her eye as she worked.

"Well, at least this groom shows some promise." The grudging compliment seemed directed to the barn in general, since the businessman had remained by the tack room, and she wasn't lowering herself to speak with Bree.

The gelding whickered and dipped its head to nuzzle its owner. Alfalfa-stained drool smeared her immaculate blouse, but the woman ignored it, running a hand down his silky, dappled flank.

"Yes, I know, Peanut." Her tone was gooey syrup. "You've been neglected of late. We're going to keep an eye on that. I promise." The gray's head moved lower, snuffling. "Did you miss Mommy?" The ice queen's face thawed as a look of delight crossed it. "You big baby, you just want a treat." She hugged the horse's neck and pulled a carrot from the back waistband of her jodhpurs. "Yes, Peanutiest, I brought you something. I swear you are the most spoiled baby on the planet."

She turned to catch Bree's openmouthed stare and looked down a nose too perfect not to have had work done. "Surely, even you have heard of using a barn name for blooded horses. His registered name is too much a mouthful for everyday use." She sniffed and gave the gray a kiss on his delicate nose.

Hard to hate a woman who makes a fool of herself over a horse. Aubrey pulled the last stirrup down with a snap, careful to hide a smile. "Is there anything else I could help you with, ma'am? Do you need a leg up?"

Her haughty look was back in place. "No. That will be all."

Bree unsnapped the crossties and handed over the reins. The woman led the horse to the businessman, who pocketed his phone and listened to her babble with an indulgent smile.

Even an ice queen like that had a love. Bree's hand jumped to her hollowed-out chest. Max's strong profile drifted through her mind before she could shut it out. She snorted to banish the silly imagining. *You're here to heal, chickie, not go all soft. You saw where being soft got you, back in LA.*

Keep things light and simple and everything will be okay.

CHAPTER 5

"You have no idea how good it is to see you, Juan." Wyatt made sure the door to his bedroom was closed before he Skyped home.

Juan's smile was wide and warm. "You look careworn. What's going on there? Is your Neanderthal brother giving you a hard time?"

"Not on purpose. Max is a good guy, but it's a simple, black-and-white lifestyle out here, and my presence brings up issues he'd rather not deal with."

"Then let him deal with himself—and the details. Why don't you just come home? After all, the will was clear. He's executor, and you get half of everything. Sounds pretty straightforward to me."

"I know, but—"

"Besides, I miss you like crazy." Wyatt watched as Juan's fingers touched his computer screen, as if to bridge the two thousand miles between them.

Homesickness opened a hole in Wyatt's chest, and he fell in. He'd looked at the local weather report this

morning; Boston would be covered in a perfect crystal-
line blanket of snow by now. "Did you go to La Vie for a
chocolate croissant this morning?"

"Is it Sunday?" Juan smiled into the camera. "Of course
I did. Celeste asked where you were. When can you get out
of there?"

Wyatt rubbed his fingers across his forehead. "It's not
that simple. The ranch is in trouble. Even if I gave Max
my half, he'd lose it in a year."

"So? Why is this your problem?" Juan leaned a bit
closer to the screen. "You've heard from him what, five
times in the past twenty years? He doesn't care about you,
Wyatt. Why are you wasting your time?"

"He does care about me, Juan. He loves me. He just
doesn't know how to reconcile loving me with his upbring-
ing. But it's more than that." He glanced out the window
that overlooked the front yard, the road, and the vast acre-
age beyond it. "I've avoided this place forever. Too long.
Dad's gone—it's too late to reconcile with him. I don't
know if it's possible to get closer to Max, but I'm not staying here for him only.

"I need to reconcile with this place, Juan. I blew out
of here and never looked back. Coming here reminds me
that I left things undone. The kind of things that eat at
the back of your mind—your self-esteem. You can understand that, can't you?"

"Sure I can." Juan's sad smile pulled at him. "But don't
forget, while you're wandering in the wilds, finding yourself, that you have a full, rich life here and a guy that's
sure missing you."

If he hadn't been breathing the past in with the cold
Colorado air, he would have hopped on the next plane

home. "I'm not likely to forget, Juan, because I sure am missing you too."

On Friday evening, Aubrey sprinted to the mess hall, attempting to dodge fat raindrops. Once under the shelter of the porch, she walked to the end to look up at the sky. Purple, flat-bottomed clouds scudded from west to east, their white thunderhead tops broiling upward. She'd seldom noticed the sky in California; why bother? It was always blue, except for the transition to a smutty layer of smog at the horizon.

The sky out here had personality. The dawn was optimistic; days like today, moody and angry. Sunsets seemed weary from a long day's labor, a misty pink edged in gold. *But the nights...* The nights were velvet. Aubrey wrapped herself in them to ward off the chilly air and the memories that dogged her steps when the sun went down and she was alone.

Her boots made a hollow thumping on the silver-gray boards of the porch. Voices trailed off when she opened the screen door. A few of the men mumbled a greeting as she passed. Brushing their cow ponies before dawn each day seemed to have broken the ice with the shy cowboys. She would never fit in, but she was getting used to their old-world manners and appreciated the deference they afforded her. They reminded her that, in spite of her job and her clothes, she was a woman.

She looked forward to a chat with Tia Nita. Being surrounded by men all day had its advantages, but sometimes she yearned for the simple company of a woman. She pushed through the door of the kitchen to see the older woman struggling to lift a huge pot from the stove. "Tia!"

She grabbed oven mitts from the counter and rushed across the room. "Let me help you." She shooed the woman's hands away and pulled the pot of beans from the stove, moving it to trivets on the counter. "You shouldn't be lifting that, especially with nine able-bodied males within earshot."

"Bah. If I wait for them, we'll be here until breakfast. Men do not belong in the kitchen."

Bree smiled at the dark-skinned woman. Salt-and-pepper hair frizzed from her kerchief, and her face glowed with moisture from the steam.

Bree picked up a knife to chop cilantro. Nita hadn't allowed her access to the kitchen until convinced that Bree was serious about wanting to learn to cook. She'd first suggested it to ease Tia's burden, but was surprised to find she enjoyed it. In her old life, cooking had consisted of reheating restaurant hors d'oeuvres. Wouldn't her friends laugh if they could see her? *Huh, friends. All those "friends" disappeared around the time that cell door slammed shut.*

"Tia? Tell me about Max and Wyatt. What were they like growing up?"

"I tell you, but cut *poquito*—small." Tia cut a stalk of cilantro to demonstrate, then handed the knife back. "See?"

Bree concentrated, trying to match Tia's example.

Tia picked up a shredder and a block of cheese. "Max, he came first. His mama was Cheyenne. Back then, it was not good to be Indian." She sighed. "His papa didn't care though. He loved that woman. Maybe too much, I think."

Bree finished chopping cilantro and moved on to the mound of tomatoes that were an integral part of every meal. "What happened to her?"

"Fever. At the end she didn't even know Angus. She had bad pain here." She touched her right side. "How you say?"

"Appendicitis?"

"*Sí*. When she died, that was the start of the bad times. Angus, he locked himself away to drink. Angry all the time." Nita's plump arms wobbled as her hands flew. A pristine industrial shredder stood on the back counter, but she insisted that cheese tasted better shredded by hand. "Max, he was a little boy. He didn't understand. Angus was too busy hurting to take care of him. I do my best, but..." She shook her head. "It was a bad time."

"What about Wyatt?"

Tia looked over with sad eyes. "That was the beginning of a worse time. But first Angus, he started to get better and take care of the ranch again. He looked around and saw Max running wild, old enough to learn." Her hands stilled as she smiled into the distance, remembering.

"Maxie looked like his mama, and Angus, he loved that boy. They were always together then." Tia chose a block of jack cheese, and creamy slivers fell on the shredded mound of gold cheddar. Her tone hardened. "Then Angus goes to Denver to buy a bull. But he came home with new cow, too. *That* was Wyatt's mama." Tia's dark eyes flashed. "That Christina, she was trouble. Angus didn't see until it was too late. She's one of those..." Tia lifted her hands to twirl them around her head. "Fancy ladies. She didn't like life on the ranch. Not a bit." She picked up the shredder once more and bent to her task. "All she wants is Angus's money. In Denver, she thought he was rich." Her eyes wrinkled with glee. "Ha! She got a surprise." Her face sobered. "Christina stayed long enough to have that baby;

then she's gone. Angus went to bring cattle from hills, and she lit out like her tail was on fire!"

"She left without her *son*?" Bree imagined a golden-haired baby lying in a crib, wailing for a mother who would never return. "What kind of woman could do that?"

"Pah!" Tia spat out. "A dog is a better mother than that one. It's good she left." Setting the bowl aside, she moved to open the oven door. As she opened it, the delicious smell made Bree's mouth water. "Then it was just Angus and the boys. Much better then." She pulled a cookie sheet of golden-brown puffed pastries out of the oven.

"Oh my God, Tia, what are those? Besides heavenly fat pills, that is."

"Beef empanadas." She placed one oven-mitted hand on her hip and turned to look Bree over. "You eat two. How you expect to get a man if you have a body like one?"

"You're assuming I want a man." Bree lifted a huge casserole dish of pinto beans as an excuse to escape before Tia got on a roll. Her life was complicated enough without adding love to the mix. She ignored the argument made by her libido and pushed the swinging kitchen door open with her butt. "Besides, if I keep eating your food, you're going to have to widen the doors around here so I can get through them. Saddlebags should only be on horses."

A half hour later, Bree addressed Wyatt, who sat beside her at the dinner table. "I'd like to take my half day off tomorrow and run into town, if that's okay." The cowboys had carried their dishes to the kitchen before gravitating to the television, as they did most nights. Only she and the two brothers remained, drinking coffee.

"Have to get your nails done?" Max asked.

Bree lifted her hand to look at her ragged nails and

reddened skin and snorted. "I only have a half day. I need to buy more work clothes." She'd washed the few shirts she owned once already, and one pair of jeans was not going to make it. She'd forgotten how filthy you could get, working in a barn.

Max's slouch belied the look in his eye, like a dog that had picked up a scent—and she was the rabbit. "I've got to go to the bank anyway. I'll take you."

Bree forced a smile, heart rate spiking. "Great." She'd have to watch herself around him, or he'd see past the Bree Tanner persona she was still perfecting. No one here needed to know Aubrey Madison. She winced as a sheet of icy shame splashed through her. No one here would *want* to know Aubrey Madison.

Carrying her plate, she pushed the door open to the deserted kitchen. Only the *swish-thump* of the dishwasher and the smell of spices remained. A fine tremor ran through her fingers as she rinsed her plate, put it in the dishwasher, then looked around for something else to do. The empty counters gleamed. The familiar jitter coursed down her legs, and she stood, gripping the stainless-steel counter, foot tapping.

How fast could she leave without being obvious? Crowds still made her jumpy. Twelve men in a room without the distraction of food left her to be watched like an odd bug in a jar. The watching made her flesh crawl. But it was the jar part that brought an animal squeal to the back of her throat, and she lived in fear that one night it would burst free. If it ever did, her past would become her present, forcing Aubrey Madison and her secrets to the forefront.

Fake it till you make it. She took a long breath. *Fake it till you make it.* She let the air leak out through her mouth, picturing the panic going with it.

When the palsy in her hands calmed, she wiped her hands on her jeans, checked to be sure the bandana covered her neck, and forced her feet across the floor. She paused, hand on the door, and forced her muscles to relax. A fear-filled face would attract more attention. *Just fake it.* She pushed through the door.

Shouts from the cowboys clustered around the TV drew her.

The youngest hand, Pedro, leaped from the couch at her approach, gesturing for her to take his seat. The last thing she wanted to do was perch on the crowded couch, but she knew that argument would be futile in the face of ingrained old-fashioned manners. *This is what a normal person would do.* Forcing her knees to unlock, she sat, scrunching herself into the corner, eking an extra inch of personal space.

The men were watching what appeared to be a rodeo. Bulls were loaded into narrow chutes, and cowboys stood on a catwalk above them. The camera zoomed in. One of the gates opened and a huge brindled bull exploded from it. A cowboy rode perched on its back, with only a rope to hold on to. The bull crow-hopped, then spun in a circle, muscles bunching as it bucked. The cowboy, one gloved hand in the rope, the other waving over his head, sat balanced in the eye of the tornado. But then the animal stopped and changed directions. The rider's feet flew behind him, his chest flattened on the beast's shoulder. The bull turned its head to come around for another spin.

Bree sucked in a breath, anticipating a train wreck. The long horns caught the rider under the vest he wore, and the bull tossed its head, flipping the man off its back, launching him across the arena to land in a heap on the dirt.

Men dressed in baggy clown-like clothes rushed in, yelling and running in front of the enraged animal. It ignored them and bore down on the stunned rider, who'd managed to struggle to his knees. The bull charged, missing with its horns but trampling the cowboy before racing off after one of the other men.

The cowboys around her groaned and shouted. Bree put a hand over her eyes, but looked through her fingers to see the bull trot out an open gate. She jumped when one of the older men patted her shoulder.

"He's okay. Just got the wind knocked out of him."

Several men entered the arena and knelt by the cowboy who was still on his hands and knees. When her lungs protested, Bree blew out the breath she hadn't been aware of holding.

"That'll teach him to keep his heels down," Armando said.

The men helped the cowboy stand and the crowd cheered. They handed the loser his hat, and he turned to salute the crowd as he limped from the area. The show cut to a commercial.

"Dear God." She glanced at the cowboys around her. "Why would anyone *do* that?"

"Do you know how much money those guys make?" Armando said from his seat on the raised hearth. "Besides, they're famous. Ah, to be young and swarmed by fans every weekend. It sounds like a pretty good life to me."

The raw brutality of the sport left Bree shaken. "You mean they volunteer for this?"

Armando shot her an incredulous look. "You've never watched the PBR?" At her blank look, he added, "Pro Bull Riders."

Max's deep voice came from behind her. "Don't you know? Our Bree's a city girl."

She ignored him, her attention pulled back to the television as the next contestant got ready to ride. A cowboy on the catwalk pulled the rope taut and the rider wrapped it around his hand. He pushed his hat down on his head, gritted his teeth, and when he nodded, the gate opened.

This time, the cowboy managed to stay in the middle of the bull, jump for jump. Like some kind of violent ballet, the man and bull both strained with all they had for opposite outcomes. A buzzer sounded, and the cowboy reached down with his free hand to release the one locked in the rope. He jumped and landed catlike, on his feet. The bull bore down on him, but he ran to the side of the arena and hopped onto the fence, and the animal passed harmlessly beneath him.

He punched both hands in the air and the crowd went crazy. As pipes on the bucking chutes shot confetti into the air, the scoreboard over the arena flashed "91," and the crowd cheered again. The camera zoomed in for a close shot of the grinning cowboy.

That kid can't be over nineteen years old!

Pedro turned to Armando. "Potato Masher's coming up. He's gonna take it all at the finals in Vegas this year."

"Nah. Wait till you see Bullwinkle in the short-go. That dude can bring it!"

"They're talking about the bulls." Max spoke low in her ear. She snapped to her feet and took a quick step away.

"It's time I got to bed. I'll see you all tomorrow at

breakfast." She turned and hustled for the door. She really needed to call her mother; she'd be worried.

Halfway across the yard, she felt a light touch at the back of her neck. She shot a look over her shoulder to see Max, arms crossed, leaning against the building, studying her.

Aubrey looked around the prison cell. It wasn't the one in the twin towers, because it held only one bunk, but the gauged cement walls were the same, as was the toilet with no lid in the corner. Something had woken her. Silence. It was never quiet in prison. Her eyes strained to penetrate the inky blackness. It was also never this dark. Then she heard his breathing. She should have been afraid, but for some reason, she wasn't.

His clothes rustled when he moved closer, and the mattress sagged as he sat on the edge. "I've come to take you from this place," he whispered. Her pillow bounced as his forearms came down to rest on either side of her head. "But are you ready to leave it?" His lips hovered over hers, his warm breath bathing her face.

"I'm ready." Want fired, hot and fast, roaring through her. She stirred, restless, craving touch. He took her lips, and she opened beneath him. The face-less man's power surged into her until she was dizzy with it. Somehow she knew she'd be safe in his arms. Saved. His hands moved over her breasts, and she arched her back, wanting more.

"You're so beautiful." Her breath came heavy as his hand slid over her belly, and down.

She pushed her hips off the mattress to press against him. "Please—" Need surged, hot and thick, like honey in her veins.

Lights snapped on. She was alone. Lupia stood in the door of the cell, a knife in her hand. "You wanna leave, puta? I can fix that."

She stepped closer.

Bree came awake with a start.

Jesus. Where did that come from?

She rolled over yet again and punched the pillow to move a few of the lumps. The sheets clung to her clammy skin. She shivered, but not from the cold air.

"Damn it." She threw the covers back and sat up. Trying to sleep was useless. As her feet touched the cold cement floor, she reached for her sheepskin-lined slippers. Wrapping the Navajo blanket around her shoulders, she switched on the lamp. She scrubbed her face with her hands hard, to pull herself back to her present batch of problems.

Max didn't trust her. She understood, having learned that lesson the hard way herself in LA, but she wondered at the brief bee sting of regret, just the same.

She hated living like a refugee, sifting her words to pull out hints of her past. It went against her nature.

How do you explain a felony conviction so it sounds like it's no big deal?

She moved to the desk and switched on the lamp, shivering when her butt touched the cold steel of the folding chair. Powering up the laptop, she thanked God that Wyatt was a software engineer in his "real" life. He'd had a satellite wireless connection installed so he could work while on sabbatical. She tapped into it.

She surfed the news. Wall Street was down, the economy sucked, and another politician was discovered accepting lobbyists' illegal campaign contributions. The usual. Sick of doom and gloom, she cast about for a lighter subject. She thought a moment then typed in P-B-R.

The link led to a professional website. Results of the night's event were posted, along with injury updates, licensed PBR gear, even a fantasy league. On a discussion board, she read a spirited argument between two fans talking trash about each other's favorite bulls.

Bree clicked on the "How It Works" link and learned that both the rider and bull are scored during a ride, and the scores combined for the overall total. The rider had to stay on eight seconds and not touch himself or the bull with his free hand. She watched a film clip of "Rides and Wrecks," wincing at the horrific crashes.

She realized that the bulls were athletes as much as the cowboys. They were varied in breed, size, and disposition. The only thing they had in common were sleek hides, strong muscles, and the burning desire to get a rider off their backs. She clicked to the "Bulls" section and was amused by the clever names: Big Bucks, Hammer, Major Payne, Cheeseburger with an Attitude.

"Chicken on a Chain? What's that about?" She chuckled and read on. This looked to be big business.

A kernel of an idea formed. She grabbed a pad to jot notes, sleep forgotten.

The fickle spring weather had turned; morning sun reflected off every metal surface in the yard. Toothpick in the corner of his mouth, Max leaned against his pickup, tipped his hat brim to shade his eyes, and waited. Wyatt might be satisfied with the new groom's explanations, but she didn't fool Max for a minute. *If this chick is a groom, I'm a ballerina.* Not that he could fault her work. The horses looked better than they had in months, and the boarders seemed to like her. Well, everyone except Janet Pearlman. She didn't like anybody.

He must have been nuts not to nix Wyatt's lady groom idea, but he couldn't put all the blame on Wyatt. Max hadn't sent her on her way because something about her attempt to be secretive made him want to know more. Well, there was also that red hair and that body a man would go to war for. Max moved the toothpick to the other side of his mouth.

Today he would get some answers. Wyatt had the theory that Bree was running from a batterer, citing her spookiness and the jagged scar as evidence. Max didn't think so. There was no doubt she'd been in some kind of fracas. But the guilty shadow in those whiskey eyes had him spending more time thinking about her than he wanted to admit. God knows, the ranch's problems were enough to think about.

The subject of his conjecture walked out of the barn, saw him, squared her shoulders, and strode over. The knit black turtleneck clung to a lightly bouncing pair of ta-tas. Wranglers were made for that kind of body, slim legs and narrow hips. *Damn nice. Pretty as a filly, all long legs and big eyes.*

She took a key from her pocket. "We can take my Jeep."

He pulled the toothpick from his mouth. "If you insist, but I've got to pick up castings for Tia's garden." He surveyed the trendy red Jeep. "I'd hate to get worm poop in your pretty—"

"Fine. Have it your way." The words hissed from thinned lips.

Ducking his head to hide his grin, he tugged the passenger door handle. It didn't budge. Damn, he'd forgotten. Last week, a bull had mistook the truck for competition and charged it. The dent was just one more in the ranch truck's collection, but now the passenger door wouldn't open.

"You'll have to slide in from the other side." She gave him a dubious stare but followed as he walked to the driver's door and jerked it open. She looked at the truck, then at him. "What?"

"Where do you propose I sit?"

He squinted into the shadowed interior and felt his ears heat. Reaching in, he pushed tools, receipts, soda cans, and bits of baling wire to the floorboard with a brush of his arm. "Well, excuse me, princess. I wasn't expecting royalty or I'd have brought 'round the Bentley."

It was her turn to redden, and he enjoyed the view as she flounced into the cab and scooted to the far door. He climbed in, pulled off his hat, and hung it on the shotgun rack in the back window.

She moved as far away as possible, cranked down the window, and rested her arm on the sill. The engine fired with only a prolonged crank. They rolled down the dirt drive, and when the truck hit the asphalt, she dropped her chin on her arm and closed her eyes.

The scattered freckles on her cheeks stood out against her translucent skin. The dark circles beneath her eyes attested to the kind of tired that comes from long nights that don't have much to do with sleep.

"I'm sorry about your dad." She sounded sincere.

His knuckles on the steering wheel whitened. "Thanks."

"You must miss him. Were you and he close?"

"Yep."

"What was he like?"

He spit the toothpick out the window. "He was a Western cattleman. Out here, that means stubborn, hardworking, and an eternal optimist."

"Wyatt says you're a lot like him, but he doesn't say it like it's a good thing."

Max kept his eyes on the road. "He was a hard man. The gene pool got watered down by the time it got to me."

A snort from his right. "Was he a good dad?"

"To me he was." Her hair swirled in the wind, bringing him the smell of lemons.

"Is your dad the reason Wyatt left?"

He reached in front of her. She started and scrabbled

back in the seat. When he tore the duct tape that held the glove box, it flopped open, spilling receipts to swirl onto the floorboard. He jerked out a hank of twine and handed it to her. "How about reining in that mop? Your hair is going to be all over my truck."

Bree perused the trash on the floor and raised an eyebrow. "Well. If it's gonna wreck your truck, by all means…"

He resisted the urge to watch. "As long as we're getting cozy in each other's business, where did you come from?"

"California." The tight in her voice drew his eyes from the road.

Small but perky breasts strained the fabric as she raised her arms to tie hair the color of fresh-cut cedar. He shifted to ease the sudden tightness in his jeans. He'd always been a sucker for red hair. Bree's was thick and curly, not like Jo's straight tresses. "Now, that fact does not come as a shock. What did you do for work?"

"Nothing special."

Out the corner of his eye, he saw her fingers trace the angry weal at her neck. "Where'd you get the scar?"

She cut him a cold glance. "I heard from John Wayne movies there was a rule in the West that people don't ask where you came from."

If the edge on her words were real, he'd be bleeding

"Fair enough." He held his hands up in surrender, then put one back on the wheel. "Then how about we play a little quid pro quo? You tell me what you're comfortable with, and I'll tell you what you want to know."

"I suppose we could try that," she said in a careful hostage-negotiator tone.

"Wyatt and my dad didn't click almost from the time

Wyatt started talking. Wyatt was a good kid and couldn't understand why Dad shied from him. Not sure my dad did either, at least at first."

"Did your dad know that Wyatt was gay?"

He thought a moment. "Satchmo said, 'I don't let my mouth say nothin' my head can't stand.' It was like that. Your turn."

She hesitated, seeming to weigh her words. "After I was born, my mom brought me home from the hospital. My dad was gone, with his stuff and anything of hers he could hock. All she had was an empty apartment, an envelope full of bills, and me. Growing up, she told me a watered-down 'You and me against the world' story. But now I understand the terror she must have felt."

And from the looks of you, you've been bunking with that terror for a while now.

"A retired neighbor lady kept me during the day, and Mom went out and got a job waitressing at The Eighteen Wh—at a local truck stop."

"Your momma sounds like a stand-up gal."

"She is."

They reached the outskirts of town. He'd save the next round of interrogation for later.

After a quick spree at the Western store, Bree carried her shopping bags to the only other establishment she knew. Max had told her he'd meet her at the trendy bar after lunch.

"Excuse me, miss. Mind if I share your table?"

Bree shifted her attention from the newspaper and her half-finished lunch to the man standing across the table from her. She glanced around. Every table in the bar was full. His hand rested on the back of the only vacant chair in the room. The needle on her worry gauge ticked from calm to concern.

Raising her voice to be heard over the babble of the lunch crowd, she said, "I guess."

"I'm much obliged."

Around her age, he was good-looking in a baby-faced kind of way. He flashed a movie-star smile. She checked out the Western-cut business suit, string tie, and expensive boots. *Probably harmless.*

"I knew today was going to be lucky." He laid an immaculate ivory felt cowboy hat on the table and sat. "Here I am, and the only open chair in the place is across from a gorgeous lady." He tossed her an "aw shucks" grin. "I'm gonna go straight out and buy a lottery ticket, 'cause it doesn't get any better than this."

Ignoring the menu proffered by the waiter who'd appeared at his elbow, the man ordered a well-done steak, then turned his soft brown eyes back to Bree. "Pardon me, miss. My mother would tan my hide. I swear she taught me better manners. My name is Trey Colburn." He extended a smooth hand across the table.

"I'm Aubrey Ma—" She sucked a breath before shaking his hand. "Bree Tanner."

"You sure now?" The corner of his mouth lifted, and he held her hand a beat too long.

"Well now, Bree, I know you're new in town because I wouldn't have missed a diamond in a drugstore for very long."

She managed not to roll her eyes. His combination of cherub and charm must slay the local female population. A little slick for her taste, though. She preferred strong features and a little less oil in her men. "I'm the new groom at High Heather Ranch."

His face sobered. "We were all so sorry to hear about Angus. He was a pillar in the ranching community, and he's going to be missed."

Something in his tone made her think that though the town might miss Angus Jameson, Trey would not. She toyed with her salad.

"Here I am babbling on, disturbing your lunch. You just go on and eat."

As if on cue, the waiter reappeared, brandishing a huge steak on a platter, still sizzling from the grill. When he left, Trey said, "You and I are neighbors, you know." He cut a piece of meat, put it in his mouth, and closed his eyes. "It's worth paying for my own beef just to taste this." He opened his eyes. "You've got to try it." Pulling a fork from an extra place setting of silverware, he cut a small piece of meat and offered it to her.

It sure did smell good. Bree took the fork from his fingers, popped the meat in her mouth, and chewed. It was tender and full of flavor. "It's—"

"Aren't *we* cozy?" Max strode to the table. "What won't work one way, you slither around to try another, eh, Colburn?"

At Max's sharp tone, Bree looked up. "Max, I thought—"

He cut her a cold look. "Are you done here? Or are you staying with your partner? I just need to know, either way."

Partner? She didn't know what was going on, but she intended to find out. Fast.

Picking up her bags, she opened her purse for her wallet. Trey's hand covered hers, and she snatched her hand back.

"Please. Allow me to buy you lunch."

Max's growl was low but more dangerous for it. "You'll never buy anything on the Heather, Colburn. I told you that." Max reached in his pocket and without looking, dropped a few bills on the table. "I'm not gonna tell you again." He turned to her but kept his eyes on Trey, as if he were a rattler that bore watching. "Are you staying, or coming?"

Colburn. The man Wyatt had said offered to buy the ranch. *Oh no.* At the closest tables, heads turned, taking in the show. Bree realized that any protest on her part would make it worse. Max's stillness didn't fool her. A storm was imminent, and she wanted to get outside before it hit. "It was nice meeting you Trey." She stood.

Trey scooted his chair back and rose. Max turned on his heel and stalked out. After a glance around to be sure she'd gotten everything, Bree followed.

First the bankers, now Colburn. Two plagues of vermin in one day. Max jammed the key in the ignition, then stopped and turned on her. "Did Colburn hire you to spy on us?"

"Are you nuts? I've never seen the man before he sat at my table today, and I don't appreciate your accusations." Bree crossed her arms and glared. "You've got to see someone about your delusions, Jameson."

He studied her.

"Not that I'd expect manners from you, but I'd appreciate your not embarrassing me in front of a roomful of people I don't know."

He twisted the key, wishing it were someone's neck. After only a few tries, the engine coughed to life. "I know it's hard for you to believe, princess, but your tender feelings aren't high on my list of concerns at the moment." He punched the clutch and shifted the truck in gear.

"What the hell is your problem, Jameson?"

He geared down for an old lady in a crosswalk who wagged a finger at him as she tottered in front of the hood. Glancing to the spitting cat next to him, he said, "Oh, I don't know. Maybe it's that the bank turned us down for a loan. Maybe it's because I may lose land that's been in my family for three generations. Or maybe it's wondering whether you're a traitor or a naive little girl."

"Where do you get off—"

"You do realize he's married, right? I should know. I attended his lavish wedding last fall, back before he got in bed with the developers." He shot her an assessing glance. "But maybe that doesn't matter wherever you come from."

"How dare you!"

He could almost feel the heat in the waves of fury that rolled off her as he punched the accelerator. "From the looks of things, his bed hasn't been empty much since."

"I wouldn't know about that, having just met the man." As she turned, the seat belt strained across her chest. "The world does *not* revolve around you, bucko. If you're so paranoid you think that I somehow—" She stopped, clearly so pissed that she couldn't get the words out. "What? My plan is to somehow dazzle you into signing away your ranch? With what, my sexy wardrobe and demure deportment?" She crossed her arms over her chest and stared out the windshield. "Butt wipe."

They drove in silence for a good five minutes. The breeze from the open window cooled his temper a bit, allowing reason to seep in. *Well, I guess my conclusion might have been a bit farfetched.* But when he'd walked into the bar and seen Colburn leaning across the table, feeding her, he didn't like it. Didn't like it a bit. And he definitely wasn't going to think about why he felt that way—angry and possessive of Bree. *Shit.*

He watched a small herd of antelope streaking through the open pasture parallel to the road, his chest aching. He missed the simple days, working alongside his father in silence. Back when the future seemed as solid as the mountains. *Double shit.*

If wishes were horses, every man would ride.

"Why are you always spouting quotes?"

He realized he'd spoken out loud. From the acid tone, she was still miffed.

"Mary Poole said, 'The next best thing to being clever is being able to quote someone who is.' "

He smiled when she rolled her eyes. Sitting with her arms wrapped around herself, frown in place, jaw clamped tight, she looked like a pouting teenager. *Nothing cuter than a het-up female.* After a quick glance in the rearview mirror, he eased the truck off the road and let it roll to a stop. Time to chew some crow.

"Aubrey?" Her head whipped up at her full name. "I might have overreacted a tad back there. I apologize. I don't think you're Colburn's spy."

"Oh, so I guess that just makes me a naive little girl, then." The frown was gone, but her bottom lip still jutted.

He bit back the obvious answer. He had some sense of diplomacy. And self-preservation. "A naive city girl— isn't that an oxymoron?"

"I accept your apology." She must have noticed his stare, because her eyes got huge and she flushed a pretty shade of peach. "Why do you always treat me as if I'm a young girl? I'm so clearly not."

"Clearly." Watching that plump lower lip, he felt something tug low in his gut. Pulling his attention back to the road, he did a quick traffic check, and then merged back into traffic. "How old are you?"

"Old enough that you shouldn't be asking." She smiled. "I'm thirty-one. How old are you, Methuselah?"

Old enough to know that what I'm thinking is inappropriate, especially with an employee. Down, Sparky. "Forty."

They kept their own counsel the rest of the way to the ranch. As he pulled up next to the house, the front door opened. Wyatt took the porch steps in one leap and trotted to the driver's side of the truck, worry plain on his face, a sheet of paper fluttering in his hand.

Max shut down the engine, opened the door, grabbed his hat, and stepped out. He wanted to be standing to face what was clearly bad news. "What is it, Wyatt?" He slapped his hat on as Bree jogged around the front of the truck.

"It's from the IRS. They're auditing the High Heather."

Max's sphincter tightened. *How much bad can one day hold?* He knew he should reach for the paper, but he couldn't seem to uncurl his fists.

"Let me see that." Bree reached around him to take the letter from Wyatt's fingers. She scanned the sheet. "They're questioning your 940 Form, Section 179, for the past two years. Providing you have receipts and adequate backup, this shouldn't be too bad." She squinted at the small print at the bottom of the letter. "I'd need to look up Publication 225 and the Tax Reform Act of 1986. I'm not familiar—"

Max snatched the paper back.

Bree looked up at him, then at Wyatt. "What?"

Max tipped his hat back. "Where the hell did you come from, lady?"

"Who cares?" Wyatt jabbed an elbow in his ribs. "If she can help, I don't care if she's Al Capone. Do you?"

CHAPTER
7

You're as good a liar as you were a detective.

After Wyatt's unwitting comment, Bree put her anger and nervous energy to good use. Grunting, she lifted the hay bale a few inches. In spite of the canvas gloves, the twine bit her fingers. Sweat tickled down her back as she shuffled the bale to the trapdoor of the loft, set it down, and with a kick, pushed it through the opening. It hit the ground with a satisfying *thump*.

Her hands were busy, but her mind wasn't. She couldn't help but think back to that day. The windowless interrogation room at the Century City Jail had been tiny, and they'd kept her there for hours.

The Federal agents only sat and looked at her.

So she started talking.

About the call from a customer, who got knockoff gaming boards instead of his ordered computer boards. Boards that would sell for eight hundred dollars a pop on the open market.

About her warehouse reconnaissance: the Taiwan

shipment of knockoff game boards she'd found in boxes labeled with the cheaper item's barcode.

About her tracking the illegal boards to an account on eBay. This wasn't her first brush with Vic's schemes. It hadn't occurred to her that the seller name, Madison Avenue Distribution, had anything to do with her.

She revealed the rest of the story: her resignation and the hushed conversation she'd overheard on the other side of Vic's closed office door. So much for amateur sleuthing. What she'd uncovered those past months was just the tip of an iceberg.

And she was the *Titanic*.

They had questions then, all right. Where was the money? Was she paying off someone in Customs to look the other way? How long had she been doing this? Where was the money?

Horror mixed with her gut load of worry and panic.

After three hours of interrogation, the investigators gave up in disgust. They turned her over to the deputies, along with a plastic bag of her possessions, and told her she'd better spend some time working on her story.

Then the nightmare began in earnest. The drunk tank. The fingerprinting. The *cavity search*.

Spit out at the end of the booking gauntlet, she was allowed a phone call. Stabbing the keys, Aubrey imagined the phone ringing in Phoenix. Her mother, stirring a pot on the stove, would put the spoon down and cross the room to answer. But she didn't. The phone rang and rang.

What now? She shuddered, thinking of calling any of her "friends." She'd be the joke of the postwork happy hour. Ignoring the shouts behind her to "Hurry her honky ass up," she scanned the smudged business cards thumbtacked to the wall. Her lifestyle left her with enough money for bail or an attorney, but not both. Wagering an attorney would help more in the long run, she dialed the number on the most professional-looking card.

That night, thoughts scrabbled in her brain like crabs trying to escape a tank. The pounding panic and cold rushing adrenaline made her sleepless night a blur: the cell, the bright lights, the noise.

The next morning, guards herded Aubrey, with other prisoners, on a bus, to court. Her cut-rate attorney showed up in large cheap shoes, looking young enough to have attended high school and law school concurrently. He listened to her babbled explanation. He didn't yawn in her face, but it was a near thing.

His interest peaked only when he explained his fee structure.

Didn't he understand that she'd been in jail? That she might have to go back?

In court, she stood on silly-putty knees as the charges were read: customs fraud, patent infringement, Internet fraud, money laundering. Her attorney's defense consisted of a bored, "not guilty." He told her that he'd hire an investigator and not to worry.

Not worry? While he investigated, she would be living with felons.

He might as well have given her water wings to face a tsunami.

CHAPTER 8

"Mom, I'm fine." Lying under the covers, Bree brushed a hand over the rough wool of the blanket on her chest. "I'm sorry I haven't called, but I've been busy. I got a job."

"Are you in Denver? How large is the company? Should I send you your work clothes?" Her mother's concern carried over the wireless, plain as if she were in the room.

She loved her mom, and after what Bree'd been through, appreciated the support. But her worry added pressure, as if Bree had to hurry and be successful, so her mother could relax. It was what pushed her to pack up her Jeep and leave Phoenix. It was also why she avoided calling her mother as often as she should.

"No, I'm outside Steamboat Springs, and my old clothes wouldn't help me a bit in this job. I'm a groom!"

"Oh, honey, you worked so hard to get your degree. Don't you want to at least try to—"

"No, Mom. I don't." Hearing the sharp edge to her words, she took a deep breath and tried again. "I chose this job on purpose. I want to rest awhile before I decide what to do with the rest of my life." She hurried on to avoid her mother's opinion. "And guess what? I like it. I'm out in the air all day, and the horses are great. One of the owners is a really nice guy, and the boarders are mostly nice too." There was no need to worry her, talking about the difficult ones.

"I'm glad, Aubrey." Her mom sighed. "You rest, hon, and put on some weight while you're at it. You're sure not going to want that job in the winter, in Colorado. You can come home to Phoenix in the fall."

"Phoenix isn't my home, Mom. It's yours and Briscoe's." Her mom had remarried long after Bree left for college, when she'd met and fallen in love with a long-distance trucker at her job as a waitress at the local truck stop. He was a great guy, and Bree was happy that her mother was happy, but Bree was way too old to see Briscoe as a step-father. "I'm going to find a new place to settle. No reason I have to be in a rush."

"Well, don't let your first experience sour you to being a controller, Aubrey. Once you explain what happened, potential employers will see how lucky they'd be to have you."

Her mom loved her daughter, so she couldn't understand why a controller with a fraud conviction wouldn't be seen as an asset to a business owner. "I know, Mom. I know. Listen, I'll let you go. I just wanted to call so you wouldn't worry."

Walking past his father's office, Wyatt glanced in. He stopped dead, the hair on his neck rising. "Jesus, Max, I thought I'd seen a ghost."

Max looked up from the piles of paper on the desk.

"You even have his mannerisms. I remember him looking over his reading glasses at me, just like you're doing now." Wyatt stepped into the inner sanctum of his childhood.

Max tore off the glasses and, tossing them on the desk, rubbed the bridge of his nose. "Well, I hope I'm better at taxes than he was. This is a disaster, Wyatt." He lifted the top page and tossed it across the desk. "What the heck was he thinking? Why didn't he turn this over to a CPA in town?"

Wyatt ignored the paper and rested one hip on the desk. "Dad was proud. I'm sure he didn't want anyone in town knowing about his losses."

Max sighed, eyeing the messy desk. "You're right. But it's not like every other rancher hereabouts is in any better shape."

Wyatt nodded toward a dusty, beat-up footlocker resting in the corner by the desk. "What is that filthy thing doing in here?"

"It came from the office your new groom cleaned out. Because it had a lock on it, the men thought it might be something we'd want." He scrubbed his hands over his face. "I haven't had the time to look at it."

"Max, why don't you just hire Bree to do this? It's obvious that she's some kind of accountant."

"Are you nuts? We hire her because she knows a couple of buzzwords? She does a good job with the horses, but I'm not trusting High Heather's future to some city girl with a black hole for a past. If you would, you've lived in Boston too long."

Some things never change. "You sound like him too, Max." Wyatt smiled. "Never trust a stranger, especially one from a city." He glanced around the office amazed to see how little things had changed in the years that had passed. He remembered standing at attention in front of this desk, speared by his father's disapproving look. "What is it about living in the country that makes people so suspicious? I never understood that."

The lines on his brother's face deepened. "What's Boston like, Wyatt? Not the city. I mean..."

"You mean my life?" Max nodded. "It's good. Juan and I have a brownstone in the North End, right in the middle of the nightlife."

"Juan. That's who answered the phone when I called to tell you about Dad?"

"Yes." He glanced at his brother. A stranger would take Max's stone face for disapproval, but he knew Max was just uncomfortable with the subject. "We've been together for five years, and I can't imagine a life without him." As if he'd walked into a fogbank of homesickness, the room seemed to recede. Home felt more real: the condo over the market street, the antiques, the dark man whose soulful eyes held Wyatt's world. The fog leached into him, a cold, aching loneliness.

"What does he do?" Max shifted papers on the desk. "For a living, I mean."

"He's a stockbroker. When you can leave the ranch for a while, we'd love for you to visit, Max."

Max worried a paper clip, twisting it. "Yeah. We'll see."

The fog dissolved in an acid bath of irritation. "Is it me that makes you uncomfortable, Max?" He stood. "Or is it that, living with Dad so long, his prejudice settled into your skin?"

He turned his back on his brother's discomfort and

walked to the wall, to the photos that had hung there forever. They were all of Max at different ages, showing sheep, on a horse, fishing. "It's funny. I'm grown now, with a life of my own. You'd think it wouldn't matter that he acted like you were his only child." He turned to his brother, who sat motionless, listening. "But it does."

Max opened the lap drawer, took out an old Polaroid photo, and tossed it across the table.

Wyatt stared at the picture, bent at the edges and yellow with age. "I remember this." The photo was of him and Max astride their horses, opening a gate. He'd been five, Max nine. They both grinned into the camera, his smile minus a front tooth.

Picking up the photo, he struggled with the familiar sadness the past always brought with it. "A single picture of both of us, relegated to a drawer. That's so typical." He shook his head and turned to the door. *What did I expect?*

"Wyatt?" His brother's voice broke into his brooding thoughts. "I'm sorry."

Wyatt stopped but didn't turn. "It's not yours to be sorry for, brother." He kept walking until he was in the privacy of his room, dialing Juan's number and reminding himself again why this didn't matter.

"If you hadn't called today, I was going to call the Mounties, Wyatt."

Juan's deep voice soothed Wyatt's rumpled emotions. He smiled. "Mounties are in Canada. We're way south of that."

"Well, the Lone Ranger, then." His voice dropped to intimate. "How're you holding up?"

"Things here never change, Juan."

"It's that bad? When can you come home? I was at the Quay last night, and everyone was asking about you."

Wyatt smiled, imagining their favorite restaurant, eating chowder at their table in the upstairs dormer. "I'd be gone already, but there are more problems. Financial problems."

"Sounds serious. Do you need money? I can wire you some. Can I come out, even if it's only so you're not the only queer in that backwater state?"

Wyatt chuckled. "Rural Colorado isn't ready for me, and I grew up here. A gay Cuban? We'd be tarred and feathered. Nah, I'll be okay. But it sure is good hearing your voice."

"Then don't wait so long to call me. I worry about you, you know." He heard Juan's sigh. "Now, let me tell you what happened with Toby and that dating service…"

After a few minutes of normal, Wyatt hung up, glanced around the bedroom that hadn't changed since he'd been here last, and brushed a tear away. Just hearing about his old life felt like he'd been tossed a badly needed life preserver.

You'll be home soon, he told himself. He imagined Juan standing, arms extended as Wyatt walked out of the Jetway. *Soon.*

CHAPTER 9

Bree pondered her dilemma as she washed windows. She sure as hell couldn't go back to being an accountant. Felonies, overturned or not, tend to be a black mark on a controller's résumé.

Getting into the bull business was going to take money—money she had, but swore she'd never touch. That "victim's stipend" from the Feds was blood money. Her blood. The thought of using it made her want to throw up.

What if I used it to do something good? This simple refuge she'd happened upon was great for now, but she knew that long-term, it wouldn't be enough. She needed to have goals.

Giving the window a last swipe, she stood back to check for streaks. A brush of pressure on her jeans made her jump, but not fast enough. "Ouch! Damn it, Charlie!" She whirled, slapping a hand to her stinging butt and glared at the dun-colored Shetland pony. He pawed the straw, not contrite in the least. "You've got to stop that." She hefted the bucket of cleaning supplies, and limping to the stall door, slid it open.

"Haven't you heard about not biting the hand that feeds you?" Stepping out, she slid the door closed, still rubbing her backside.

"Looked to me like he didn't bite your hand." Max stood in the aisle, watching her with a lopsided grin.

A spear of sunlight from one of her clean windows highlighted a narrow slice of his stubbled jaw. Masculinity rolled off the guy like cologne off a So-Cal yuppie.

She ignored the twitch of desire low in her belly. "He needs to learn some manners." She brushed past Max to return to the tack room.

"Hey."

His low voice sounded the way sex felt. Languid Sunday-morning sex, with light slanting over a rumpled bed and a lazy day that stretched on forever. She turned.

"Do you want to go for a ride?"

His long legs in snug denim hugged all the right places as he stood leaning against Charlie's stall, a cocky smile on his face.

Boy, do I. I'd love to throw a leg over you.

"I need to get out of here for a while, and you've been here three weeks and haven't seen much of the ranch."

Her heart took a happy skip. She'd been dying to ride, but had been hesitant to ask. "I'd love to."

He stood frozen for a heartbeat, then strode to Trouble's stall. "Why don't you tack up Smooth? He needs the exercise and he's a good mount."

He must have read her mind. The big bay Tennessee Walker was one of her favorites. "Who does he belong to?"

Max slid the stall door open and caught Trouble's halter. The stallion rushed to muscle him out of the way. "Whoa, big fella. We're going. Hold your stockings on."

She handed him a rope crosstie to snap to the horse's halter.

"A dot-com exec left him in lieu of back stable fees. Dad took a shine to him and rode him most days. Said the gait was easy on his arthritis." He ran a hand over the paint's gleaming coat. "I should sell him. Last thing we need around here is another animal eating his fool head off. Just haven't had the heart to yet."

As she scratched under the stallion's forelock, the horse grunted with pleasure. "Smooth. Is he named after the Santana song?"

"You didn't know Dad. He's named for Johnnie Walker whiskey." He bent to run his hand down his horse's foreleg, giving her a close-up of one damn fine rear end.

"Oh, I see." She gulped, ducking under the crosstie.

Fifteen minutes later, she led Smooth from the barn to where Max sat astride his restless horse. He looked over her mount. "I should have told you. We don't use the boarders' tack."

She yanked the stirrup on the English saddle down with a snap. "I didn't. This is the saddle I used on Trouble that first day." Rounding the front of the horse, she pulled down the other stirrup. "It was filthy, so I assumed it belonged to the Heather." She touched the supple leather, shoulder aching remembering the hours of elbow grease it had taken to restore it. She gathered the reins, put a foot in the stirrup, and swung into the saddle.

Trouble danced and Max had his hands full. The paint lowered its head and crow-hopped across the yard, snorting and squealing. Max kept his seat, giving the stallion its head. When the horse had settled a bit, Max reined it to her side. Smooth stood calm, like the gentleman he was.

"He always does that." Max straightened his hat. "It's easier to just let him get his ya-yas out at the beginning." Trouble took mincing steps, his rear swinging out as Max led the way to a well-worn trail leading out of the yard.

God, it felt good to have a horse under her again. She felt the flow of muscles beneath her and relaxed into Smooth's rhythmic walk. "He wouldn't be so fractious if you'd turn him out during the day. I've wondered why you don't."

"I should. It's just that he's so dadgummed hard to catch. It takes me a half hour in the morning and with the men waiting, it's time I don't have."

"Do you mind if I try? He and I get on pretty well."

"Be my guest. It's your time to waste."

The smell of sage wafted from scruffy bushes disturbed by the passing horses. The sun warmed her shoulders through the jean jacket. Delicate spring flowers sprouting from dusky green plants waved in the breeze. As she peered into the distance, a haze of lavender seemed to hover over the landscape like an aura.

Max pointed out Rabbit Ears Peak, standing at the gateway to the Yampa Valley. He put names to the plants they passed and explained their medicinal qualities. The stallion had calmed and they walked side by side in silence.

He looked even better astride than he did on foot. The Western saddle cupped his hips, and his wiry body moved as if part of the horse. In profile, the line of his chiseled face did something to her insides. Something good. *Don't even think about it. He's the boss.* "Do you mind if I ask you a question?"

"Depends." The tilt of his hat shaded his face, making it unreadable.

"I just wondered. Is there something more between you and Trey Colburn?"

Cold brown eyes cut to her. "You mean besides the fact that he's a philandering pig?"

With effort, she held his stare. "Yeah. Besides that."

He broke eye contact first. "The Colburns have been here almost as long as my family, but they weren't happy just ranching. Trey's dad was in the Senate. His brother Merle went off to law school and is a big mucky-muck attorney back East. Brother Brian is the CEO of the family holdings, pulling the strings from Denver. Even his sister, Daphne, married the head of a hedge fund in New York and has a summer home in the Greek Islands." Trouble threw his head up, spooked at nothing, and Max checked him.

"Trey's always been the runt, running the home place. He wants more but doesn't have the brains or mettle for it, so he set his sights on being the big fish in Steamboat's little pond. He bought Rowdy Jackson's ranch at the base of that mountain." He pointed to a peak to the east. "Told him he needed it because he didn't trust the government not to close grazing on public lands. Granted, Rowdy was broke and looking to get out of ranching, but Colburn didn't own it a month before he sold it to a conglomerate to build a ski resort." He glanced from the mountain to her. "They paid four times what he'd paid Rowdy."

"Yes, but just because he—"

"Rumor has it that the conglomerate wants to open a guest ranch so they can make a profit in the off season. Colburn's offered to sell them his land, but the Heather stands between his spread and the land they already own— and they don't want his unless they can have ours. They say, 'Character is what you are in the dark.' I don't think I'd want to see what Colburn looks like after the sun goes down."

"I guess I see your point." *But where I come from, that would be considered smart business.* She watched a muscle flex in Max's hard jaw.

But this ain't Kansas, Toto.

They topped a rise above a small valley. Herefords grazed in belly-high grass, and to the east, a stream bisected the pasture. Vivid color assailed her: deep green grass, rust-colored cattle, and the white snow on the mountains. "A high-priced photographer would make a killing in this state."

Max would have to take her word for it. She should have looked silly in a baseball cap, perched on that English saddle, a rein in each hand. But she didn't. Gazing into the distance, heels down, head high, back ramrod straight, she looked like she belonged here.

"Let's give 'em their heads." With just a touch of heel, Trouble laid his ears back and galloped down the hill. By the time they'd reached the bottom, Smooth had pulled alongside. Bree flowed over the horse's neck, baseball cap tucked into the waist of her jeans, hair streaming. Laughing, she urged her horse on with her heels.

The little brat is trying to beat me! He leaned forward, and Trouble surged under him.

Cud-chewing cattle watched as they tore across the meadow. Max pulled up at the stream's edge. Bree didn't. She gathered the horse with her hands, and Smooth took off from the bank. The stream was too wide—no way she'd make it. Max's brain registered the image: Bree, hair flying, a look of bliss on her face as the horse sailed over the creek in a graceful arc. His hands tightened on the reins as Trouble fought for his head, wanting to follow.

Smooth touched down on the other side without wetting a hoof. Max released the breath he wasn't aware of holding. He dismounted as she cantered in a circle. Smooth splashed through the water at a sedate walk. Bree laughed down at him, her eyes shining.

"Did you see him? What a great horse—he sailed over that water like it was a puddle." She reined in, kicked her feet out of the stirrups, and leaped from the horse to land beside him.

He was still breathing hard when he grabbed her arm above the elbow and yanked her to his chest. "That was the stupidest stunt I've ever seen. You could have broken your neck, you little fool."

He looked down at her wide, bright eyes and her breasts, rising with her rapid breathing. "You don't know the terrain, the horse…" Lord help him, he couldn't take any more. He bent his head, his lips smothering her laugh. Desire hit him hard. When her mouth opened in surprise, he deepened the kiss. He'd wanted to do this since he'd first laid eyes on her, and the reality of those lips was even better than he'd imagined.

She tasted clean and tart, like lemons and chill wind. Once over her surprise, her tongue met his in greeting, then settled down to get better acquainted. This girl didn't do anything by halves; when she kissed, she was *there*. Her soft mewling woke him like a slap. He hadn't been invited, and she was an employee. He broke the kiss and backed up a step.

Bree's face registered shock, her cheeks on fire with a blush.

Now I'm in for it. He tipped his hat. "I beg your pardon."

Her eyes narrowed to slits as her gaze raked over his face. "I'd like to see you beg for something, Jameson." Looking him straight in the eye, she snaked her hand around his neck, knocking his hat off as she pulled his mouth back down to hers.

Sweet Jesus. Max forgot his good intentions. He hauled her off her feet, flattening her breasts against his chest as her hair fell around them. He let her slide, slow, down his body. When she stood on her own feet, he fisted her hair in his hands and tilted her head to give him better access to that willing mouth. *Hot.* He reached down with one hand to cup her backside and snuggle closer. She shifted one leg between his and slid across him with a sinuous twist of her hips. *Damn.* She might look like the girl next door, but she sure hadn't learned that move in the Girl Scouts.

Behind him, Trouble nickered and pawed the ground. The beast tossed its head and bolted, ripping the reins from his hand. Max tore his mouth free and turned, but it was too late. He stood, catching his breath, and watched the black-and-white rump retreat into the distance to the thumping cadence of hooves.

"That cayuse is dog food this time, I swear to God." Dazed, he bent to pick up his hat.

Grinning, Bree tugged her cap from her waistband and snugged it over her hair. She cocked her head and fluttered her lashes. "Need a lift, Cowboy?"

God, he'd love to do things that would wipe that smug smile off her face.

"I need to be getting back anyway." She turned to check Smooth's girth. "I've got this slave-driver boss. If he knew I was out here wasting time, he'd can me for sure."

He chuckled. "Sounds like a real butt wipe."

"He is." Bree gathered the reins and mounted, throwing him an impish smile. "Sometimes."

He ignored her extended hand, grabbed the cantle of the saddle, and vaulted up behind her.

Despite her casual words, Bree worried over the kiss on the ride to the ranch. She tried to ignore the wall of solid cowboy at her back: the hands at her waist, the muscled thighs bracketing hers, the prominent lump brushing her backside.

Where did he learn to kiss like that out here in the boonies? He'd made her want to pull him into the grass and do what came natural. It had been a long time since she'd even thought about sex, much less contemplated how to get it. She shook her head to clear the estrogen fog.

"I have an idea that might help the ranch, Max." His fingers tightened at her waist. "I've done research, and I believe we could make good money raising bucking bulls for the pro bull-riding circuit."

He was quiet a moment. "Hang on a minute. We?"

He *would* pick up on that part first. "Well, yes. My proposal is that you, Wyatt, and I incorporate."

She rushed on before he could object. "You have the land and the know-how to raise cattle. I know how to run a business and I have some money to invest." She snuck a glance over her shoulder. One raised eyebrow—not as bad as she'd feared.

"There could be a lot of money in this, Max. The industry is taking off, and there's a demand for good bucking stock." She took his silence for attention, glad she didn't have to say this face-to-face.

"We wouldn't even need to sell all your stock. The breed of bull doesn't matter, only that he bucks. We'd just inseminate your bucking cows with semen from retired PBR Champion bulls."

"Bucking *cows*?"

"Well, yeah. We'd have better odds of producing good buckers if both parents like to buck, see?"

He shook his head. "I don't—"

"Of course, I'd expect you to do due diligence. If you stop by my room sometime, I'll show you my research. I've played with some spreadsheets and pro forma budgets."

"Going in partners with you is out of the question." His hands dropped from her waist.

"Why?"

"I don't know a thing about you, Bree. You can't expect me to trust my family legacy—"

"Oh really? You didn't seem worried about where I came from, back there." She jerked her head, indicating the trail back to the stream. "Look, Max, I'm only asking that you check it out before you reject the idea. Discuss it with Wyatt. This could be a good thing for all of us."

She nudged the horse into a trot. Smooth gait or not, riding tandem was a precarious proposition, one that discouraged conversation.

CHAPTER 10

After spending an hour chasing down his stubborn, flea-bitten excuse for a mount, Max was tired, hot, and hungry. He strode across the yard to the house, ignoring the sniggers of the men who lounged on the mess hall porch, waiting to be called to dinner. The cowboys had been riding in when he and Bree had returned and they'd stared like they'd never seen a cowboy left afoot.

Max wiped his boots on the back porch mat and opened the screen door. A quick, hot shower and one of Tia Nita's good suppers would go a long way to improving his attitude.

"You look grumpy for someone who just returned from a cozy ride." Wyatt sat tipped back in a chair, laptop computer in his lap, grinning like a fool.

"Y'all are only jealous." Max stomped to the kitchen to grab a beer.

"There's some truth to that, brother."

Max tipped the longneck back and drank deep, the bite making inroads in his dusty throat. He ran the sweating bottle across his hot forehead. "You're not going to believe the hair-ball idea that crazy redhead came up with today." He walked to the kitchen table, set his beer down, and leaned his palms on the edge. "She wants to go in partners with us. No. Scratch that. She wants to incorporate."

Wyatt shifted his attention from the screen, one eyebrow raised. "Incorporate what?"

"A bucking-bull operation. She watched one night of the PBR, got online, and went loco." He picked up his beer and took another swig. "She thinks we could make enough money to put this place in the black."

"Well, how do you know we can't? I would have never thought of that."

"I'll check it out. Raising bucking bulls may make some sense. But you and I going into business with *her*?" He snorted. "Not in my lifetime. This is a family business, and I intend to keep it that way."

Wyatt threw his head back and laughed.

"What's so funny?"

"Oh, now I understand." Wyatt smiled into the distance.

"Are you going to fill me in, or keep braying like an ass?" People around here were starting to get on his nerves.

"Bree came to me a few days ago, asking how much we'd charge her to put a bull in our pasture."

"What did you tell her?"

Wyatt looked at him like he'd lost his mind. "What's a little summer grass? I told her it was no charge. But I wondered what she was up to." He grinned. "She must've guessed what your reaction would be and decided to jump in. With or without us."

"Why, that scheming little—"

"Just a minute, Max." His boots thumped to the floor. "You turn down her proposal, and then she's at fault for doing it on her own? What kind of pretzel logic is that?" He ran his hand over his chin and squinted. "I know you, Max. You're not upset with the idea. You're upset because it's hers."

That fried it. Max glared at his brother, spun on his heel, and stomped off to the shower.

Bree concentrated on cleaning the large hoof wedged between her knees. A featherlight touch roamed across the waist of her jeans. "Sorry, Peanut. I don't have anything for you. Your mom will be here in a few minutes. She'll bring you something." Bree brushed a few cedar shavings from the polished hoof, dropped it and straightened. The silver-gray coat shone, not a hair out of place. The horse's nicker told Bree that they weren't alone before the sound of footsteps behind her did.

"Who gave you permission to braid his mane and tail?" The imperious voice announced the arrival of Peanut's mistress.

Bree straightened her shoulders. This was a game she played—a challenge, to wring a grudging compliment from the barn's toughest boarder. "Good morning, Janet. You're right on time."

Looking like she'd stepped off the cover of *Town and Country*, Janet ran a gloved hand over Peanut's shiny flank. She eyed the fancy running plait Bree had spent a half hour braiding. She sniffed. As the big gray's head came around to nuzzle her, Janet's stern face melted to a child's delight. Pulling a carrot from the waistband of her jodhpurs, she addressed the horse. "Yes, I know, honey. It's a bitch to be all dressed up with nowhere to go, isn't it?" Janet rubbed the velvet nose, then turned to Bree, haughty expression back in place. She reached in her pocket, pulled out a sheaf of cash, and thumbed through it.

Bree shook her head. "Oh no, ma'am. Thank you just the same. It's all part of the service here at High Heather." She unsnapped the short tether at the bridle's bit and handed the reins to Janet. "Have a nice ride."

Fifteen minutes later, Bree stood before the battered armoire that had been delivered from the big house the week before. Leave it to Wyatt to notice that she'd been living out of boxes under her bunk. Bree wondered again at the glaring disparity between the brothers' personalities. She hadn't seen much of Max the past few days, but when she did, he was frowning.

Reaching past the work shirts, Bree retrieved a satin hanger. She held the blouse up, surveying herself in the mirror inside the wardrobe door. The off-shoulder peasant blouse in pink cotton, finished below the breasts with smocking, left her waist bare.

Completely inappropriate. But I want to feel like a girl for a whi—

Her glance fell to her neck. The graceful blouse showcased the scar, making it more obscene. A bubble in her chest burst, sheeting her gut in shame. Her hand strayed to her stomach, to warm it. Wearing the blouse would be a travesty. A frilly felon.

The cold receded, leaving a tarry oil slick that clung to her insides. Bree swallowed the bitter residue in her throat, turned to the closet, and buried the blouse in the very back.

She chose a collared black fitted blouse with cap sleeves and denim short shorts instead, a watered silk scarf for her neck. She took a swig from the prescription antacid bottle, then gathered a fresh pair of fancy underwear and the flat, jeweled sandals she hadn't been able to pass up the last time she'd been in town. She tugged a canvas bag full of dirty laundry from the bottom of the wardrobe. Might as well kill two birds.

It was one o'clock by the time she walked to the main house. Catching movement from the corner of her eye, she glanced up and stopped in her tracks. Max and Tia Nita were working the garden. Well, Max was, anyway.

Tia lounged in a webbed lawn chair, shaded by an umbrella anchored to the arm. Max was shirtless, hoeing in the hot sun. His jeans, farmer's tan, and cowboy hat should have looked silly. Instead, he looked like Mr. July in a beefcake calendar, sweat glistening on his chest and biceps. Even his torso, usually hidden from the sun, was a warm bronze, reminding her of his Native heritage.

Tia pointed to something between the rows and Max set his hoe to it. Then, as if sensing her gaze, he looked up. He straightened, and leaning on the hoe, thumbed his hat back. Bree's skin heated as a stab of lust shot through her. *Wow, that sun is hot.*

Except the sun didn't touch the part of her that burned. She felt like a rabbit in a snare, unable to look away. Tia followed the line of Max's interest, saw Bree, and waved. With effort, she returned the wave before she hurried to the house and a cold shower.

Later, she lingered in the bathroom, hair in a towel, checking her face in the mirror. Thanks to the baseball cap, she hadn't collected many more freckles. As she slathered on moisturizer, she wished for at least a cover stick for the dark circles, but her makeup had been gathering dust in the bottom of her suitcase since she'd arrived.

She smoothed vitamin E cream over the scar. *Damaged goods*. She shook her head to dislodge the thought. *Only the guiltless get to whine*. The past was gone; all she could do was make better decisions for the future. She tied the scarf over the abomination and stuffed her discarded clothes into the laundry bag.

After starting the first load, Bree wandered to the great room, intending to find a book to read from the shelves flanking the massive fieldstone fireplace. It was a handsome room. Sunlight streamed in the tall windows and French doors, highlighting the huge chocolate leather couches and bright Navajo rugs on the polished oak floor.

She paused at the sight of Tia Nita sitting in an overstuffed chair, knitting.

"Ah, Miss Bree, come sit." She patted the arm of the chair next to hers. Bree crossed the room and sat. "Today you look like a *chica*—very pretty." Tia touched Bree's cheek, frowning. "Why you don't sleep?"

Bree's conscience squirmed. "I sleep." She glanced to the pile of yarn in Tia's lap. "What are you making?"

"I make scarves for the cowboys, for winter." She picked up the needles, and her fingers flew.

"The colors are beautiful." Bree touched the soft strip of alternating copper and turquoise blue. "But why do you bother? The men can buy warm clothes in town."

"I do it for me. When I knit, my troubles go." Tia glanced up from her needles. "I can teach you."

"Oh, don't bother. I'm a klutz with that kind of thing."

Tia reached into the cloth bag at her feet and brought out another pair of needles and a ball of blue yarn. "It will give you something to do when you don't sleep."

Tia had a point. She sure could use something to occupy her mind at night, when memories lie in the dark, waiting to pounce. She'd finished cleaning every piece of dirty leather in the barn and needed something else to do with the smallest hours of night.

Bree picked up the needles. "Okay, but I hope this yarn isn't expensive. It's going to end up in a hopeless knot."

An hour later, Bree took a break and stretched cramped fingers. Following Tia's careful directions, she'd produced a small swatch of uneven stitches. As long as she didn't put it next to Tia's, she was pretty pleased. "I was surprised to see Max gardening with you this morning, Tia. Can't one of the hands help you?"

As Tia looked up, her needles stilled. "My Maxie. He started gardening with me when he was little. I think he missed his mama, and it reminds him of her. When he was in school, it was something we did together. Now? I think he does it so I don't work so hard." A proud, maternal smile crossed her face. "He's a good boy."

Not knowing what to say, Bree laid the needles beside her and stood. "I'll get us some iced tea."

Rounding the corner of the kitchen, she saw the man himself, standing in front of the open refrigerator. He must've just come from the shower. His hair was slicked back, his feet bare. Pushing away the picture of Max as a little boy, missing his mom, she walked to the cupboard. "Hey, Max." She reached on tiptoe to get two glasses.

A low whistle came from behind. She whirled around, nearly dropping one of the glasses.

"Damn, you clean up nice." His eyes roamed her body from head to freshly painted toe. "Please tell me you're

not wearing that to dinner. We'll have a riot on our hands."
He gave her a big-bad-wolf smile that made it plain that he
could eat her up.

"Thanks. I think." He looked good enough to eat
himself—and lately she found herself hungry for more
than just Tia's meals. She kept from touching him as
she reached around him to put the glass under the ice
dispenser in the door. "As long as you're standing there,
would you mind getting the tea out for me?" She took a
deep breath. The ice in the glasses clinked in her shaking hands. She took the two steps to the counter, set them
down, and wiped her hands on the back of her shorts.
"Have you thought at all about my proposal?"

He carried the jug to the counter. "I have. I have only
one question."

She relaxed. Business questions she could handle.

"Why did you go behind my back and ask Wyatt about
putting a bull in our pasture?"

Her stomach clenched. She'd known he'd hear about
that. "Maybe because I knew how you'd react." She raised
her chin and tried the imperious look that worked so well
for Janet. "I was right."

He leaned against the counter and crossed his arms.
"You don't think you were a bit...underhanded?"

Her skin heated. She'd only been covering her bases.
And buying a bull was a sound business decision. *Damn
him.* "Look, bucko. I don't need yours or anyone else's
permission to buy cattle. Or to go where I please. Or to
do what makes me happy. Ever again." She was flat done
with being judged, formally or otherwise. "Max Jameson,
you are an insufferable curmudgeon." Stepping up, she
poked a finger in his chest. "You're a bully, and everyone

kowtows to your foul moods. Well, I've got news. It takes a lot more than the likes of you to scare me."

She lifted the full glasses. "Maybe people wouldn't feel the need to do things behind your back if you were just a bit human, instead of two-thirds grizzly and the rest—" She sputtered, unable to think of anything bad enough. "Snidely Whiplash!"

With a head toss that flipped her hair over her shoulder, she stalked from the room.

Max cocked his head. "Snidely Whiplash?"

"Here, give me that. You never could dig postholes for crap." Max took the double-bladed implement from his brother's hands. "I'll bet you have blisters inside those gloves, don't you?" He rammed the digger into the rock-hard soil. God they needed rain.

"Well, excuse me. There aren't many barbed-wire fences in Boston to keep the calluses up."

Wyatt stepped to his horse and pulled the canteen strap off the saddle horn. He took off his hat and took a long drink, then handed it over. "It's almost worth the blisters to be out here, though. I'd forgotten how beautiful the mountains are."

"Hey, that was your choice. The mountains haven't moved." Max sipped metallic-tasting water and eyed his brother. "And grab the sunscreen out of your saddlebag. You're getting burned."

Wyatt put his hand on his hip, like a girl would. Max turned away and rammed the blades into the ground.

"Yeah. My choice. A pretty easy choice it was too, given the circumstances."

"Oh, you know Dad—"

"Dad was only part of the problem, as you very well know."

"I'm not saying I'm blaming you for leaving, Wyatt. But you understand what it's like here. You were raised in the country." He pushed on the handles and lifted out dirt, then rammed them into the ground again. Sweat rolled down his bare back and into his eyes. He didn't want to talk about this.

"I understand better than you, Max, how the homophobes in town feel about my lifestyle. What I want to know is what *you* think."

Max looked up. "You best to put on that sunscreen, I'm telling you." He looked down the row of new fence posts—nowhere near enough to quit for the day. *Shit.* "Look, you know I love you. We grew up together. You're my brother." Another clump of dirt hit the ground, and he stopped to wipe his brow.

"Yeah, I know you love me. I don't know what you think of me, though."

Max threw down the post-hole digger. "What, Wyatt? You want to know what I think of your lifestyle?"

Wyatt nodded.

"I hate it. Okay? Is that what you want from me? I hate that you're different. I hate that because of who you love, you don't fit in." He stomped to where the horses stood, snatching mouthfuls of prairie grass. He reached into the saddlebag and pulled out the sunscreen. "And I hate that it hurts you so much."

He tossed the plastic bottle to Wyatt, walked back to the hole, and picked up the digger. Blood pounded in the veins of his neck, and his head throbbed in the same beat. "Now, can we just get this done so we can get back to the house and get a shower?"

"Okay, Max, we can let it go for now. But you're going to have to find a way to deal with this, if we're to have a relationship going forward." He popped the top on the sunscreen and dabbed it on his palm. "Because I can't change who I am, even if I wanted to." He spread lotion on his face. "So that leaves only one of us to do the changing."

CHAPTER
11

Saturday night, Max sat stewing at the empty dinner table in the mess hall. Wyatt had excused himself after dinner, saying he planned to work for a few hours. Max scowled at the men—and one stubborn woman—huddled around the television, watching bull riding. He remembered how shy the cowboys had been when Bree first arrived. What a difference a few weeks made. Now, aside from polite deference, the men showed no sign they noticed she was female. Bree had changed too. She'd been so skittish at first. Now she sat, hip-to-hip on the crowded couch with four men, cheering for the bulls.

She's doing this just to get me to change my mind about the business. But if that were true, why was she ignoring him? Bree asked Armando a question, one Max couldn't quite hear.

Armando laughed. "The flank strap doesn't hurt them. It doesn't even make them buck. That's in their blood. All it does is get them to kick out their back feet, see?" He pointed to the screen, and Bree leaned in, intent.

"How do they—"

The rest was lost in the squeal of Max's chair on the linoleum. No one noticed when he walked out.

At the main house, Max gazed out the window of the great room, a cut-crystal glass of whiskey in his hand. Actually, he was seeing himself; the lamplight turned the dark pane to a mirror. Wyatt was right; he did look like the old man.

Been behaving like him too.

He'd told Bree to examine her motives. Maybe it was time he did the same. Hell, probably past time. He paced the length of the room, his boots making a hollow thumping on the pine floor. Each lap granted new insights. The bull operation was a good idea, and he'd been too stubborn to admit it.

But he did have some questions. He recalled the horrific ropy scar on Bree's neck. The shadows in her eyes. He still didn't know who this woman was, or where she came from. And it rubbed him like a foxtail under a saddle blanket. She could be a running from the law, for all they knew. He snorted. Maybe Wyatt had a point about small-town paranoia.

Wyatt was right about something else too. He'd nixed Bree's idea at first because it had come from a woman. When had he turned into his father—discounting women for anything more than their obvious charms?

He took a sip from the rocks glass and winced, only partly due to the liquor's bite. It wasn't that he thought women weren't smart or capable. It's just that it was a man's job to work things out. He made a sound of disgust. Did he believe that? Or was it just a part of the cultural pool he'd swum in since he was a kid? After all, he didn't buy into his father's opinion of Wyatt, or his lifestyle. At least, he didn't think he did.

He glanced at his reflection in the mirrored window once more. It was as if a younger version of his father stood before him. "Yeah, well, if you had all the answers, old man, we wouldn't be in this fix to begin with. Maybe it's time to try something different." Setting the half-empty glass on the coffee table, he walked to the door.

Looked like it was going to be crow for dessert.

"Much as I've eaten of it lately, you'd think I'd have a taste for it." The crisp night closed around him as he stepped out of the house. The light in the barn window told him Bree was still up. He crossed the yard to slip in the side door. Horses rustled in stalls as he passed, casting lighter shadows in the gloom of the unlighted breezeway. He followed the beacon of the tack room light. Stepping in, he glanced around. Considering this room an extension of Bree's quarters, he hadn't been here in a while.

No more snaked pile of leather in the corner. Clean bridles hung from pegs, each labeled with a horse's name. Saddles straddled sawhorses, supple leather glowing. Even the linoleum floor shone. He inhaled the smell of rich leather and warm horse.

How many hours had she spent on this room alone? Max knew other responsibilities kept her busy all day, so that only left—He imagined her, late at night, cleaning leather all alone. He swallowed the stab of guilt.

Jesus, if she works this hard for someone else, how hard would she work for herself?

He might not have known Bree long, and he might not know her past, but he felt like he knew her. He noticed a hand-lettered sign, thumbtacked on the wall by the door.

High Heather appreciates your patronage! This is a good, hardworking, caring woman.

He stepped to the inner door and knocked.

"W-who is it?"

"Bree, it's Max. Can I talk to you for a minute?"

The door opened the length of the safety chain and a tawny eye appeared in the crack. The door closed, then swung open. She stood in a spaghetti-strap cotton top and some kind of stretchy pants that hugged her legs, ending midcalf. A space heater rattled in the corner, making the room cozy-warm. He glanced to the bed, where a contorted mass of yarn lay, knitting needles sticking out of the middle.

"Do you mind if I come in?"

Her eyes darted around the room as she considered, then stepped back. She gestured to the only chair, but he stayed where he was. *Easier to do this standing up.*

"Bree, I've been an ass, and I'm sorry." He raked his hand through his hair. "You've done nothing but work hard and try to help since you got here, and I've been taking out my troubles on you."

Her jaw dropped in surprise.

I guess I've got a longer fence to mend than I thought.

Her eyes narrowed. "Have you been drinking?"

He smiled. "Yes, but only half a glass."

"In that case, I accept your apology. Now, will you sit down? You're making me nervous."

He crossed to the chair. It looked like one of the leather ones from his office. Wyatt's doing, no doubt. *Danged brown-noser.* "Are you comfortable out here? Is there anything you need?"

She sat on the bed, the only other seat in the room. "No, I'm good. Thanks for asking."

He forced himself to meet her eyes. "This idea of yours. Wyatt's high on it. And if it would be a way for me to keep ranching..."

Her eyes lit up. "I think it's a viable solution, Max." She reached for the laptop. "Let me show you. I've worked up some spreadsheets."

A half hour later, Bree straightened and rubbed her lower back. Standing bent over Max's shoulder, squinting at data had taken its toll. He'd offered her the chair, but imagining his solid chest leaning over her, his face next to hers, she knew she'd never be able to concentrate on numbers. She had to hand it to Max. Once he opened his mind, he opened it all the way. He'd listened closely and asked educated questions.

He looked up at her. "Sit down, will you? I'm getting a crick in my neck." He closed the computer. "I think I have all the facts I need, anyway."

Bree perched on the edge of the bed, their knees almost touching, waiting for the verdict.

Forearms braced on his thighs, he took one of her hands. Habit forced her spine straight, and she leaned back. Holding her hand in his rough one, his thumb rubbed the back in a soothing motion, like he would with a skittish horse. "I'm going to think hard on this, Bree." He glanced up. "Either way, I want you to know how much I appreciate you trying to help. We were pretty lucky the day you saw our ad in the paper."

"Who are you?" She tilted her head. "And what have you done with Max?" She smiled to cover her discomfiture. "Are you *sure* you didn't tie one on, back at the house, cowboy?"

His eyes roamed her face to settle on her lips. "I feel a buzz, but booze doesn't have a thing to do with it." He tugged her hand, and before she knew it, she was settled in his lap, his arms around her. "You've got a lot stronger kick than Johnnie Walker." He reached up to smooth her hair, trailing the back of his fingers down the side of her face. "Smoother, too."

He waited, still holding her gaze, giving her the choice. She leaned in, lips just above his. "Let's hope there's no hangover."

The kiss started sweet, but a spark struck when she took in the smell of him: the scent of outdoors, an undertone of booze, and *man*. A tendril of smoke unfurled in her chest. From the cold campfire ring of burnt-out relationships, tinder burst into a small hot flame.

She grabbed his shirt, pulling him closer. She opened her lips and he was there, meeting her halfway. *It's been too long.* Craving fired in her chest, making her breath hitch. His hands held her, cradling her face, his tongue exploring. He lightened the kiss; then his lips were gone. She groaned, wanting more. He covered her face in featherlight kisses, touching her eyes, her chin. She tipped her head back as he trailed down her neck.

My neck. Reality crashed in like cops at a drug bust. She jerked away and sat up.

He let her go. "Won't you tell me what happened, Bree?" His dark eyes shifted from her neck to her eyes. His look was open and vulnerable, as if he actually cared. "Not because of business, but because I want to know you. Like it or not, your past is a part of who you are."

And he'd almost made her forget that. She recalled his reaction to Trey Colburn. Max's black-and-white morality.

He'd never understand. It made her sadder than it should have. Sliding from his lap, she stood and stepped away.

He sat a moment, watching her with sad eyes. "Well, I'll say good night then." He retrieved his hat from the desk and stood. "You lock the door behind me, now, hear?"

Boots on the railing, Wyatt tilted on the back legs of the porch chair, admiring the yellow cast of midmorning light on the porch. *There are a few advantages to country living. I wonder what Juan would think of Colorado. If he came out for a visit, maybe he would like it.* Wyatt tipped his hat back as his brother charged out the screen door, briefcase in hand.

"It must be nice to sit on the porch like a hound. Some of us have to work for a living," Max snarled.

Wyatt yawned and stretched. "I am working, just on a different shift. I was up until two this morning fixing an application error. Where are you off to?"

"Taking the calf crop to the sale barn. The men rounded up the calves in the pen that fronts the road, and they're meeting me there to load them."

Wyatt pulled a nail file from his back pocket.

"And what are you going to do? Get a manicure?" Max spit the words like they were a piece of bad meat.

"What does a *real* man clean his nails with, Max? A bowie knife?"

"I didn't mean—"

"You're nervous about today. You're not comfortable with the emotion. So instead of dealing with that, you pick a fight with me. Nothing much changes on the Heather."

"Well, thanks for the insight, Dr. Phil." When Wyatt didn't return the smile, he turned away and settled his hat. "Sorry, Wyatt."

"No problem, bro. Actually, Bree and I are taking a ride out to check herd in the far pasture. I heard wolves howl last night."

They both glanced up as Bree rounded the corner mounted on Smooth, leading a saddled broomtail and Max's pinto dancing at the end of a short halter rope.

Max mumbled under his breath, "Here comes trouble."

Wyatt dropped his feet from the rail and stood. "Which one?"

Max snorted a laugh. "Both." He walked down the porch steps. It looked like Trouble was going out for the exercise, since he wore only a halter. "How long did it take you to catch him this morning?"

"He came when I called."

"Yeah, right." When the pinto head butted him, Max scratched him under the jaw.

"No, really, he came right to me," she said in a little-girl, I-have-no-idea-where-the-cookies-went voice.

Wyatt walked down the steps to take the broomtail's reins. "Good luck with the calves, Max." Leather creaked as he mounted and settled in the saddle. "We'll see you at dinner."

"I just hope the price is up today." Max threw over his shoulder as he strode to the ancient cattle hauler parked in the dirt drive.

Wyatt nudged his mount to a walk and Bree kept pace, Trouble taking mincing steps beside her. She wore the same fancy shirt she had on when they'd first met. But instead of a country-dressed city girl, she now looked like a dressed-up country girl.

"Do you miss this when you're in Boston?"

"Yes and no. I miss the land." He looked to the snow-dusted mountains at the horizon and pulled in a lungful of scent-laden air. Summer had finally made its way to the high country. This was the first shirtsleeve day they'd had since he'd arrived.

"It must've been hard for you, growing up here."

Maybe it was her casual attitude that loosened his tongue. Or maybe it was just time. The feel of the past returned the empty separateness he'd lived in back then. With puberty came the first kernel of understanding. A terrifying kernel that he'd shoved to a dark place inside.

"The worst were high school mouth breathers. Like a pack of wolves, they scented out that I was different." The memories were well worn. They shouldn't still have sharp edges. But they did. "There were some dicey moments in the locker room after gym class, I can tell you that."

She winced. "I'll bet."

"One day after school, Max took on the alpha wolf. I wasn't there, and Max never talked about it, but the kid ended up in the hospital." He remembered his horror at the violence, then at himself for being happy about it. "They were dumb, but they had long memories. It was bearable after that."

They rode in silence for a while, stirrups bumping occasionally, watching the purple martins dart after cabbage moths.

Bree said, "My best friend in high school was the quarterback of the football team. He was all state, the darling of the town. His safety as well as his future depended on no one knowing he was gay." She glanced over at him. "Such a great guy. He had it all: brains, talent, killer looks. He was what every other kid in that school wanted to be, with one exception."

"This story doesn't end well, does it?"

She grinned. "Are you kidding? He's in the NFL now, happy, well adjusted, and in love with the greatest guy. I fly out to see them once a year." She sobered. "It doesn't have to end badly, Wyatt."

"Oh, I'm not complaining." He tipped his straw hat to block the sun as the trail turned. "My life is wonderful. It's just that coming home stirs the silt at the bottom of the tank, you know?"

"Boy, do I."

From her pained look, he could see that she did. "What about you? Are you going to tell me about your personal drama?"

Bree tilted her head, considering. "Nope." She laughed. "But if I did, you're who I'd talk to, Wyatt. Thanks." The paint had calmed as they walked, and she loosened his lead. "I'm sorry you didn't get a chance to talk to your dad before he died."

"I'm not." The moment the words left his mouth, he realized it was true. "Oh, I'll admit to fantasies of coming home and having him actually *see* me. To look at me, just once, like he did Max." *Jeez, I sound like a guest on* Oprah. The saddle creaked as he straightened.

"But it's not too late with Max. I'm not giving up what's left of my family. In a twisted way, it's good that we've got money problems. It puts us in the traces together, and like it or not, we'll have to work things out."

Bree rubbed her palms together. "I understand that Max talked to you about my bucking-bull business idea. I've been dying to ask what you thought about it."

He smiled. "Now, keep in mind, my area of expertise is about as far from bucking bulls as is possible, but I like what I've heard so far." He reined his horse to a halt. "I'll be honest with you, Bree. For me, it isn't about the land, or the money. I've gotten along all these years without either and done just fine. It's about Max." He tipped his chin to the meadow before them. "This is more than his career. It's who he is. It's where he was meant to be." He shook his head. "Sorry to sound all dramatic, but he's my big brother, and I owe him. A lot." He leaned his forearm on his saddle horn and watched her. "And unless I miss my guess, you care for him as well."

Bree opened her mouth, then closed it.

"So if you've found a way to help, you can count me in."

She cleared her throat. "I think the next step is to sit down and discuss a business plan."

Max reclined, feeling downright smug, arms draped across the metal bleacher at his back. He listened as the auctioneer droned on. The price of beef was still dismal, but thanks to their reputation, the Heather's calf price held better than most. He scanned the crowded sale barn as the next lot of yearlings was herded into the auction pen.

A raucous laugh overrode the babble of conversation and the bawling of cattle. Trey Colburn stood next to the pen, holding court over a group of "gentlemen ranchers"—rich men who wanted to play at what men here took dead serious.

"Kinda makes you sick, don't it?"

Max looked up. Slim Tanton, a local rancher and friend of his father, stood next to the bleachers. "Like Frank Zappa said, 'There's more stupidity than hydrogen in the universe, and it has a longer shelf life.'"

Slim's wrinkles lifted in a smile. "Stupidity's sure been running wild here the past few years." He rolled the auction schedule in his fist. "I've been meaning to get out to see you, Max."

"What can I do for you, Slim?" Max sat up.

"Nothin'. That's what I wanted to tell you. I'm selling out." He raised a hand to halt protest. "I'm tired, Max. Tired of the long winters, the politics, the changes." He waved the paper tube toward Colburn's group. "Tired of that."

"Damn sorry to hear you're leaving us, Slim."

"My Tracy's asked me to come live with her down Abilene way. Since I lost Maggie, it hasn't been the same. I want to get to know my grandkids 'fore I die." His washed-out blue eyes hardened. "Just wanted you to know, I ain't selling out to no yuppie. Justin White, next to me, is gonna lease my land to run cattle."

Max whistled through his teeth. "Does White have that kind of money, Slim?"

"He don't need money. Not now, anyway." The old man's shoulders straightened as he looked across the ring at the men in expensive slacks and string ties. "He'll make payments as he can. Hell, I don't need the money. When I'm gone, Tracy can decide what she wants to do with the land."

"I understand, but I wish to hell you weren't doing this. You and my dad went back a long ways. I'll be sorry not to have you for a neighbor." Max put out his hand. "Are you sure there's nothing I can do to help?"

He shook. "Nothin' to do, Max. I'll stop by the Heather before I leave town."

"Be sure you do that, Slim." As he watched the rancher walk away, Max's celebratory mood vanished. Acid gnawed at the wall of his stomach. Reality gnawed at the edges of his mind. *Hell, I'm gonna be in the same place if something doesn't change...soon.*

Two hours later, the empty trailer rattled over the Heather's gravel drive. As Max pulled up and shut off the ignition, dust billowed in the cab. They sure could use some rain. He cranked up the window and grabbed his briefcase. Stepping from the cab, he noticed the hands clustered around the front paddock.

They didn't notice his approach. Their focus was on a pint-sized bull, chewing cud in the center of the paddock, looking bored. A mixed-breed, charcoal gray with black spots—so many that they smeared together in places, lending it a mottled, unbalanced look. One short horn tilted skyward, the other at the ground.

Max tipped his hat back. "What the hell is that?"

Luis said, "That's Fire Ant, boss. Bree's new buckin' bull."

He snorted. "That little thing?" *God help us. She may know business, but we're going to have to keep her away from the sale barn.*

Armando stood, arms draped on the top of the fence, one boot on the bottom rail. "I don't know, boss. Some of the best bulls in the PBR are small."

Max shook his head. "Maybe, but I've seen horseflies bigger'n that."

The men chuckled.

Armando said, "There's Little Yellow Jacket. He retired the best in the business."

Luis broke in. "Yeah, but give me a big, slab-sided bucker like Mudslinger. He looks scary just standing there."

"Standing ain't what they're paid to do," Armando said. "PBR isn't a beauty contest."

The clang of the dinner bell ended all conversation. Max followed the crowd that hustled up the steps and into the mess hall.

Bree stood at the top of the porch steps, hand on the bellpull. "Well, Max? What do you think of my bull?"

He opened his mouth to tell her, but seeing the pride shining on her girl-next-door face, he didn't have the heart. His hesitation gave him away.

Bree sniffed and lifted her freckled nose. "Well, you haven't seen him buck."

Dang, she's cute when her back's up. "And you have?"

"Of course." She flipped her hair over her shoulder. "Well. Not in person, but I watched video clips, and he's got potential."

"Oh. Well. In that case..." He climbed the steps and ducked his head to hide a smile.

"I've got a couple of big three-year-olds coming that you'll like the look of." She raised her chin. "But I'm telling you, Fire Ant is going to sire a famous line of PBR bulls."

"Hey, lady, you say it, I believe it." His stomach growled. Ignoring it, he added, "I've been thinking on your idea. Wyatt and I talked, and we're ready to sit down and meet when you are."

Her face lit up like a little girl at Christmas. And it made him feel like Santa. Well, a younger, randy Santa.

"How about if I cook you two dinner at the main house sometime next week? That way we wouldn't be interrupted."

"You can cook?" He dodged a slap. "Sounds good to me." He opened the door and held it for her, but she hung back.

"You go ahead. I've got to make a call." Bree waited until the screen slapped behind Max, then reached in her pocket to pull out her cell phone.

She hit speed dial. "Mom? I need some help."

At her mother's anxious reply she said, "No. No, Mama, I'm fine. I didn't mean to scare you. Everything's great." She walked to the end of the porch, out of earshot. "I need some emergency recipe therapy, Mama. What do cowboys eat besides Mexican food?"

Bree dragged another bale of alfalfa from the outside door of the hayloft to where Max was stacking them against the wall. She'd objected when he offered to help, but looking at the growing pile, she knew there was no way she could have put away the latest delivery without him. She put a fist to the small of her back as she straightened. "Unh."

Max dropped the bale on the rising pile and turned. "Let's take a break."

"No, I'm okay—"

He caught her arm just above the elbow and led her to the doorway, where a blessed breeze lifted the wet hair off her neck. "Your face is beet red, and you're sweating. You sit here. I'll be right back." He strode to the hayloft, snatched up the bale she'd struggled with, and tossed it on the pile as if it weighed twenty pounds rather than a hundred twenty.

She admired the way his Wranglers pulled taut over his backside when he bent. She appreciated the heavy muscles of his shoulders and back when he lifted. But when he turned and walked toward her, she treasured one of his rare smiles even more.

"You and Wyatt. Take the gloves off. It'll help with the blisters." When she pulled off her gloves, he sat on the bale next to her and examined her palms.

"It's all right. I need to develop calluses. They'll make me look tougher." She tried to ignore the tingle that spread from her palms up her arm, as if his touch had mainlined into her blood.

Max snorted. "His boyfriend will probably have a fit about it."

She studied his face, gauging his mood. "Would you mind a piece of well-meaning advice?"

His expression was hopeful, but there was reserve in his dark eyes. "Bill Cosby says, 'A word to the wise ain't necessary—it's the stupid ones that need the advice.'" He dropped her hand and heaved a sigh. "All right. Hit me with it."

"Do you love your brother, Max?"

"What do you mean? Who told you I don't?"

"Then why do you make those little offhand remarks about him?"

He shifted on the bale, and his eyes skittered away. "We always pick on each other. It's just how we are."

"But it isn't loving if it hurts." She smiled to soften her words. "Can't you see on his face that those jabs hit home?"

Max's face got red. He opened his mouth, but nothing came out.

Instead, he looked out the window at the view of the meadows and the foothills beyond them. Slowly, the taut muscles in his jaw relaxed. Still, he said nothing.

Bree sat in the quiet with him, waiting.

"I don't know how to deal with it—his gayness—if that's even a word. It's one thing to know about it when he's in Boston, but now that he's back, it's impossible to ignore. I can't help but imagine him and his boyfriend..." He flushed even redder.

"But, Max, it's like your Cheyenne blood. He can't change it."

He got to his feet and looked down on her. "Save the lecture. I know the facts. It's living with them that I'm not so good with." He stepped to the door and leaned a fore-arm against the edge, staring out. "I've never known how to handle that part of him. It's like someone telling you to get used to someone walking around with no skin. You know you shouldn't stare, but it's so foreign to you, you can't help it." His words came out tortured in spite of the fact that his face showed no emotion. "I don't want to react that way. I know it hurts when I tease him about it. I think I do it to try to find a way around the elephant between us." He ran a hand through his damp hair, leaving tracks. "I don't know how to get past it."

She stood, walked to him, and ran the backs of her fingers down his cheek. "You just love him, Max. That and time will make it better."

"Your mouth to God's ears," he whispered, and he turned to look out the doorway again, shutting her out.

CHAPTER 13

Thursday evening, when Max met Wyatt at the head of the stairs, they both stopped short and looked each other over. Max wore tan dress pants, Wyatt's were blue, but they both had on white, collared dress shirts. Wyatt raised an eyebrow.

Max shrugged. "Hey, it's a business meeting." They started down the stairs. "I sure hope Bree can cook. I could eat two-day-old roadkill right about now."

"In that case, it really doesn't matter how well she cooks, does it?" They turned into the front hall, boots loud on the wood floor. They jostled at the door to the kitchen, both trying to get through first. They burst in to find the table in the nook bare, pans bubbling on the stove.

Wyatt shrugged. The swinging door between the kitchen and the formal dining room opened, and Bree swept in.

Wow, Max thought, what a difference a day made. Their stable hand had morphed into a businesswoman, and by the look, one to be reckoned with. Her hair was up in a fancy French twist, and she wore an ivory silk blouse and a camel pencil skirt. She was all business. His fingers itched to mess her up a little.

Wyatt looked down. "Nice shoes."

"Thanks. They're last year's Jimmy Choo's, but I love them."

Jimmy chews? Max looked down. He didn't know about shoes, but he sure could recognize a great pair of legs in silk.

"Dinner will be served in the formal dining room, gentlemen." When she smiled, Max glimpsed his Bree under the makeup. Well, not *his* Bree. *Not yet anyway.* Before he had time to herd that stray thought, Wyatt stepped in front of him and bowed, offering her his arm.

"May I escort you, *jeune fille*?"

Max was left to follow.

The dining room appeared a combination of board room and high-class restaurant. The lace-covered table was perfectly set with what he recognized as Wyatt's mother's china and sterling silver. A flip chart on a stand took up one corner, and a pad and pen lay next to each place setting. Wildflowers spilled from the silver-plate centerpiece, and the sunset tinted the room in amber.

"Have a seat. I'll be right back with the salads." She disappeared through the door to the kitchen.

"Wow, that's some groom you hired, Wyatt," Max said, pulling out a chair. "Doesn't mean she can cook, though." He chuckled.

"You're such an ingrate, Max." Wyatt took a seat, but they both jumped up again to help when Bree came back through the door, arms laden with salad dishes. When her arms were empty, she reached for the sideboard to retrieve an open bottle of red wine.

She grinned at Max's long face. "I know you'd rather

have a beer, but push the envelope a little, dude. This is a 2006 Sonoma Coast Failla Pinot Noir, one of the best reds around." She poured them each a half glass, crossed the room to the flip chart, and tossed back the cover to the first page of marching numbers in neat rows. "Here's the plan."

Max tasted the wine, managing not to wrinkle his nose as he put it down. "I figured it out. You were Madoff's personal accountant, weren't you?"

Back to him, she froze, arm half raised. The marker in her hand shook.

It was quiet enough to hear the clock in the kitchen ticking. She lowered her arm, then turned. "No. I—"

"All right, Max, that's enough." Wyatt threw his napkin on the table and stood. "I'm not going to let you bully a lady anymore. You were brought up better than that. You either trust Bree enough to go into business with her, or you don't. And if you've let her cook this big dinner with the intent of turning her down, you and I are going to step outside." Shoulders squared, hands fisted, he loomed over Max. "You'll kick my ass, but then you'll have to feel bad about that, too." Wyatt's soft, reddened cheeks and pursed lips made him look like a sulky five-year-old, but Max wasn't about to tell him that. Besides, Wyatt was right.

"I apologize for my lack of manners, Bree."

Her face went still like she was waiting for a "But."

"I would much rather go into this venture with all my questions answered, but I guess you have a right to your privacy." He looked up at Wyatt. "Sit down, John Wayne."

Wyatt sat.

"I do have one requirement. It's a deal breaker for me." Max wiped his lips on the linen napkin. "High Heather is not part of the deal. We can have a partnership, or a corporation, or whatever, but the land stays in Jameson hands."

Bree turned back to the chart and circled points as she made them. "I have no problem with that, Max. It makes the startup more even. I'll contribute my three head of bucking stock, which will bring in working capital. You throw in your breeding stock. We'll all contribute whatever money we can spare for hauling expenses and to fund a trainer, who we're going to need, at least in the beginning."

They discussed the budget over a roast that had been marinated in something wonderfully spicy, mashed potatoes with rich brown gravy, and flaky biscuits that melted on the tongue. An hour later, they sat drinking coffee, the table strewn with crumpled paper and pages of notes. Max sat back and unhooked the massive silver belt buckle that dug in his gut. He'd even tasted the after-dinner cordial. A sissy drink, but one that packed a surprising punch.

Bree said, "I'll handle getting the articles of incorporation drawn up and filed with the state. There's only one more thing to agree on." She tossed her napkin on the table and stood. "What are we going to call this venture? It should be catchy. Something that relates to what we do, but something that people will remember."

Max spoke up. "High Heather Bucking Bulls."

She walked to the easel and turned to a white page. "I thought more along the lines of using our initials." She wrote, W-A-M. "Wyatt, Aubrey, and Max." She drew a flourish beneath it. "As in Wham! Get it?"

"What's wrong with High Heather?" Max grumbled.

"High Heather's not part of the deal, remember?"

"Well, yours is just dumb. It sounds like a name a girl would think up."

"You're just mad because your name comes last. We could change it to M-A-W, but that is *really* stupid. If you'd get your ego out of it—"

"Oh, now, that's total bull." Max glared across the table at her.

"No, it's fact." Chin stuck out, she glared back.

Wyatt jumped in. "That's brilliant!" They both blinked at him. "Total Bull. That's the name." He tipped his chin to Bree. "It's catchy." Then at Max. "It's manly."

"I like it." Bree beamed.

"I can live with it," Max grumbled.

Wyatt dusted his palms together. "Now, wasn't that easy?"

Bree tossed a dish towel over her shoulder and stood. "I'm glad that's settled. I'll get dessert to celebrate."

"Oh good," Max said. "What are we having?" He took a sip of coffee.

She smiled sweetly. "Orgasm pie."

Max choked. He slapped a hand over his mouth and scooted his chair back.

Bree tossed him the dish towel. "You'd better not ruin Tia's company tablecloth. She'll wear your guts for garters, cowboy." She turned on her heel and sashayed out the door.

Max caught his breath and laughed. "I don't know if this venture is going to make money, but it sure won't be boring."

In moments, Bree was back with a gooey plateful of chocolate heaven. *Those legs, a businesswoman's brain, and she cooks, too.* Max couldn't help but stare.

When Bree poured another cordial, Max raised his glass. "Beauty is worse than wine. It intoxicates both the holder and the beholder." He tossed back the contents of the tiny prissy glass. "Aldous Huxley."

Bree flushed prettily.

Wyatt beamed. "There may be hope for your black soul yet, brother."

Max lowered the chair back on four legs. "Stick around, little brother. I may teach you a thing or two."

Bree held up a hand. "You'd best quit while you're ahead, Max."

The next morning, saddled ponies milled in the corral and cowboys lounged against the fence awaiting orders when Max and Wyatt walked up.

"Mornin', boss."

"Mornin', Armando, men." Max shot a glance at Wyatt, then began. "The Heather is taking a lead change. You all know the beef market is in the toilet. We've seen ranches around Steamboat failing, one by one.

"That's not happening to the Heather if we can help it." He slid his hands into his back pockets. "We—well, Bree—came up with the idea of raising bucking bulls. Wyatt and I have put a lot of decidin' into it, and it just might work. Bree has two more bulls on the way, but we're gonna need more.

"So today I need you to go up to the west pasture and bring down the bulls. Even the one and two-year-olds that didn't go to market."

Wyatt shifted next to him and mumbled out of the side of his mouth, "And the cows."

Max turned and stared him down.

"And the *cows*," Wyatt spread his arms and shrugged. "You know what Bree said. We've got to find out which ones will buck."

Max looked skyward. *Lord, I know you're testing me, but can't you leave me just a bit of dignity?* He'd been a bull rider in high school. No self-respecting cowboy on the planet would be caught dead riding a cow. It just wasn't seemly. He sighed and turned to face the men. "And the cows."

"Have any of you ever ridden a bull?" Wyatt asked.

Armando leaned forward to look down the line of raised hands. "Pedro, mechanical bulls in a bar do not count." The cowboys laughed and elbowed the youngest hand.

Max said, "We're gonna have our own buckin' contest, just like the PBR. Any man that can go eight seconds gets an extra day off and a little cash to take to town."

CHAPTER 14

A week later, Bree hesitated in the aisle of Walmart, eyes on a skein of hot-pink eyelash yarn. Tia wouldn't find a taker for that on the Heather. She'd have to knit something for herself.

Bree put two skeins in her basket and walked to the checkout line. Families crowded the aisles. Kids darted around their parents' shopping carts like hummingbirds around a feeder. She relaxed, leaning her forearms on the cart. Today was the first day that a crowd hadn't made her feel jumpy.

Wyatt walked up and dumped an armload of jeans, work shirts, and socks in the cart. "I ran into my high school English teacher in the underwear aisle! You have to love small towns."

"This place is a zoo. Are they giving away free beer?"

"It's like this every Saturday," Wyatt said, unloading the cart onto the conveyor. "It's like the old town square—as much a place to socialize as a marketplace."

Out of the corner of her eye, Bree caught a flash of

gold on blue serge. She stiffened and whipped her head forward.

Behind her, two policemen stood in line.

Sweat gathered under her arms.

Taking her items from the basket, she tried to ignore the men's heavy presence at her back. Her fingers fumbled, and she dropped several metal knitting needles. They tinkled as they hit the floor and rolled. Bree bent, but the cop was quicker. He squatted and retrieved them, reaching under the candy display for the last one.

"Thank you." She accepted the needles with a shaking hand and stood.

She felt the hot laser of professional scrutiny slide over her body. "Are you all right, miss?"

She ducked her head and looked away, to hide the scar. "Fine. Thanks." She spun back to Wyatt's raised eyebrow. She knew she was behaving oddly, but her sluggish brain couldn't conjure normal.

Dammit, Bree, settle down. You don't have "convict" stamped on your forehead.

Her palsied fingers slipped off the closure on her wallet. Wyatt pulled the cart through and then stepped between her and the cops. His solid presence and steady touch at her elbow calmed her enough to pay the cashier.

Finally, she was free to go. She forced her feet to a sedate pace to the parking lot.

"Bree, what's wrong?"

She sped up, leaving Wyatt's question behind. At the car, she juggled the keys, almost dropping them. When she got the door open, she tossed the bag on the floorboard and relaxed the frozen tendons in her knees enough to sink into the seat. She jammed the key in the ignition and waited for Wyatt.

There is no reason to get riled up. It's not like you're wanted for something. But the rush of adrenaline negated logic. Her heart raced and blood pounded in her ears.

"Bree, you're obviously upset. Why don't you let me drive?" She jumped at Wyatt's voice, her butt actually leaving the seat. He stood, hand on her door, frowning.

She put up a palm, as much to halt argument as to hide from his worried gaze. "Please. Wyatt. Just get in."

He didn't look convinced, but complied.

When he was in, seat belt fastened, she wheeled out of the parking space and sped to the exit.

"Bree, talk to me."

"Give me a minute here, will you? Traffic is nuts." What was she going to tell him, that she had a phobia for cops? Thoughts scurried through her brain like panicked mice.

At the main street, she signaled left and pulled out. A horn blared. She whipped her head to the right. A truck bore down on them too fast. Its tires locked and squealed, laying rubber.

"Shit!" Wyatt flinched back.

She floored it. The engine roared and the Jeep sprang into traffic, the rear fishtailing as the tires found purchase.

Oh my God. She'd totally misjudged the oncoming truck's speed. Blood throbbed in her head, louder than the engine whine. Keeping the accelerator buried, she shot a look in the rearview mirror, expecting blue strobe lights. All she saw was the truck she'd cut off, retreating behind them.

"Take the first turnoff you come to." Wyatt's voice squeaked like a stepped-on mouse. He pried his fingers from the dash.

"I'm okay, Wyatt. I just—"

"I think I need to unload my pants."

Seeing his clenched jaw, she decided not to argue.

On the outskirts of town, she took a right onto a narrow dirt farm road. She drove several hundred yards, pulled over, and shut down the engine.

Wyatt let out a long breath.

The wind hissed through the curtain of oats on either side of the road. Cawing crows argued on the barbed-wire fence, voicing their displeasure at the disturbance. The sounds leached into Bree's mind, smoothing her roiled thoughts. Her shoulders had dropped below her earlobes when Wyatt spoke.

"I know who you are."

In her core, a gut bomb of acid exploded. She wanted to see his expression, but her neck muscles wouldn't obey. She saw only her fingers, thin claws, whitening on the steering wheel.

"I have a friend. He manages the IT department for the State of Massachusetts."

Massachusetts? That couldn't—

"He has access to the DMV records."

I've never even been that far Eas—

"For the entire country."

In her narrow field of vision, her fingers loosened and then disappeared as her hands thumped into her lap. Fingerprints smeared the steering wheel, and a thin layer of dust covered the dash. Funny, she'd never noticed that.

"You changed your name on your driver's license. But the Jeep's plates are registered to Aubrey Madison. Once I had the name, Google did the rest."

The wind died. The crows fell silent. The world seemed

to stop as her mind snapped a picture. No doubt it would be added to the nightmarish film that ran through her head before sleep most nights.

When had she let down her guard? Somewhere in the comfortable routine of days, denial slipped in unnoticed. Now she was going to pay. What had she been thinking? She'd known she was different. An albatross hiding in a flock of sparrows.

Idiot.

Nothing to do now but drive home, pack, tuck tail, and run.

"Talk to me, Bree."

Home? When had the Heather become home? Thoughts blew through her head, but she was too discouraged to chase them down. It didn't matter when, anyway. Shame bloomed in her chest. Her heart pumped billows of it, coursing through her body. It burned.

"Trust me, Wyatt, you don't want to know."

"Yeah, I do."

If his voice had been demanding, torture wouldn't have pulled it out of her. But it wasn't. It was soft and cool like butter on a burn.

"I know what old secrets can do, Bree. You bury them in the back of your mind and try to forget. Yet they sit there, like a nugget of radioactive plutonium. Poison leaks into everything." He rubbed his forehead like it hurt. "Until it takes you over. It becomes the sum total of what you are, until you forget you were ever anything more. You *are* the secret. You need to tell someone. I'm here. Talk."

She dropped her head to the steering wheel.

She was so damn tired. Tired of running like a manic hamster on an exercise wheel. Tired of not sleeping in a futile effort to keep the memories at bay. Maybe if she just let the damn things come, she'd get some peace. Besides, now that the cat was out, she had nothing to lose. For the first time since her release, unconsidered words fell from her mouth.

The Feds had played hardball. She'd told them to investigate Vic, but he'd covered his tracks well. He'd gone to ground, leaving the eBay account untouched since her arrest. All roads led back to her. Feds traced the money to an offshore bank account in Mexico, but without the number and password, they couldn't get to it. Aubrey wanted to help them, but she didn't know the number. The account wasn't hers.

Intimating that she'd change her mind soon, the agents left. Not an hour later, a guard came to her cell, ordering her to collect her things as he unlocked the door. They were moving her into the general population. No more single-cell, solitary exercise time, or meals alone.

Arms full, her too long orange prison pants slapping with every step, he led her through locked doors to another wing of the jail. A cacophony of catcalls rained on her as she strode the gauntlet between the rows of cells.

"Fresh meat!"

"Oohh, isn't she a pretty one?"

"I see you later, *puta*!"

They wouldn't really *leave her here, would they?*

They did. She was locked in a ten-by-ten cell with three women who terrified her with their prison tats, tough talk, and hard eyes. Bree took the only open bunk on top and tried not to cower.

On the call with her attorney the next day, Aubrey was frantic when he promised to look into it. Look into it?

This wasn't a research project, for chrissake. It was her life! In hindsight, maybe a jail wall hadn't been the best place to look for an attorney, but she'd paid him a huge retainer and didn't have money for a better one.

Before she hung up, Aubrey asked him what *La eMe* was. Her cellmates spoke mostly Spanish to each other, but this word came up several times, and it sounded important.

His hesitation told her she wasn't going to like the translation.

The Mexican Mafia.

He rushed on to placate her with assurances that he was busy preparing for the trial. He said there was no way the jury would convict her on the meager amount of evidence the Feds had. All she had to do was hold tight, be safe, and stay out of trouble.

She'd wrapped her heart in that flimsy blanket of hope and hung up.

The prisoners were allowed out twice each day, once for showers, once to "exercise" in the yard, a hard-packed dirt square surrounded by guards and razor wire. Day after day, Aubrey kept to herself, trying to perfect her dismal attempt at invisibility. Her thoughts ran in an endless, useless loop, never coming any closer to a solution.

Her cellmates didn't address her directly, using English only when they wanted her to overhear. Aubrey wished they'd left her ignorant. She learned that the smallest of them, Lupia, a pretty Latina with a tattoo of an eagle and a snake in a flaming circle over crossed knives, was the girlfriend of one of the Mafia's top lieutenants.

They called Aubrey *carne ratón*—mouse meat.

One night, a week into her personal hell, Lupia's whisper cut into Aubrey's feverish thoughts. She said Aubrey would be getting a conjugal visit from her "boyfriend" soon. He would give her drugs. She was to stash them in her *almeja* and bring them to Lupia.

Maybe it was the darkness that emboldened Aubrey. Or maybe she was losing hope.

She just said no.

Her cellmates laughed. She didn't need to worry about being caught. Her boyfriend would be a gringo, and the guards would never suspect a *princesa* like her. Aubrey should thank Lupia; she'd even get laid!

Aubrey bit her tongue until the iron taste of blood filled her mouth. Giving in to hysteria wouldn't get her anywhere with the guards, and the scent of fear would only frenzy the pack. Aubrey knew if she were caught with drugs, any chance she had of walking out of this hellhole would vanish.

Turned out, she'd been naive to think things couldn't get worse.

Two days later, Aubrey was showering with seven women she didn't know when Lupia's soldiers came. As she turned to rinse soap from her face, she was grabbed from behind and wrestled to the floor.

Her head cracked on rough cement, leaving her dazed for precious seconds as water pelted her face. Her hair was caught in a viselike grip as a brown face filled her vision, features contorted with hate, waving what looked like a toothbrush in her face. Light glinted off a wicked shard at the tip. Panic surged, but fear immobilized her.

The girl's wet hair hung in a curtain, cutting off Aubrey's peripheral vision. "You can let go," she'd growled. "She won't scream. Will you, *ratón*?"

The weight on her limbs lifted. Aubrey felt a prick at

her throat and jerked. A sticky warmth trickled down her neck. She was going to die on this filthy cement floor.

Screw that! Fueled by desperation and the adrenaline held inside since she'd been dumped in this shithole, Aubrey clubbed the girl's temple with her fist. She collapsed, unconscious, on Aubrey's chest, but before she could scrabble from under, the others were on her.

A dark-skinned, pockmarked girl straddled her chest. "You wanna play, *puta*?" She spit in Aubrey's face. "You don't even know the game." She cocked her head. "I tell you what, white girl. I give you a necklace to remember me by." A laser of molten pain burned an arc down Aubrey's throat.

The artery pumped straight up: a geyser of crimson, spraying them all. Aubrey screamed in pain and horror, blinded by blood. She heard scrabbling and then they were gone. Aubrey slapped her hands to her throat, frantically trying to hold the gaping skin together and stop the heat of blood sheeting down her neck.

She was alone, with the sound of water drumming on the floor, the coppery smell of blood, and the chill of shock and cold cement seeping into her bones.

Bree lifted her head from the steering wheel to stare through the windshield. "I woke up in the prison infirmary. What passed for a doctor there told me the artery had only been nicked, that I was lucky to be alive. I was on the fence about that. My attorney assured me that I'd be returned to a solitary cell, and even if I were convicted, the judge would grant leniency due to the 'incident.'" As if the words were emptying her, her voice diminished to a breathy whisper.

"I got four years, to be served in a Federal penitentiary. Club Fed may not have been up to Martha Stewart's standards, but it looked like heaven to me."

She reached to trace the scar, surprised to find it wet. When Wyatt handed her a tissue, she glanced in the rearview mirror. Her face was mottled, and a red weal stood out on her forehead where it had rested on the steering wheel.

"Feel better?"

She ran a gut check as she dried her face and blew her nose. "Maybe." Both her body and mind quieted, calm after the storm.

If you're going through hell, keep going.

She turned to face Wyatt and what came next.

He gave her a shrug and a slow smile. Something twitched in her mind. "You knew." She snatched the random thought before it was gone. "The first meeting of Total Bull, when you stood up for me. You knew then, didn't you?"

"Yes."

"Then why...?"

"I know it *all*, Bree. I know that the judgment was dropped when your boss got caught."

And she'd thought she was ready for anything. Anything but kindness.

"You're no threat to the Heather. In fact, as a controller and businessperson, we're lucky to have you."

The wind started in the oats again and another crow flew in, to join the group on the barbed-wire fence, setting off a cawing gossip chain. Bree took what felt like her first breath since she'd parked.

"But you're still a threat."

Seeing Wyatt's tight lips, her stomach clenched for the next blow.

"To Max. He cares for you. I haven't been around in years, but I know my brother, and I've never seen him look at a woman before the way he looks at you."

She squirmed in the seat. This was getting complicated.

Wyatt leaned forward, intent. "I'm not going to tell him, Bree, but you have to."

"I know, Wyatt. I will." *Somehow.* "Soon." She started the car and executed the three-point turn that would take them back to the main road. "Oh and, Wyatt? Thanks."

They rode in silence, the secrets on both their minds swirling in the cab of the Jeep. Bree lowered the window to let the wind blow them away. She couldn't wait to get back to the cocoon of High Heather and settle back into her simple life.

Wait. Her life wasn't so simple anymore, was it? She pictured Fire Ant standing in the corral. She owned livestock for cripes' sake!

Her gorge rose. *Total Bull.* What had she done? She'd stopped here, looking for a haven of anonymous mediocrity. Somehow she'd jumped right back into another high-profile business. Hadn't she learned from her last experience? Hadn't she learned the hard way not to trust her own judgment?

"Hey, isn't that Max?" Wyatt pointed to a solitary horseman trailing a few head of cattle in the pasture fronting the road.

When the cowboy lifted his hat, a silly thrill burst inside her, remembering Wyatt's earlier words. Max kicked the horse and cantered up to the fence, matching the speed of the Jeep as she slowed. She pulled over and let the engine idle.

"Hey, guys, where've you been?" He shaded his eyes against the glare of the sun.

In spite of her worries, his broad grin was contagious. "Walmart."

"Well, you know what they say. If they don't have it, you don't need it." He snuck a glance at the cattle, which had stopped to graze. "Hurry up and get back to the house. Tia's making chili rellenos for supper!" He smiled a carefree boy's smile, wheeled his mount, and slapped his hat to its rump. The horse bounded away, scattering the cattle.

Wyatt watched him go. "That's our Max, the sophisticated businessman." He turned to Bree, a fond smile still in place. "I have to admit, even if he is my brother, he's kinda cute, isn't he?"

"Too cute for his own good." Glancing in the rearview mirror, she pulled back onto the road. *And mine.*

How could she possibly worry that a venture with the Jamesons could end up like one with Vic Christakos?

Remembering Max's guileless smile, Bree shook her head. She might not be able to trust herself, but she knew she could trust him.

"Wow, Wyatt, I'm impressed." Max leaned over the desk in Wyatt's bedroom, peering at the corporate website Wyatt was creating for Total Bull.

"Back up, Max. I can't see what I'm doing." Wyatt's fingers flew, and a new page opened. "We'll have a page for our bulls, showing lineage, stats, photos, and semen prices."

A photo popped up. It was of Fire Ant, chewing grass in the field. He looked as scary as a milk cow.

Max snorted. "I hope we're not leading with this one. Maybe we can get some action photos of him when we have the Heather bull-riding event. If he doesn't look better when he's bucking, we're dead anyhow." He leaned in again. "You're a guru at this, Wyatt. Where did you learn to do this?"

Wyatt rolled his eyes. "What do you think I do for a living?"

"I thought it had something to do with writing software, not designing websites."

"That's the advantage of having an IT geek on the team. A software engineer can do lots of stuff. That's what's so fun about the career. Aside from the fact that it makes me a sex magnet. Damn, Max. Will you quit hovering?"

Max got an elbow to the gut, and he sat back. "Not my fault—your typeface is so small, I can't read it!"

Wyatt frowned at him. "Next time you're in town, you need to buy some stronger reading glasses at Walmart, old man."

"There's nothing wrong with my eyes. I'm telling you, the type is tiny."

"Max, there's no shame in needing glasses. This happens to men around your age. It's perfectly understandable." Wyatt's lips quirked. "While you're down there, you may want to pick up some Viagra, because I've heard that about the same time the eyes go, the—"

Whap! Max smacked his brother on the back of the head. "Bro, when I have problems in that department, you can have me put to sleep."

"Well, I can get a rifle out of the gun case and take care of that anytime. You just let me know."

Max chuckled. "You worry about your own little trouser snake, and I'll worry about the mighty Sparky."

Wyatt shook his head. "We're both talking big for two guys not getting any."

"Yeah, how pathetic is that?" He grabbed the mouse and minimized the website. "Hey, Wyatt, do you have that game on here that we used to play in high school?"

"Are you talking about Pong?"

Max nodded, searching the dozens of icons on the desktop.

"You're kidding, right? That was DOS-based Stone-Age stuff!"

"So? I liked it. I was pretty good at kicking your butt on it, too, if I remember right."

"Max, I don't even have a system that would play that crappo game anymore. But I'll tell you what I do have..." He reached into a duffel beside the desk and pulled out two wireless joy sticks. "*Call of Duty*," he said in a reverent tone as he handed one of the sticks to Max.

"What's that?" Max played with the stick. "Hey, where'd you get this? This is cool."

"It's only the best Black Ops game out there." Wyatt clicked on an icon, then sat back, stick clutched in his hand. "Prepare to be blown away. Pong, my ass."

The screen exploded with light and sound.

Max straightened in his chair. "Duuuude."

Three hours later, they took a break. Max walked out the back door and flinched when Slim Tanton's pickup tires crunched on the Heather's gravel drive. It was as if the nightmare of his future had just rolled into the present. Boxes full of Slim's life filled the bed to overflowing. Ropes crisscrossed a green tarp, edges flapping in the wind.

Max walked slowly to the truck. "Looks like you're ready to go, Slim."

"I am. Promised I'd stop on my way out of town, so..."

"Well, come on in and sit a spell. I've got coffee on, and Tia made churros."

The old man stayed put. "I've got to get on the road

before it gets much later, Max, but I'm obliged." His face wrinkled as he squinted up, looking foreign without his ever-present Stetson. The skin of his forehead shone white and vulnerable above his tan line and a few wispy strands of hair that crisscrossed his liver-spotted pate. It seemed only a few years ago his dad and this man were the superheroes of Max's childhood.

"I stopped by the Grange, and they told me what's going on. I have to tell you, I don't envy any of you who are going to try to ranch around here. Just as well that I'm getting out."

Max's stomach did a roller coaster dive—without the thrill. "I've been shorthanded around here and missed the last Grange meeting, Slim. What's going on?"

The old man threw him a pitying look, his jaw working a wad of chaw. "Word is there's big money pushing congress to get the BLM land on the lower slopes closed to open grazing. Someone is throwing serious money around, and legislators are swarming." He spat a stream of tobacco juice out the window. "Greedy bastards. We voted them in to see to our interests, and now they're seeing to their own."

Colburn. This has his greasy fingerprints all over it. Without free summer grazing in the meadows, it would be impossible to turn a profit ranching in Steamboat. *Scritch!* When Max recognized the sound of his molars grinding, he made himself stop. "Surely we're lobbying too?"

Slim snorted. "Yeah, and the money ya'll got is a fart in a windstorm compared to theirs."

Maybe Slim was taking the right way out. *But he has somewhere to go to. You don't.* He managed to say goodbye to his dad's friend without getting maudlin, but when the pickup hit the road, Max turned away, his spirits lower than a snake's belly.

His feet led him to the barn without his say-so. Bree stood tippy-toed in the aisle, sweet-talking a chestnut gelding through the bars of a stall, kissing his muzzle and whispering to him. He smiled. "Is there a line I can use to get me a little of that?" She turned on him with a frown, but seeing his face, hers went all soft and worried. "What is it, Max?" She walked over to stand before him.

He took his hat off and swiped a sleeve over his forehead. "I just said goodbye to an old friend. Guess it made me kinda melancholy."

"Aw, poor fella," She reached up, pulled his head down, and gave him a kiss on his forehead. "I'm sorry you had a bad day, Max."

Up close, he saw the shadow of pain in her eyes. "Looks like I'm not the only one who had a rough day."

"Nah, I'm fine." She trailed her fingers down his face.

He watched her eyes darken. "Yes, ma'am, you surely are." He lowered his head to brush her lips in a soft, tender kiss. Letting up before he lost control, he backed away. "I've got work to get at before dinner." He put his hat on, turned on his heel, and walked away.

CHAPTER
15

A few days later, Max glanced out the window of the mess hall as the men filed out to saddle their mounts for the day. The barn's silhouette was only a darker shadow against the murky charcoal predawn sky. He sat with Wyatt and Bree, making plans and drinking a last cup of coffee.

Armando walked up, hat in hand. "Boss?"

"Yeah, Armando?"

"I was thinking." He turned the hat in his hands. "I would like to learn to train the bulls. I'm good with the horses, and I've worked cattle my whole life."

Max looked to Wyatt, who just shrugged. Then to Bree. "I gather from her squirming that our partner has an opinion."

Straightening, Bree pushed her hair behind her ears. "I've been talking with several trainers online, doing research. I asked a couple of them to come out and train our bulls, but they've got obligations elsewhere." Something niggled at the back of Max's brain. He knew someone who trained bulls... A picture flashed in his mind of a sale ring. "JB Denny! I met this guy at a Kobe beef auction once. He trained bucking bulls for a living."

Bree shook her head. "He's one of the top trainers in the PBR. I e-mailed him. He's too busy with his own operation to fly out."

Max rose from his seat. "Maybe he will if I ask him. I've got his business card back at the house somewhere."

"I've got another idea." She put her elbows on the table, cradling the coffee mug between them. "What if we sent an apprentice to him? Denny might agree, if he could do it without leaving home. It would be cheaper for us that way too. We'd have the expense of Armando's travel and room and board, but the training fees would have to be less."

Max could almost see numbers racing through that pretty head like a ticker on Wall Street. They really had been lucky that day she'd showed up in his filthy barn. He studied her features in the hard fluorescent lights. Under the excitement, she looked beat. The circles under her eyes were darker today, and her face showed strain.

What kind of roads had you been traveling before you hit the Heather, Bree? Will you ever trust me enough to tell me?

She held Max's gaze, chin outthrust, high color in her cheeks. "What do you think?"

"I think it's a brilliant idea." He cleared his throat and looked at his head wrangler. "Would you be willing to do that, Armando?"

"I don't know. I have my job here."

Wyatt broke in. "Max and I could handle the day-to-day supervision. Couldn't we, bro?"

"Sure we could."

When Armando nodded his assent, Max shook his hand. "Thanks, Armando. I can't think of anyone on the Heather who'd be better for the job." The man flushed, settled his hat on his head, and walked out, screen door slapping behind him.

"We'll need to talk about something else." Max sank onto the bench, worry gnats swarming his brain. "The calves brought a good price at market, but training fees will take a bite out of it. There's no money coming in until we've got buckers on the road to events. And it's going to be a long, cold winter."

Wyatt spoke up. "I've got a little money to throw in, but it's not going get us far."

Bree put her mug down with a decisive thump. "Fire Ant will bring in cash. We'll need to train the other two-year-olds I bought—" She broke off as she noticed her partners' hidden smiles. "You'll be sorry you maligned my bull. He'll be a hit on the circuit. You just wait and see."

She's cute when she gets all huffy. Max studied the indignant set to her shoulders as she flipped her hair with an irritated snap of her head. How he'd love to lean over and kiss the pout off those lips. Her delicate lemon scent drifted to him, and he recalled that proud head thrown back, eyes blurred with want. He watched color rise from her collar and realized he was staring.

"Well, by all means, I didn't mean to *malign* your bull." He held up a hand and really tried not to smile. She looked like a little cat, spitting and fluffing her tail. "I think we'd better work out a plan B, just in case."

Wyatt kept his face carefully neutral. "You have to admit, Bree, it's the fiscally responsible thing to do."

Max enjoyed the view of that heart-shaped butt in snug jeans as she stomped to the door.

She turned. "I think a closed mouth gathers no boots." Lifting her chin, she sniffed and flounced out.

Max swore she twitched her tail.

A half hour later, he sat at his desk at the main house, digging through the flotsam in the lap drawer. "Aha!" He pulled lint from a dog-eared card announcing, "Denny Bucking Bulls," and dialed the number.

"Denny Bucking Bulls, Charla Rae speaking." The chirpy woman's voice was a surprise.

"Yes, ma'am. I'm Max Jameson, from the High Heather Ranch, in Colorado. Could I speak with JB, please?"

"Sure thing; hold tight." The phone rustled. "Hon? There's a Max Jameson from Colorado on the line."

A click. "Well, if it isn't the beef masseuse—how you doing, Max?"

Max laughed. He'd been looking over a lot of Kobe beef at auction when he'd met the East Texan. "I told you back then, anything gets massaged on this ranch, it's gonna be me."

"And how's that going for you, Max?"

A still photo of Bree's strong, capable hands drifted in his mind. "Well, let's just say I'm working on it. How about you? That wasn't your ex who answered the phone now, was it?"

"Sure wasn't. Charla Rae and I remarried six months ago."

"Well, JB, I'm damned tickled to hear that."

"How about you, Max? Beef prices getting any better up your way?"

"Hell no. Things are getting more dismal by the day. Which is why I thought to call you. I was hoping you wouldn't mind helping out a brand-new bucking-bull operation."

JB laughed. "You? A stock contractor?"

"Well, me, my brother, and a certain lady..."

"Lady? Oh, let me sit down. This I've got to hear."

Bree watched as Tia surveyed her sitting area that evening, her face glowing with a quiet pride. High wingback chairs faced the fieldstone fireplace, soft-toned Navajo rugs underfoot.

Tia occupied the largest bedroom of the sprawling main house. The only one on the ground floor, it had belonged to the elder Jameson until his death, when Max insisted Tia move from the small cubby off the kitchen. She'd protested, saying being close to the kitchen made it easier for her, but her boys wouldn't hear of it.

Bree glanced beyond the sitting area to the cast-iron bed with the old-fashioned white chenille spread. Framed photos of the boys growing up covered the walls. Crossing the room, she was drawn to a large photo that dominated the mantel.

A beautiful, dark-skinned woman sat bareback, astride a flashy paint horse, her long black hair caught lifting in the wind. Fierce pride shone in her eyes, and Bree had the unnerving feeling the woman was staring at her. A solemn child sat before her on the horse.

"That is Ameo'e." Tia's softly accented voice broke into Bree's thoughts. "It means Sacred Road Woman in Cheyenne." She bent to her knitting once more. "Angus called her his Amy."

Bree studied the photo. The toddler was Max, so small and serious. Amy's hands held the reins, her son's pudgy hands grasping her forearms. The raw power of the portrait sucked her in. Max couldn't have been more than three; his chubby legs dangled. A sadness in his solemn eyes pulled at her chest.

Tearing her focus away, she turned. "How did you come to High Heather, Tia?"

"My father, he came north to work as *jefe del caballo*. He broke horses for Señor Angus. I was nine. My mother helped in the kitchen." Tia's needles clicked as she stared into the fire. "I was eighteen when my father was killed by a horse."

Bree walked the few steps to Tia's chair and knelt to rest a hand on her arm. "Oh, Tia, I'm so sorry."

She gave a shake of her head. "It was many, many years ago. My mother went back to live with her people in Mexico. She wanted me with her, but this was the only home I knew. So I said no." There was a twinkle in her eye. "Girls didn't do that then. My mother was angry, but I set my feet like a burro. Besides"—her smile flashed in the firelight—"there was a boy."

"Ooh, this is going to be a good story. Spill it, Ms. Nita."

"Later, maybe." Sharp sparrow eyes bored into Bree. "You tell me about you and my Maxie."

Bree sputtered, a flush of heat spreading up her neck. "There's nothing to tell."

"I know what I see." Tia gave a sage nod. "My Max, he's happy. Different than I've ever seen him."

Bree jerked back, settling on her heels. It was as if the woman had reached into her head and pulled out a secret that Bree had only begun to flirt with. "Tia, you don't understand."

"I understand. You are falling in love with Max. And him you." The older woman's smile slipped as her brows came together. "But I know also that you have much sadness." She reached up to touch Bree's cheek. "And much pain. I am sorry for that." Tia let her hand fall. "I hope you do not let your ghosts come to haunt him too. He carries so much already."

Bree stood and crossed to her chair to retrieve her knitting as silence fell. She'd been wandering through her days, not considering where they led. Glancing to Ameo'e's fierce gaze, she couldn't ignore the ramifications any longer. Was she ready for a relationship? Especially one with a complicated, conflicted cowboy?

Tia, like any mother, had made her alliances clear. And Bree didn't blame her one bit.

CHAPTER 16

In honor of High Heather's first rodeo event, Bree threw a Western saddle over Smooth's broad back. English tack would probably push Max over the edge. She chalked up his black mood at breakfast to his indignation at riding a cow. The cowboys were in the bunkhouse, bragging and preparing to ride in equal measure.

A thrill of anticipation shivered up her spine. Today would be the maiden event of the partnership as well as Fire Ant's debut. She threaded the cinch, then hesitated. Why couldn't they use a buckle like normal people?

"Here, let me do that." Max's deep voice rumbled from behind her.

She jumped. "Jeez, you could give a girl some warning." She put a hand to her stampeding heart. Tanned arms came around her to take the leather strap, and Bree leaned into the comfort of his broad chest.

"You pull it across the front." His breath tickled her ear as he demonstrated. "Now watch. You should be able to do this in your sleep."

She watched the strength in the rough hands that pulled the strap through the D ring before slipping it through the loop.

He snapped the leather tight. "See?"

See? How was she supposed to pay attention with him this close? She took a deep breath. The unique scent of leather and cowboy cologne did good things to her insides. Turning in his arms, she tipped her head to look into his eyes. "God, you smell good, Jameson."

He shifted focus, his gaze homing in on her lips. She held her breath as he leaned closer, his face filling her vision. He hovered there, his dark eyes speaking of things his lips had never said.

The banked flame in her belly flared. With a groan, she grabbed his lapels and fused her mouth to his. No gentle kiss was this. She nibbled his lips, demanding admittance. His ragged breath thrilled her, and his hat fell off as she tangled her fingers in his hair. She wasn't a small woman, but she felt so in his arms. They tightened, flattening her breasts against his chest, sending delicious signals south.

He slowed her in his lazy way, taking his time as his tongue delved. This man did nothing in halves, and everything else faded as she basked in his sharp focus. His hand slid to the small of her back, the other tightening on her butt to press them center to center.

"*Tsk.* Why don't you two get a room?"

Squeaking in surprise, Bree sprang back to see Janet's haughty look.

"It's a sad day when I have to saddle my own horse while the owner has a go with the hired help." With a sniff, she and Peanut strutted by.

Bree gawped.

Max chuckled, sounding pleased with himself. "Don't let her get your goat. She's like that to everybody." He bent to retrieve his hat.

Bree watched Janet stroll out of the barn. "I'm just amazed she knows how to saddle her own horse." Janet must have been in Peanut's stall the whole time. *Of all the people to catch us making out.*

Smooth stomped a hoof, reminding her of the business at hand. She turned to Max. "You'd better go do some stretching. Are you sure you want to do this?"

"Think I'm too old, do you?" One side of his mouth kicked up in grin. "I'll show you what a bit of maturity does for a man." He pulled her into his arms again, and her mind spun away in the sweet demand of his mouth.

The pilot light he'd fired that day at the stream flared faster each time they came together. His lips were firm and knew what they wanted. She ached to give it to him.

"Max?" Wyatt's voice echoed from the end of the aisle. "Where's the—oh. Sorry."

Max growled.

Bree patted him on the butt, relishing feeling sexy and desired. She whispered, "Later, cowboy," in his ear and slipped out of his arms.

A half hour later, Bree leaned an elbow on the top slat of the corral fence, studying the new Stetson in her hands. Max had presented it to her at breakfast, saying that he wasn't going in partners with a city girl who didn't even own a decent hat. She fingered the band, loving the contrast between the creamy white and the narrow woven hatband of bright turquoise and purple. When she'd wondered aloud how he got the size right, Max had flushed and admitted to measuring her baseball cap.

She smiled down at the hat. Maybe she'd managed to work her way around the thick wall of gruff that Max used to keep people away. Or maybe his abrasiveness no longer intimidated her. In any case, she was looking forward to exploring this softer side of Max Jameson.

"Oh, quit your mooning." Wyatt sidled up with a knowing smile.

She put the hat on, ducking her head to cover her blush, wishing her face didn't read like a freeway billboard.

"Okay, we're about ready!" Armando yelled as he entered the opposite side of the corral astride Smooth. Bree had argued that she should work as the safety roper, but the cowboys overruled her, saying the job was too dangerous. She'd grumbled, but knowing it was an argument she wouldn't win, settled for cheering from the sidelines. Armando had chosen Smooth for the job, to see if a Tennessee Walker could work cattle.

"Who's up first?" Wyatt asked.

Bree glanced at the roster she'd printed out. "Pedro. I think he was afraid if he watched everyone else ride first, he'd be too scared to try it himself." She had doubts about letting the youngest hand on a bull. "If he gets hurt, I'm not going to forgive myself."

Wyatt snorted. "You don't understand cowboys. I guarantee you Pedro would rather have a bull stomp his guts than to chicken out."

She shook her head. "What is wrong with you men?"

He put up his hands. "Hey, you won't see this butt anywhere near a bull." He shuddered. "Juan would pass out."

Max yelled from atop the bucking chute. "I declare the First Annual Total Bull Bucking Event officially *begun*!"

The squeeze chute used to confine Heather stock for

vet exams was pressed into duty as a bucking chute. The bull inside it looked even larger with little Pedro perched on top, one hand in the air, the other in a death grip on the rope, his hat jammed so far down that his ears stuck out sideways.

The gate swung open into the arena. Bree squinted in case she had to close her eyes quickly to block out the wreck. Nothing happened. Max leaned over and swatted the bull on the rear with his hat, and it exploded out of the chute. Running, it sped to the exit gate, crow-hopped a couple of times, and then stood, waiting to be let out.

Armando trotted over and grabbed Pedro by the collar. Smooth backed up, pulling him to safety. He dropped the teen at the bucking chute, where the cowboys atop the fence yelled and hooted.

"Whooeee! Guess you showed him what for, Pedro!"

"That one's a Big Mac for sure, boss."

"We'll run a better 'un under you next time, *pequeño vaquero*."

Pedro, flushed and smiling, climbed the fence. "Not his fault. I just scared him." The cowboys roared and pounded his shoulders.

"Well, that one was a bust." Bree crossed the bull's number off her sheet.

The sun beat down as the event progressed through five more bulls. None bucked well enough to be considered for training. Bree was hot, dusty, and discouraged.

"You knew the odds of finding a good bucker in our stock were slim, Bree." Wyatt took off his hat and wiped a sleeve across his sweaty forehead. "It'd be like winning the Kentucky Derby with a cart horse."

"I know, but I'd hoped." She put the clipboard down

to climb to the top rail. "Fire Ant's up next. Those four-legged wannabes will get a lesson on what a buckin' bull is supposed to do."

"Who's the rider?" Wyatt's eyes widened. "Tell me it's not Max."

"No way." She chuckled. "This is a job for somebody young enough to think he's invincible."

Wyatt put a hand to his chest. "Oh, thank God. His rodeo days are ancient history, and I was afraid he was going to pull some hairy caveman routine to try to impress you. I've only begun to get my brother back, and it wouldn't do for him to get killed just yet."

"Miguel is giving it a try. His was on his high school rodeo team, so he's got some experience."

"Miguel? Isn't he a bit ... *large* for Fire Ant?"

She knew he turned his head to hide a smile. "Dammit, why do you all make fun of my bull?" She crossed her arms. "You'll see."

Across the arena, she watched Miguel lower himself onto the bull's back. Fire Ant stood calm in the chute, looking bored, his head turned to look through the slats.

Bree cupped her hands around her mouth and yelled, "You go, Fire Ant. Kick butt, baby!"

The cowboys laughed.

"If you get in trouble, Miguel, just stand up. He'll run right out from under you!"

"Cross your spurs under his belly, *amigo*!"

Miguel nodded. The gateman pulled the chute door wide. Fire Ant went ballistic. He burst out of the gate and bounced straight up, all four feet off the ground. He landed stiff-legged with a bone-jarring thump, and started bucking and spinning. Miguel's weight shifted to his back pockets in the first leap, and the bull spun faster with every revolution. Miguel tried to adjust to the centrifugal force pulling him to the outside, but slid farther and farther off his rope, until he lost his grip entirely. He was slung off the bull and hit the corral fence with a crack, landing in a heap in the dirt.

Armando trotted in on Smooth, herding the bull to the open exit gate. The men vaulted off the fence, running to Miguel, who lay flailing like a turtle on its back.

Wyatt grabbed Bree's arm to keep her from jumping into the arena. "Stay here."

"But he's hurt."

Max was the first to kneel by the fallen cowboy. He talked to him calmly, then stood. The cowboys surrounding Miguel helped him up.

Max looked to where Bree wriggled, held back by Wyatt's restraining arm. "He's okay," he shouted. "Just had the wind knocked out of 'im."

Bree climbed down outside of the fence and stood on mushy knees. "I've been so involved with the business that I forgot how dangerous this sport is. I don't know if I can take it."

Max jogged up. "Hell, Bree, Miguel gets hurt worse than that squatting with his spurs on."

Glancing across the arena, she could see the cowboy moving under his own power, dusting himself off. When Pedro handed Miguel his hat, he jammed it on his head and swaggered to the gate.

Bree and Wyatt trotted the outside perimeter to stand behind the cowhands.

Max said, "Okay, men, we're down to the cows. Who's first?"

Silence.

"Oh, come on. You guys were rarin' to go a few minutes ago." He shoved his hands in the pockets of his jeans. The cowboys found important things to catch their attention. Everywhere else.

He made a disgusted sound. "I guess it's gonna be me, then." Bree reached for his arm, but then let her hand drop. She might not know everything about cowboy law, but she did know it would belittle Max in front of the men if she tried to stop him.

He settled his hat a bit tighter on his head. "Remember one thing." He hesitated until, one by one, he held the men's attention. "If it gets back to town that I rode a cow, somebody's gonna be stringing fence for a month."

"You go, Maxie," Wyatt said under his breath.

Max glared at them all, then stomped to the chute, spurs jingling.

Bree swallowed audibly. "I think I'm going to throw up."

Wyatt laughed and threw his arm around her shoulder. "He's gonna be fine, Bree. Didn't you know Max rode the Colorado circuit back in the day? Used to piss my dad off, too. He said the only reason Max rode bulls was to meet pretty nurses."

She shook her head. "Maybe so, but that was many moons ago, Tonto."

"True, but Max's head is too hard to get hurt. You, of all people, know that."

Yeah, but there are parts of that body I'd like to become fond of.

The men had brought the three- and four-year-old cows from the mountain pastures, and they were wild. When Max lowered himself onto a black cow with

wicked long horns, she reared, trying to climb out of the
tight box. Max backed up in a hurry. Pedro strung a rope
through the slats over the cow's neck to keep her from
rearing again. Armando pulled the bucking rope taut as
Max lowered himself again. He shoved his hand into the
loop in the rigging, took the tight rope, and wrapped it
around his hand, locking his fingers over it with a pound
of his fist.

Wyatt leaned on the fence, a twitching muscle in his
jaw belying his assurances. Bree sat, elbows on knees,
hands covering her eyes, peeking through her fingers.
She swallowed again, her queasy stomach churning like a
washing machine.

Max nodded. The gate swung.

The cow burst from the chute, grunting and bucking. Saliva flew from the animal's mouth as it spun in a
frenzied attempt to rid itself of the weight. Max caught
the rhythmic pace perfectly, rocking forward and back to
negate the animal's power.

Time slowed for Bree as the image burned in her mind:
Max in a red shirt and leather chaps, balanced like a gym-
nast on the straining animal, his face a mask of concen-
tration. Churned dust shimmered in the air as the hands
yelled, cheering their boss on.

Tonio blew a shrill whistle when the eight seconds
were up. Nobody explained it to the cow, though; she
spun, getting stronger with every rotation. Max wrestled,
trying to get his hand out of the rope. As Armando trotted up, Max finally freed himself and was launched. He
landed on his feet, but the forward momentum made him
stumble. He ran a few steps and fell forward, flat on his
face, raising a cloud of dust.

Armando and Smooth cut the cow toward the gate. The minute the animal cleared the corral, Bree and Wyatt were off the fence, running across the arena. The cowboys were faster.

Bree broke into the circle of shouting men to see Max, sitting in the dirt, grinning like a little kid, a smear of green cow poop spread from his hat brim to his waist.

Wyatt burst out laughing and slapped his brother on the back. "That one's a keeper."

Max looked at the men around him, a swagger in his voice. "Okay, you pussies, who's next?"

Bree slapped her hand over her mouth and ran, barely making it out of the corral before upchucking her breakfast in the dirt. Sides heaving, she leaned her hands on her knees and tried to catch her breath.

Max's arm came around her waist. "Bree? What's wrong?" He pulled a clean handkerchief from his back pocket and held it out to her.

She wiped her mouth, then whirled to face him. "You idiot! You could have been killed! I don't care about your stupid cowboy code. I'm *never* watching you do that again."

His cocky grin pissed her off even more. "Darlin', a bull is like a dancing partner—you have to let him lead."

Her stomach lurched. She pushed him away, being careful where she put her hands.

"Come on. Let me help you."

She sagged against the fence, head between her knees, pictures of what could have happened to him whirling in her mind. She waved her hands at him. "Do me a favor and stand downwind, will you?"

• • •

Max smoothed his hands over his hair, squeezing out the last of the water. Turning off the shower, he stepped out and grabbed a towel from the rack.

Bree was irked with him. *Nothing new there.* Although, looking back, he had to admit he'd been a bit rough around the edges when she first met him. Between Jo's quitting him, his father's death, and the ranch's problems, he'd been on a six-month streak of foul mood. He now regretted the bad impression he'd made. He'd been touched by her misguided worry this afternoon. And then there was that smoking kiss in the barn.

So what're you gonna do about it?

If she were a country girl, he'd know what to do. He'd take her to the Double Z for a beer and some slow country songs to snuggle up and dance to. But Bree wasn't a country girl. He remembered her, perfectly coiffed, discussing wine with Wyatt at dinner while Max sat there like a clueless hick.

He pulled on his jeans and jerked open the door. "Wyatt!" He padded down the hall in his bare feet. "Where the heck are you?"

Wyatt's bedroom door opened and he stuck his head out. "Is the house on fire?"

"No. I need your help."

Wyatt stepped aside and waved him into the room that Max hadn't been in since his brother arrived. A huge computer monitor with two towers on either side took up most of the desk space, wires snaking everywhere. Max noticed a framed photo centered on the nightstand. Wyatt grinned into the camera, his arm around a shorter brown-skinned man. Max's face heated, and he averted his eyes, feeling like he'd just seen his brother naked.

"What wouldn't wait until you fastened your jeans, Max?"

He looked down. "Oh." He buttoned his Wranglers. "I need the name of a good wine."

Wyatt looked over his reading glasses. "*That's* what you're in an all-fired hurry about?"

"I want to make up to Bree for scaring her this afternoon. I know she likes wine, and I thought I'd take her a bottle."

"Let me get this straight. You're asking me for dating advice?"

Max felt the tips of his ears heat. "You're right. Bad idea."

Wyatt grabbed his arm as he tried to brush by. "Hold on, now. What did you have in mind?"

Max looked at his still wet feet. "I don't know. I thought I'd buy a bottle and give it to her."

"Oh, that's smooth, Max." Wyatt rolled his eyes. "Sit down. This may take a while."

Max hesitated outside Bree's closed door, a handful of wildflowers wilting in his sweaty hand. *Come on, Jameson. You're not in junior high, for chrissake.* He forced himself to knock.

"Hang on." Her muffled voice came through the door.

He heard the chain drop and the door opened. She looked great in a business suit, but this was his Bree: smiling, no makeup, hair barely restrained in a ponytail. Her creamy skin glowed smooth and perfect. Well, except for the scar. She wore nothing but a sports bra and a tiny pair of spandex shorts, her feet bare. A pink crystal in her belly button winked in the light. He swallowed. Audibly.

She smiled. "Come on in, Max."

He thrust the flowers at her. "These are for you."

Looking down at the ragged bouquet, her face flushed. Then she beamed up at him, as if he'd given her a winning lottery ticket. "Thank you." Sniffing the air, she cocked her head. "Max Jameson. Are you wearing cologne?"

"I wanted to make a better impression on your nose

than I did this afternoon." Not knowing what to do with his hands, he slipped them into his pockets, hopefully disguising the tent between them. He'd never understood body piercings, but he was starting to warm to the idea. He leaned against the doorframe. "Whatcha doing?"

"Yoga. It relaxes me."

Funny, it's having the opposite effect on me.

She poured water from a pitcher into a glass on the desk and settled the flowers in it before picking up an oversized denim shirt from the bed and shrugging it on.

What a shame to cover all that pretty skin.

"Aside from the finale, I think today went pretty well. I'd have liked to discover a bucker in your bull stock, but we did find quite a few good cows."

He grinned. "The women on Heather tend to be feisty."

"Good thing for you that they are." She dropped onto the bed. "That solves half the equation. I'm going to use the last of my savings to send off for some semen straws, but we're going to have to decide which PBR bulls we want to sire our string."

He crossed the room to take her hand. "I didn't come here to talk business, Bree."

"You didn't?"

"Come with me." He led her to the door.

She tugged at his hand. "If we're going somewhere, I need to put some clothes on."

"You meet the dress code just like that." He took his time, his glance wandering over her body. "Okay, maybe some shoes."

He waited while she reached under the cot. When she straightened, she had loafers in one hand and what looked like a prescription bottle in the other. Before he could ask, she dropped it in the trash can and dusted her hands. She stepped into the shoes. "I'm ready."

Offering his arm, he led her around the rear of the stable to a grassy area between the building and the pasture fence. It was full dark and the damp grass released a cool, fresh scent. Hundreds of crickets chirped backup to a single locust's solo. He heard her breath catch when she saw his surprise: a round café table for two, covered in white linen, and a vase full of wildflowers. All illuminated in the flickering light of half a dozen votive candles.

He escorted her to a chair and settled her in before pouring the wine.

No, decanting. That's what Wyatt called it. He sank into his chair.

Her smile was luminous, as if he'd poured her the moonlight. "This is some surprise, Max." She sighed and reclined, tilting her head back. "I'd never seen stars like they are here. I go outside nights just to stare at them."

Max pulled his focus from her lean abs and tilted his head back to share the view. "I go to nature to be soothed and healed and to have my senses put in order." He dropped his gaze to find her studying him. "John Burroughs."

"Yes. That's exactly right."

He raised his glass. "May the saddest day of your future be no worse than the happiest day of your past."

The crystal rang as she touched her glass to his. "Amen to that."

He'd seen a wince lots of times, but he'd never before heard one.

She swirled the wine, sniffed it and then took a tentative sip. "Hmmm. This is lovely. What is it?"

"Storybook Mountain Zin. I know you like Napa Valley

wines. It's aged in barrels stored in caves on the side of a mountain." Max took a sip. It would never replace a good Rolling Rock but he could choke it down.

They spoke of inconsequential things—the weather and local gossip. He discovered they both loved football, were ambivalent about baseball, and were bored to death by NASCAR.

Her eyes glinted like chips of topaz as she raised his dad's cut-crystal wineglass to take another sip. He decided she belonged in the candlelight. Her peach-tinted skin glowed. The fine bones of her face and hands reminded him that she no more belonged in his stable than Ivana Trump. But just for tonight, he didn't care what had brought her here. He was going to relish his good fortune.

They laughed, reliving the pratfalls of the day. When he picked up the bottle to fill her glass once more, he was surprised to find it empty.

She gave him a wistful smile. "It's for the best anyway. We've both got to be up early."

She reached a hand across the table to cover his. "Thank you, Max. This has been a perfect evening." She closed her eyes and he watched her breasts rise with her deep breath. "And I haven't had one of those in a long, long time." After a handful of heartbeats, she stood and blew out the candles.

Somehow this woman had burrowed into his world and turned it inside out. Studying the silhouette of her face in the dark, he was overcome by a sense of rightness. She belonged here, with him. When he held his hand out to her, she entwined her fingers in his. She *fit* him.

They strolled in companionable silence to her room.

She stopped in the doorway. The light from the tack

room bathed her face as she turned to smile up at him. To say good night.

It was his move now, but for the first time since high school, Max didn't have a smooth line. All the ones he used to charm buckle bunnies and barflies sounded to him like a fist against meat. Blunt. Wrong.

So instead he blurted the first thing that came to his wine-dampened brain—the truth.

"Bree, you've never gotten to see the good side of me. I've been mad at the world for quite some time now, and Jo's leaving capped it all off. I realize that I took all that out on you. Because you were there, with your beauty, your red hair, and your sophisticated ways." He took her hands in his. "I'm sorry, Bree. Sorry for all of it. If you'll let me, I want to show you that there is a good side to Max Jameson."

Her lips turned up, but when she would have spoken, he put a finger to them. "I've been thinking about your kiss all day." Her smile slipped. "The feel of you through your jeans. You looking at me like you are now." Her whiskey eyes darkened to molten honey, and her mouth opened a bit. "The truth is, since that first day, when I saw those long legs walking toward me, I just wanted to wrap them around me." As he lowered his head to kiss her, he recalled her promise. "Is it later yet, Bree?"

He could hear her breath in the hushed barn. She stood on tiptoe and touched her lips to his. "Oh yeah, Max. It's definitely later."

The anticipation in her kiss granted him admittance. A surge of joy hit his brain even as a lust spread downward. Kissing her, he nudged her farther into the room and kicked the door shut with his heel. Now that he'd gotten through the part of the date he'd rehearsed, he felt twitchy. "It's been a long time for me, Bree. I want to make this special—for both of us."

The corner of her mouth lifted in a sexy smile as she reached up to unsnap the top of his shirt. "I'll try to go slow, Max." The second snap popped. "But it's been a long time for me too." She grabbed his lapels and with a sharp tug, the remaining snaps cracked like pistol shots. "I'm not promising patience." Her lips closed over his as she slid his shirt down, trapping his arms. The sexual tension that simmered in the air all day boiled up. He allowed her to lead the way for only a moment before he fought his arms out of the sleeves and tossed the shirt aside.

Her nails lightly raked his back as his tongue wrestled with hers, their breathing loud in his ears. Using his thumbs, he tipped her head back and trailed kisses over all that exposed tawny skin. As he approached the ropy necklace of scar tissue at the base of her neck, she jerked away.

His gut tightened. That this vibrant, beautiful woman would believe that a scar made her less gorgeous somehow made him want to go pound someone to mush.

He caught her chin, bringing her gaze to his. "You're exquisite, Bree," he whispered, "Every inch of you." Her sad eyes told him how badly she wanted to believe, but didn't. He lightly kissed the edge of the scar and then moved on, to run his tongue over the delicate ridge of her collarbone.

Bree closed her eyes and was lost. Her body now existed only where he touched it. He lightly nipped her shoulder, pulling her into the circle of his arms. Her skin, her lips, her heart, ached to make him hers, this cowboy who'd put the ground back under her feet.

Her shirt disappeared and then her bra. His strong, gentle hands rested on her waist as his gaze took her in. There was a look of wonder on his face and, for the first time since waking up in the prison infirmary, she felt whole.

His light touch smoothed over her rib cage to cover her breasts, palms sliding over her hard nipples. Electric signals shot through her as she arched to his touch. She wanted to bring this man pleasure. Wanted to give him—everything.

Suddenly he was gone. She opened her eyes to see him leaning to turn on the desk lamp.

"I want to see you." His eyes were black smoke where they grazed her body. She reached for him, but he backed away. "Just let me get rid of some extra stuff." He put the heel of one boot to the toe of the other to pry it off.

The last time she'd seen him shirtless, he'd been in the garden with Tia. She hadn't been able to do any of the things she'd imagined. Now...she knelt, and when he pulled off the other boot, she unbuttoned his jeans. He went still and looked down at her. As she released the last button, his hard length sprang into her hands.

I should have known a cowboy would go commando. She tugged his jeans down his muscled legs and he stepped out of them. Running her fingers lightly up and down his length, she reveled in his velvet hardness. It had been so long since she'd caressed a man. She'd almost forgotten...

He bent and lifted her to her feet. "Hon, if you want this to last any time at all, you don't want to be doing that." Cradling her to his chest, he ravaged her mouth, then settled her gently on the bed. She chuckled, reclining on one arm, watching the man who was about to become her lover as he divested himself of clothing. Desire pooled in her belly as she took in the warm-toned skin sculpted by the harshness of working the land. Muscle corded his arms and legs, his stomach flat and taut.

A muscle deep in her core jumped as she melted in molten anticipation. *"Hurry."* She stripped off her shorts and scooted to the far side of the narrow bed.

As he lowered himself to lie next to her, the heat of his skin seared her where it touched. Max's eyes followed the path of his hand as it skimmed her torso. "God, you're lovely." He bent to whisper a kiss across her forehead; then he lowered her lips to hers.

The hot kiss sizzled as they lay plastered together on the narrow cot. Even on their sides, Max was perched precariously on the edge, not an inch between them.

Raising his head, he murmured, "I've got a better idea." He pulled her over him to straddle his waist, and she moaned as her wet core made contact with his hot, smooth skin. The yellow light from the desk outlined the sharp planes of his jaw, his shoulder, his bronzed chest. She delighted in the change in texture as she ran her hands over as much skin as she could reach. Her skin tingled where his gaze roamed. His hands skimmed her ribs, encouraging her to raise her arms. She stretched, understanding that he wanted to see her that way.

"Free your hair," he growled.

Bree tugged the band at her nape, and her hair tumbled down her back and, with a whispery touch, over her breasts. His hands tightened at her waist.

Modesty had no place here. She held his gaze as she leaned down to run her tongue over his nipple.

"Bree." He brought her face to his to kiss her frantically. "Wait." He stretched to reach his pants on the floor and pulled out a condom. She took it from him and ripped it open with her teeth, hurrying to slide it over his pulsing erection.

"Bree, please..."

She smiled. Heady with the power she held over this hard man, she leaned down to tease his nipples with her own. She'd thought only to arouse him, but as her body glided, fissures of pleasure exploded between her legs. She moaned, sliding down until his jerking erection demanded entry.

His fingers squeezed her thighs, but he held himself still, jaw clenched, letting her take the lead. "Is this what you've been wanting, Max?" She slowly lowered herself and felt the head of him glide into her.

"Sweet Jesus," Max growled as he grabbed her bottom, and bucking his hips, plunged into her.

Bree cried out as he filled her, the pressure of him making her frantic for more. As he massaged the sensitive bud in her soft folds with his thumb, bursts of pleasure shot through her. She leaned back and ground against him, to pull him deeper. Faster than she thought possible, an orgasm rocketed like fireworks through her body to explode in her brain. She swayed, keening, as her muscles clenched, milking him, unwinding her. He held her hips as he bucked, once, twice, and let out a hoarse shout.

She collapsed on top of him, dragging air into her starved lungs. She continued the lazy rocking, knowing the shocks that coursed through her traveled through him as well.

As his breathing calmed, the galloping heartbeat beneath her ear slowed. Her muscles were liquid. If she never moved from this spot, she'd die happy. He brushed her hair back for a kiss. A sweet, tender kiss that touched her in places his fingers couldn't. She folded her hands on his chest, resting her chin on them. Smiling, she said, "Well, now, cowboy. I'd say *that* was worth waiting for."

His arms enveloped her, and the warmth lulled her into a dreamless sleep.

Bree was alone when she opened her eyes to morning sun streaming through the high window above her bed. *Sun?* She glanced at the travel alarm on the desk. Six o'clock. *The boss probably won't fire me for being late this morning.* She felt more refreshed than she had in—forever.

She turned off the desk lamp that had burned all night before flopping onto the tousled bed that smelled of Max. Her and Max. She stretched like a house cat in the sun. Muscles she'd held taut for a year and a half now hung slack off her bones. She wallowed in liquid laze, replete.

Max's lovemaking opened a door so long closed that she'd forgotten what lay beyond it. They'd spent the entire night discovering, using all their senses to enjoy each other. After their initial rush, they'd caught a rhythm. Max was strong and patient, reveling in her satisfaction as much as his own. Her last waking memory was of lying on top of him, his arms around her, his heart strong and steady under her ear. "Who knew? All I needed for a good night's sleep was a new pillow."

She smiled, climbed out of bed, and reached for her clothes, then extras, for after her shower. She dressed quickly and as she grabbed the knob, noticed a white slip of paper tucked into the doorjamb.

Good morning, Sleeping Beauty. See you at breakfast. Max.

She hummed a happy tune as she opened her door to a new day.

An hour later, showered and refreshed, Bree walked into the mess hall as the cowboys were finishing breakfast.

"Buenos tardes, chica," Miguel hailed her. "Did we sleep late?"

Surveying the group, she spotted Max sitting at the far end of the table, hands wrapped around a coffee mug. His private, knowing gaze reminded her that he knew what she looked like with her clothes off.

Trying not to blush, she lightly cuffed the back of Miguel's head on her way to the coffee. She batted her eyelashes. "Watching all you big, strong men yesterday flat wore me out." After pouring a cup, she hesitated, unsure of where to sit. Everything seemed different today.

Max was deep in conversation with Wyatt, who was sitting across from him. Without looking up, he patted the bench beside him.

A thrill went through her. *God, Madison, you're acting like a smitten seventh grader.*

Maybe. But this morning hope sang in her blood, and all seemed right with the world. Her body felt clean and light, like the first hot day of summer, when the chill of winter finally leeches out of your bones. She strolled to the table, taking a seat next to her cowboy.

Max turned to her, "We're going over our plans for the Fourth of July." His eyes were full of promises that his businesslike tone belied.

As Wyatt's gaze bounced back and forth between her and Max, a lopsided grin spread across his face. Bree's face heated. His tone was all innocence as he asked, "Do you think Fire Ant is ready for his debut?"

She raised her voice to address the table in general. "That bull was born ready, as yesterday proved. Maybe he'll get a little more respect around here from now on."

She sniffed at the men's chuckles and turned to Wyatt. "So what goes on around here for the Fourth?"

"Only the best celebration in the state. There's a Pro Rodeo all weekend, but Saturday's the big day." He picked up the *Steamboat Pilot* folded at his elbow and shuffled pages until he found what he wanted. "We begin with the Lions Club pancake breakfast down at the Little Toots Park." He said in his best drawl, "That's followed by a five-K run down Lincoln Avenue. Then there's an art festival, barbeque, and of course, fireworks." He looked up. "And that's only the stuff we'd be interested in."

She swiveled her head to Max's deep voice. "Then on Sunday morning, we drive a hundred and ten pair of cattle down Lincoln Avenue, right through town."

"You're kidding me. More than two hundred cattle herded down Main Street?"

Max said, "One pair for every year the town's been in existence, as a reminder of the town's heritage. One that certain people need—especially this year."

Wyatt broke in. "Now, Max, don't get on a rant. The girl wants to know about the Fourth."

Max frowned across the table, then glanced at Bree. "We drive them to the rodeo grounds to be used in the pro events."

Bree perked up. "Pro Rodeo?" At the brothers' nods, she continued. "Why not take Fire Ant and let him decimate the ranks of local bull riders?"

Max said, "I already took the liberty of signing him up. I didn't think you'd mind."

"Mind? Think of the publicity!" She cocked her head. "I don't suppose they'd allow us to enter some of our cows?" She laughed at Max's horrified expression. "I'm just kidding." She patted his hand. "Your secret is safe with us, big guy."

The cell phone in Bree's shirt pocket vibrated, and she jumped. It was early for her mother's daily call. She pulled the phone out. The number on the display wasn't familiar. Flipping it open, she stuck her finger in her other ear. "Hello?"

"This is Estella Estavez, with the IRS. Is this Aubrey Tanner?"

Break over, her muscles snapped to attention. The familiar buzz of adrenaline shot beneath her skin as her heart stuttered and then steadied into a gallop.

"It is." It came out squeaky as a stepped-on mouse.

"I have your application for a Corporate Federal Employer ID number here, but there seems to be an irregularity. We've run a routine criminal history, and I'm picking up a Federal charge under the other name you listed—Madison—but no further information."

Bree cut her eyes to the table, relieved to find Max and Wyatt still engrossed in conversation. "Could you hold just a moment? I can hardly hear you." She stood on shaky legs and strode quickly to the door. Thankfully, the porch was deserted. "I can explain everything."

CHAPTER 18

The pool balls clacked and scattered as Max broke. He rubbed chalk on the tip of his cue and waited for the balls to stop rolling. Wyatt stood across from him, leaning on his stick. After dinner, they'd pulled the dust sheet off the pool table in the corner of the great room.

Wyatt's golden hair gleamed at the edge of the pool of light. "I'll bet this table hasn't been touched since you and I last played."

Max lined up his first shot. "Not much, that's for sure." He snapped it off, wide of his intended target. "Evidenced by my ability, or lack thereof."

He straightened, watching as Wyatt circled the table, moving like a cat stalking a sparrow. The bar-style light above spotlighted emerald felt and cast the rest of the room in shadow.

How many hours had they spent around this table as kids? Years melted away, as he compared the man in front of him to the boy he remembered. Same gold hair and soft features, but somehow so different. Max took a pull from the longneck on the edge of the table.

Wyatt's shot was better. The red three-ball snicked into the pocket, and he ambled to the other end of the table. "I've been meaning to talk to you about something, Max." He sighted down the cue to his next target, the five ball. "Since it looks like I'm going to be here awhile," His elbow jerked and the five was history.

"Yeah?"

Wyatt surveyed the table, eyes darting from one angle to the next, bouncing the cue in his hands. "I'm thinking about inviting Juan out for a week."

Shit. The beers Max had drunk soured in his gut. He and Wyatt had fallen into the habits of the past over the last couple of weeks, rediscovering the closeness they'd shared as kids. *I should have seen this coming.* In all fairness, half the ranch belonged to Wyatt. His home, if he wanted it to be.

Max glanced at the pool table, avoiding Wyatt's eye. *Wyatt and his boyfriend under this roof? In the same bedroom?* He scrubbed a hand across the stubble on his chin. *Damn it, why can't he just leave that crap in Boston?*

Even as he thought it, Max knew he wasn't being fair. But fair wasn't the way the world worked. "Can't we just let those dogs lie, Wyatt?"

His brother speared him with a hard look. "Yeah, we could, Max, but you and I can't go on like this forever, going about our business, acting like we're still kids. Like you don't know I'm gay." He snatched his beer and took a long swig.

Max winced. "Believe me, Wyatt, that is a reality I'm not likely to forget."

The cue clattered as Wyatt tossed it in the middle of the table, scattering balls. "Well, good for you, Maxie."

"What the hell is wrong with you?"

Wyatt paced in the edge of the pool of light. "I'm not that kid anymore. I have my own life. My own love." He strode to the table, leaning on his hands at the edge. "You don't get to be in charge of everything in this sheltered little world, Max. This is who I am." He raked his hands through his hair. "Just try to put yourself in my shoes for a minute."

"I wouldn't have any idea of how to do that."

"I know you don't." He put his palms on the edge of the table and leaned in. "Imagine that you and Bree are a couple. You go places together, but people can't know you're more than friends. Everyone would see your relationship as shameful."

Wyatt started pacing again, his words speeding up. "No, it's worse than that. Everyone thinks you're twisted because you love Bree. Like you're a freak of nature. You try to ignore them, to tell yourself they can't dictate your life, but it's so insidious—that judgment. Like water in a flooded basement, it seeps into everything and ruins it."

Max squirmed. Half of him wanted to tell Wyatt to man up and deal with it. After all, he'd been gay his whole life. But the other half wanted to hunt down those people who hurt his little brother and pound them to dust.

Wyatt continued. "Eventually you end up dealing with it one of a couple of ways." He ticked off the points on his fingers. "Either you act out, figuring if they don't like it, you'll shove it in their faces." He raised another finger. "Some people can't stand the pressure and kill themselves." He raised a third finger. "Or you run away.

To somewhere where you can be accepted for who you are, somewhere you don't need to hide anymore." His brother's sad eyes were a rebuke. "You know which one I chose. And now you know why."

Max forced himself to hold Wyatt's stare. "I was proud of you when you left."

Wyatt stopped pacing. "What?"

"You put up with so much crap, from the kids at school, from Dad, but it never broke you." Wyatt shot him a shocked glance. "Instead of fighting a battle you couldn't win, when you'd had enough, you took yourself out of it. That takes guts, and I've always admired you for it." The cue stick flexed in his white-knuckled hands. *Why is it so hard to say the truth?* "I should have told you long before now."

"I've always felt like I took the coward's way out."

In his small voice, Max felt the huge shame his brother lived with all these years. "Look at me, Wyatt." He waited until his brother's head came up. He willed his fingers open and the cue clattered onto the table. "I *am* trying, even if it doesn't look like it. This is a gut-level reaction for me. I know it hurts you. I'm struggling to figure out how to get around it.

"Look, I realize we're not kids anymore. I guess I keep going back to that because that's when you and I were comfortable with each other. Like if we start there, maybe we can build a bridge to now and it will all work out." He put his hands in his pockets. "I know it must look like I'm ignoring the fact that you're . . . Shit, Wyatt, I don't even have the vocabulary to talk about this." He reached over to mess up his brother's perfect hair.

"Can you give me some time to figure out how to handle all this? You know people around here, and we are trying to start a new business. I promise I'll think about what you said. And about having Juan visit."

"I'm not going anywhere, Maxie." Wyatt raised his beer in an insolent salute.

Max whipped out a hand to cuff the side of his brother's head. "And quit calling me Maxie, you little punk."

A week later, in the kitchen of the main house, Bree shuffled through the pile of paper on the kitchen table.

"What are you looking for?" Wyatt asked from behind his laptop.

"I just had that darned schedule." She looked up as Max stomped in.

He hung his sweat-stained hat on the rack beside the door and wiped his face on his sleeve. "Damn, but it's hot out there."

"I'd kick off those boots, bucko. If you track that"—she wrinkled her nose—"stuff all over Tia's clean floor, she's gonna tear strips off your hide."

Max sighed and toed off his boots, then padded to the refrigerator to get a beer. Twisting it open, he gulped half of it in one swallow.

She'd barely seen him the past few days. He'd worked from before dawn until dark, shouldering Armando's duties as well as his own. "This will all pay off when Armando's home in a month. Thanks to your buddy JB, he's going to be the best apprentice trainer in the business."

"Yeah, keep telling me." Max padded to the table to drop a quick kiss on her lips. "You're fresh as a cool breeze." He pulled his damp shirt away from his sweaty chest. "Thought about you all day." He smiled down at her. "Well, you and that beer."

"That's my brother." Wyatt chuckled. "He'd charm the socks off a snake."

Max leaned over to peer at the computer screen. "Whatcha doin'?"

She closed the laptop. "Nothing we need to discuss right now."

His look hardened. "What is it?"

She hated to put more weight on those broad shoulders. But he'd need to know eventually. "I'm signing Fire Ant up for the PBR Challenger Tour." She picked up the schedule. "It's expensive, though. Even if I only enter him in the events closest to the Heather, there's travel expense, gas, and hotels. Add to that the expense of Armando's training." Her voice tapered off. "We'll run through the proceeds from the calf sale by fall."

Max dropped into the chair next to her.

She rushed on. "Now, there is an upside. Fire Ant *will* win." She glanced at the spreadsheet on her laptop. Coward that she was, she couldn't stand to see his face while she told him the rest. "But that won't do much more than offset the costs. To really make money, we've got to be taking a full trailer of bulls to an event." She pooked. Weary lines cut deep on his chiseled face. She lifted her hand to cover his, then let it fall back to the keyboard. He wouldn't accept comfort now. Better to just get it all out.

"We're going to need more working capital. I've run through all my savings, inseminating the cows. I have no doubt that we're going to have a promising crop of calves next spring, but…"

"They're not going to start working for three years. We've got to survive until then."

"Yeah."

Wyatt cleared his throat. "I can get us money." He had their undivided attention.

"I've talked to Juan about our corporation, and he's intrigued. He'd like to buy stock."

"I don't know about that, Wyatt." Max's face was as stony as any on Mount Rushmore.

Wyatt ignored him and addressed his comments to Bree. "I'm not talking about a partner. He wants to buy nonvoting stock as an investment."

"We don't need your boyfriend's charity." His voice sounded like a peach pit in a garbage disposal.

"Charity?" Wyatt ran a hand through his hair, mussing it. "Jesus, Max, will you pull your head out? He's researched the industry. He knows what he's getting himself into. Do you realize that bull riding is the fastest growing sport in America? There's lots of money to be made here, and he knows it."

Bree broke in. "I could run some numbers."

"This is moving too fast." Max shook his head. "The corporation has barely been formed, and already we're looking for money."

Bree broke in. "You saw the budgets. You knew that this was a possibility."

"I know. But the reality of going deeper in debt to pull ourselves out—"

"It's not debt, Max; it's stock. That's on the equity section of the balance sheet, not liability side. Corporations do this all the time."

"Yeah, but Jamesons don't." Max ran his fingers through his hair.

Wyatt's concerned gaze raked his brother. "Are you

sure this isn't about offering stock, but about who wants to buy it?"

Max lifted his beer and drained it. "Of course not. I told you I was working on that, Wyatt, and I am." He looked at Bree. "I don't care where you put it on your pretty balance sheets. It's money someone's banking on getting back, and I'm not comfortable with the risk." He slammed the empty bottle on the table and stalked out.

Bree surveyed the milling cattle churning dust in the stockyard corral, pride swelling in her chest. Half of the herd for the parade through town sported the Heather's double H brand on their flanks.

She'd looked forward to the Fourth of July celebration for weeks. They'd gotten up well before dawn, loading the cattle and trucking them to town. After the roping and steer wrestling events at the rodeo, they'd be trucked back to the sale barn and sold.

"Let's head 'em up and move 'em out!" The hoarse shout of the elected trail boss overrode the bedlam of bawling calves. A frisson of excitement shivered through her as Bree tugged the reins from the hitching post, put her foot in the stirrup, and mounted.

She tugged the brim of her Stetson to block the horizontal rays of the rising sun. Not a cloud in the sky. It was going to be a perfect day; she could feel it.

Catching quick movement out of the corner of her eye, she jerked her head up. Trouble exploded across the yard, bucking and squealing, leaving Max grabbing for leather.

Cowboys shouted as riders scattered.

Wyatt trotted up on a buckskin cow pony. "Quite

an entrance. I don't know why Max brought that ill-mannered beast to town."

Trouble calmed a bit, having made his point. The big paint pranced in place, head thrown up, fighting the rein.

"Oh, he's full of himself; that's all." Bree thought the pair magnificent. She longed for a camera to capture the flashy horse and the lean cowboy in the morning light. As if sensing her gaze, Max glanced up, and smiling, tipped his hat to her.

"Looks to me like they're both pretty full of themselves," Wyatt said.

"Yeah, and neither you nor I would have it different." She touched the Walker with her heel and took her place in the phalanx of riders skirting the corral. As the gate opened, they herded the cattle out of the yard, onto the asphalt of Lincoln Avenue, and turned right, toward town.

When the herd settled to a sedate walk, the riders relaxed, throwing jibes at one another.

Bree couldn't wipe the silly grin from her face. As they neared downtown, crowds lined the road. Kids waved American flags, and the outriders had their hands full as a few cows spooked, their hooves clattering and slipping on the asphalt. Bree eyed the edge of the herd warily. Unfenced cattle and little kids made a combustible mix. All senses on alert, the cowboys tightened the herd as they broke into a trot. She urged Smooth next to a white-eyed steer, nudging him into the fold. Four blocks farther, Bree was glad to see the turnoff to the rodeo grounds and an open holding pen.

She drew a heavy sigh when the last steer cleared the fence, and the gate swung closed. Taking off her hat, she swiped her sweaty forehead.

"Every year I forget how hairy that can be." Max ambled up on Trouble. "We've never had any accidents, but there have been a couple of close calls."

"Are you guys ready for breakfast?" Wyatt reined up next to them. "I've been thinking about those pancakes since before sunup."

CHAPTER 19

Max nudged Bree's elbow and rattled a sack of popcorn. She took a handful and turned to the arena. They sat shoulder to shoulder in the packed metal bleachers, waiting for Miguel and Jesus's turn in the team roping competition. The midday sun blazed, and the still air was full of smells of cotton candy, cologne, manure, and human sweat. Bree lifted her ponytail and turned her face to a puff of breeze. Max blew lightly on the back of her neck.

"Hmm, that feels good." He'd been solicitous all day. A touch at her waist here, a warm look there, each subtle reminders of the tectonic shift in their relationship. *How could a woman's heart not melt at soft displays of affection from a hard man?* Distracted, she forced herself to check the program in her lap. "I think they're up next." She watched the end of the arena, where a steer waited in a squeeze chute, restrained only by a rope strung across the front. Miguel and Jesus sat mounted in open stalls on either side, horses dancing in anticipation.

Suddenly, the rope was gone and the steer shot into the

arena as if released from a bow. The horses galloped in hot pursuit, ears laid back, the cowboys' lassos spinning. Miguel let his fly first, and it settled over the steer's horns. He took a quick twist of the rope around the horn of the saddle and his horse sank on his haunches. As the steer hit the end of the rope, his head came around and his hindquarters swung out. Jesus released his lasso underhanded, and when the animal stepped neatly into the noose, he jerked it taut.

Bree jumped up cheering as the announcer called over the PA system, "Torres and Moreno, best at nine point five seconds." The grinning pair tipped their hats to the crowd as they trotted by the grandstand.

Max stood and reached for her hand. "Let's go check on your midget bull. I'm about cooked." They squeezed their way to the end of the row, where Max jumped to the ground, then grabbed her waist and swung her down beside him.

Bree preened inside, knowing that by their clasped hands, Max was staking his claim.

The rodeo grounds were packed for the Rancher's Rodeo, and they were stopped every few feet by the greetings of friends and neighbors. More than one puzzled glance fell on Bree when Max introduced her as his "partner."

They finally reached the show barn. Fire Ant stood in a stall, chewing cud, oblivious to the bustle around him as hands arrived with stock for the Pro Rodeo this afternoon. His cockeyed horns lent him a dumb-as-dirt look that his relaxed attitude reinforced.

Max leaned on the top rail of the stall. "You couldn't have picked a bull that looked a bit more intimidating?"

Bree smiled fondly as the bull turned away to give

them a view of his backside. "Oh, I think he's adorable." She turned to Max. "And you'll agree when he brings home the purse tonight."

"Your mouth to God's ears, honey." He reclaimed her hand and they walked into the blazing sun. "Let's grab some lunch. Watching people work makes me hungry."

"How can you think about eating? I'm still stuffed with pancakes."

Max headed for the impromptu food court cordoned off on a grassy hill next to the parking lot. Blue plastic awnings shaded the vendors, mostly students and members of local civic organizations, selling everything from churros to watermelon. The Rotary Club's half-barrel barbecues were going full blast, throwing off delicious smells and billowing smoke in equal amounts. The Chamber of Commerce beer truck did a booming business under a tree. Max made a beeline for it.

In line, Max went still beside her and his hand tightened on hers. She followed his gaze, but saw nothing untoward in the passing crowd.

"Grab me a beer, will you, Bree? I'll be right back." Without waiting for an answer, he stalked off.

Max kept his eye on the group as he dodged running children and picnic tables. Several large, ham-fisted men stood in a semicircle around his much smaller brother.

Déjà vu. Max recognized Wyatt's tormentors from high school. Their leader, Stan Pruitt, still ran his father's hardware store in town. Max forced his fists to relax. Maybe he could talk Wyatt out of trouble this time. But knowing these men, he doubted it. He sidled up to the group, taking a stance behind his brother.

"What's going on, Wyatt?" He surveyed the men's intent expressions.

Wyatt turned and smiled. "Hey, Max. You know everyone, right?"

Stan Pruitt leaned in, and Max tensed. "Yeah, I go to the 'Tools' menu. Then what?"

What the hell?

"Scroll down to 'Customize.' It'll allow you to make almost any changes you want." Wyatt reached to his back pocket for his wallet. He pulled out a business card and handed it to Stan. "Call me if you have any questions."

Stan studied the card, then glanced up at Max. "Did you know your brother wrote the POS program I use at the store?"

Bubba Wright asked Wyatt, "Do you have anything for inventory control? I've got about five thousand SKUs and my software sucks."

Well, he obviously wasn't needed here. Max backed away, shaking his head as his brother launched into a detailed explanation. Wyatt was right. Max was still trying to solve his brother's problems the way he had when they were kids. Given what just happened, things had changed. That bore thinking about.

Maybe times had changed. Maybe the town was ready to accept Wyatt for who he was. After all, if he'd have made a list of those least likely to change, the guys in that circle around Wyatt would have been on it.

And if those guys could change, maybe there was hope for him. He should tell Wyatt to schedule a trip out for Juan.

He wandered back to the beer truck, where Bree still stood in line.

"Is everything okay?" she asked.

"Things are good. Weird, but good."

Full dark descended as Max and Wyatt skirted the huge crowd that sprawled on the grass for the fireworks show. Max neatly sidestepped two boys who chased each other with sparklers. Wyatt followed, carrying a bag of hot dogs.

Max kept his eye on the too-full plastic cups of beer as he walked the uneven ground. "Okay, so consider me a member of the Fire Ant Fan Club."

"Jeez, what a zoo," Wyatt grumbled as he stumbled in a gopher hole. "Do you believe our little Fire Ant bucked off a Pro Bull Rider? As far as I'm concerned, Bree is our stock buyer from now on."

The hillside was a crazy quilt of blankets, lawn chairs, and beach towels used by families to mark their territory. Loudspeakers blared "The Stars and Stripes Forever" as a baton troupe from the YMCA did a synchronized routine on the lighted stage. At least Max supposed it was intended to be synchronized. The crowd competed with the PA system as kids yelled, babies cried, and people talked as they waited for the show to begin.

"Well, howdy neighbor."

Max shifted his focus from the beer in his hands to Trey Colburn's sardonic smile, noticing a slight sway to his stance. He was "duded up" as usual, his dress pants and golf shirt a step above the Wranglers and T-shirt uniform of the crowd.

"Y'all look downright domestic." He took a few steps into the deeper shadows of the trees. "Max, I need to talk to you." Max took two steps, far enough to drop out of the stream of people who walked the edge of the crowd, then stopped.

Wyatt followed. "What do you want, Colburn?"

Trey glanced left and right, to be sure passersby weren't eavesdropping. "I want to ask you one last time to reconsider selling."

Max tried to judge Colburn's expression through the gloom. Gone was the rich man swagger. He seemed almost afraid and about half drunk. "What's the matter, Colburn? Having a bit of trouble, are you?"

Colburn paced two steps, but then turned. "You don't understand." He rubbed his palms on his pants leg. "I've got to have that land. Goddammit, with the consortium's money you could buy another ranch somewhere else."

"I could, but I like it here. You tend to get fond of the land your parents are buried on. You could say it's gotten in our blood." He glanced to Wyatt. "Isn't that right, brother?"

"Max." Wyatt's quiet voice held a warning.

Max wanted more information, and Colburn appeared desperate enough to give it to him. "How much trouble are you in, Colburn?" Max handed the beers to Wyatt. You didn't face a rattler with your hands full. "If you need money, why don't you tap one of your rich friends?"

"It's never been about money." His shoulders slumped as he deflated like a balloon in the hot sun. "I'm as good as any of my brothers. I'm Andrew the Third, no less, *and* the oldest. Yet here I am, surviving on the crusts that Brian lets fall through his fingers." His eyes glittered as a flash of headlights from the parking lot struck him. His face was a mask of fury. "It's not fair."

This guy is pathetic. Max fought the urge to shake his head. "Let me see if I've got the picture." Max pushed the brim of his hat back with one finger. "You expect us to sell our family's legacy to the vermin you call friends who intend to ruin the land by covering it with condos and estates for ski bunnies. All so you can play big man for your family? And you think that's going to make you a success?"

With a squeal of rage, Colburn lashed out. His fist caught Max square on the chin. Wyatt dropped the beer and raised his fists, but Max shook his head to clear it and put out a restraining arm.

"Now, Wyatt, you know that fighting never solves anything." Max swung, his uppercut coming from knee level. There was a loud crunch as it connected with Colburn's jaw. The man stood a moment, a confused look on his face. Then his bones seemed to dissolve as he crumpled into the grass. "But it feels good, don't it?"

Wyatt said, "It sure does, brother." Several men jogged over.

Max rubbed his knuckles. "Don't worry about this, gentlemen. The city will be by later to clean up the trash."

A hollow bang of percussion thumped as a fountain of magenta shot into the sky. Max put his arm around his Wyatt's shoulders. "Let's go find Bree and watch the show."

Max glanced at the clock on the wall of the study. One in the morning, and he had to be up at dawn. Bree had nodded off against his shoulder on the drive home, and Wyatt had crashed in the jump seat of the truck, but Max couldn't sleep. His brain ached from wrestling with Total Bull's cash-flow problems.

His glance fell on the scratched metal footlocker next to the desk. *Probably full of old feed store receipts.* There was no telling, given his dad's weird accounting habits. He leaned over to study the ancient lock, more to distract his thoughts than out of curiosity. He pulled a letter opener from the lap drawer of the desk and knelt on the floor.

The lock was sturdier than he thought. It took ten minutes and a bloodied knuckle, but when it finally gave, Max lifted the lid. He chuckled as he lifted a bundle of feed store receipts off the top pile of papers. *Well, at least these should put me to sleep.*

Next in the stack were pedigree papers of bulls long dead, the great-grandfathers of some of the cows slumbering in the Heather's meadows right now. Thirty-year-old tax returns, a blue ribbon from a local stock show... *yada, yada.* As he lifted a handful of paper to throw in the trash, an ivory envelope fell to the floor. Fancy writing on the outside caught his eye—*Angus.*

Max pulled out a piece of ivory card stock, monogrammed **CEJ**, and opened the card.

Angus. Your instincts were right. The boy isn't yours. I'd hoped to find somewhere to be safe, somewhere to start over. But this isn't it. You know it. I know it. Where I'm going is no place for a baby. He's better off with you. I'm sorry.

Christina

CHAPTER 20

Bree stuffed a beach towel into the packed saddlebag. *Lunch, sunscreen, paperback novel, blanket.* "Whatever is missing, we'll live without it." She patted Smooth's rump, unsnapped the crossties, and led him out of the barn.

At breakfast Max had assigned the men to ride fence and move cattle to a new pasture, but she was taking the day off. She'd invited Wyatt to come along, but he chose to work. Just as well. She could use some alone time. She mounted Smooth in the empty yard and set off at a sedate walk, the Walker's signature rolling gait melting the tension in her muscles.

Summer had finally settled into the high country. Grass stood knee high, and gravid honeybees courted the wildflowers in a lazy dance. The snow had retreated to the highest of peaks, seen through the shimmer of heat at the horizon. Bree took a deep lungful of clean air. LA seemed like a mirage from the distant past. Funny how quickly this land had become home.

Not only the land. She smiled. What if Tia was right,

and she and Max were falling…into a relationship? That hadn't been the plan. Smooth's ears twitched at her snort. The grand plan had been her downfall.

"Trust me, Smooth, planning is overrated."

Her smile slipped. It was time to tell Max about her past. She knew she had to. If she didn't, the omission would look like a lie. God knew she, of all people, understood the damage lies could do.

"I'm going to tell him. Soon." She took heart at the firm tone of her voice. Smooth was the best kind of listener. He didn't judge. "After all, the only thing I did wrong was to not bust Vic's ass the minute I found out what a scumbag he was." Well, that wasn't exactly true either. Here, alone with her horse and the wide summer sky, she admitted to the shame that had dogged her for so long. She'd known Vic had been cheating Customs for a year, but hadn't seen it as her problem until the agents arrested her.

Bree remembered Max's cold stare when Wyatt mentioned Juan's offer to buy stock. It was the same look he'd given her on this very path, when he'd talked about Trey Colburn's manipulations, something that would have been judged good business where she'd come from.

She imagined telling Max about OCT and the Twin Towers jail, picturing the unforgiving lines of his face, his downturned mouth, the judgment in those dark eyes. Max had a rigid code and a moral compass chipped out of stone. If she could hardly live with the knowledge of her past, what could she expect from a Boy Scout like Max?

A photo album of memories flashed through her mind. Max, astride a nervous Trouble, sitting tall in the saddle, big hands relaxed on the reins. The sun glinting off his naked chest in the garden, the bead of sweat rolling down.

That same broad chest under her hands. Bree shifted in the saddle.

Things were going so well between them. Surely after all she'd been through, it wouldn't be wrong to find solace in Max's arms. She remembered his dark eyes, looking at her like she was a goddess—scar and all.

But it would be taking a huge risk. She wouldn't only be staking their relationship and her job. He could make her leave High Heather.

She'd found the stability here to shore up her badly shaken underpinnings. More than that though, the good, honest, hardworking people had taken her in—accepted her for who she appeared to be and liked her for it.

Somehow that acceptance allowed her to see the old Aubrey Madison clearly. A slick, hip, social climber whose career trajectory was more important than her morals.

Bree Tanner was about as different from that woman as possible.

And she liked that. She was proud of this Bree Tanner.

Max knowing her past could end all that. She imagined packing her things in the Jeep and driving out to the road, leaving her heart on the stable floor of High Heather.

"I *can't* tell him. I love him too much."

But if she loved him, how could she not?

Max took the left fork in the trail, waving the rest of the men toward the ranch. It had been a good day. The cattle were sleek and fat from gorging on new summer grass. He pushed his worries to a corner of his mind and focused instead on the clop of Trouble's hooves, the creak of saddle leather, and the swallows keening as they flew overhead.

God, he loved this ranch. But even if the bucking-bull idea didn't work and he lost everything, he knew he'd find a job on another ranch, somewhere far away. He was born to spend his days in the saddle, chasing cattle and mending fence. It was all he'd ever wanted.

Trouble splashed across the stream, and Max reined him left, toward a copse of trees. A quick dip to wash off the dust would be just the ticket before heading for home, for dinner. *And Bree.* He felt his mouth stretch in a goofy grin. He should be embarrassed of his calf-like behavior, but he couldn't seem to—*Goddamn!*

The subject of his thoughts splashed in the pool formed by a deep bend in the river, naked as a babe. *Babe is right.* He reined up and leaned his crossed arms on the saddle horn. Her back was to him, and the sunlight filtering through the swaying branches overhead sent shadows sliding over her skin. When she walked to the shallows on the opposite side, more of her delectable body was revealed with every step. Water sluiced off her shoulders, her sculpted waist, that cute rear. This day ratcheted up to the list of top ten of all-time great days. "I see you found our swimming hole."

Water flew from her hair as she whipped around, crouching and covering herself. When she saw who it was, and that he was alone, she relaxed, stood, and dropped her arms. Her breasts were full, but not too large, their apricot nipples puckered in the cool air. He remembered the skittish girl who'd applied for the job all those weeks ago and understood what it meant for her to stand before him, naked and unashamed.

"Don't move. I'll be there in a minute." He dismounted, grateful for the extra room in his Wranglers. He loosened the cinch and retrieved the halter from his saddlebag. Replacing Trouble's bridle, he led him to where Smooth grazed a few hundred feet away and tethered him. Stripping quickly, he stepped up to where the grass ended at the undercut bank. No way to do this slowly. He jumped in. The water was chilly and over his head. He pushed off the bottom to shoot out of the water, yelling.

"Cowboy up, big guy. It's not *that* cold," Bree taunted, hip deep in the shallows.

He swam to her, dove under the surface, grabbed her ankles and jerked. With a "Whoop!" she lost her balance and fell backward. He walked his hands up her body, until she lay cradled in his arms.

She laughed up at him, water sparkling on her skin. As she sobered, her whiskey eyes grew dark. He bent to taste the water and sunlight on her lips. No reason to rush. They had all afternoon. She opened to him and his tongue met hers in a greeting that sent shivers through him.

She asked, "Are you cold?"

He growled out, "Not with you in my arms, darlin'." He lowered his head once more. She wrapped her arms around his neck and moaned into his mouth as his hands wandered over her submerged breasts. He pinched her nipples, and she squeaked, but then arched to his hands for more.

God, I don't know what I did to deserve a woman like this, but I promise to do more of it in the future.

She struggled, fighting her body's buoyancy.

"Just relax and float, honey." He smoothed his hands over her arms to encourage her to relax. As she put her head back, the rest of her body rose to the surface. He scooted closer to the shallows, where he could prop her buttocks on his knee. She sculled with her hands, hair moving in the current, watching his every move.

Her smooth alabaster skin was cool beneath his hands. His fingers stroked her nest of auburn curls, searching for the swollen bud at the center. Slow, lazy circles with his thumb made her body arch. When he heard her respiration speed up, he slowed and replaced his thumb with his mouth. Bree whimpered.

That a woman as private as this would open herself to him made him feel humble, even as he throbbed to take her. Her legs parted slightly as he slid his hand under, letting his fingers tease her opening. As she moved restlessly, he steadied her with his other hand.

He closed his mouth over her and suckled, plunging his fingers into her. She moaned, and the muscles rhythmically clenching his fingers were almost his undoing as well. He lost himself to the water nymph before him and her pleasure as her nails dug into the skin of his upper arm.

He blew gently across her curls. Her muscles spasmed again, the pulses becoming farther apart as she relaxed.

She reached for his shoulders to pull herself up. She straddled his lap, her legs bracketing his. Wrapping her arms once more around his neck, her kiss imparted a closeness that seemed somehow new. He deepened the kiss, hoping she would understand what he offered.

Bree sensed a difference in Max today. He seemed more open, more vulnerable. Using that term to describe a cowboy was an oxymoron, but that's what it felt like. His face was relaxed and, for once, unguarded. She shifted in his lap. "What is it, Max? What's wrong?" His gaze searched her face, looking for, what?

He dropped his head to lean his forehead against her chest. "I'm just so tired. Life has gotten complicated, and I can't even pretend I know what to do anymore." She put her arms around him. "When I'm with you, I can put all that down for a while." Max lifted his head, and his eyes bored into hers. "I need you, Bree."

Nothing is going to hurt this man on my watch. She cradled his face in her hands to lift his head. "Forget everything for a while, Max." She bent to kiss him gently. "Just let me love you." She settled onto him with a sigh. Still holding his head in her hands, she spread kisses across his face. Her muscles spasmed—an aftershock from before or a precursor to what was to come, she didn't know.

He groaned, and his arms tightened around her.

The water made this effortless. She slid up his length slowly, teasing herself as well. "Shhh. Let me…" Emotions flickered across his face as his dark eyes slid shut in pleasure. When she lowered herself, he filled her once more. She held still, but her internal muscles fired again, and she raked her nails up his back. His fingers curled over her shoulders, holding her down as he ground into her. She wanted to take everything this man could give, and then take more. She wrapped her legs around him, bringing him closer yet.

He growled as she rose and pulled her down again. Like a seesaw, they rose and fell, passion ratcheting higher each time. Max gritted his teeth and squeezed his eyes closed, his face taut as they strove to bring each other to the jumping-off place.

"Bree, honey." His hoarse shout echoed off the water and the entreaty in his voice pushed her over the edge. She bit his shoulder as if it would somehow keep her anchored to earth as she came apart again.

They floated, loosely holding each other, catching their breath as the gently lapping water rocked them. When his breathing calmed and they lay languid in the shallows, Bree tugged his hand. "Let's get out. I'm going all pruny." She ignored his groan of protest. "Come on. I've got a blanket." When he didn't move, she said, "And a soda."

He cracked one eye. "A beer?"

"You wish. Come on. You're going to fall asleep and drown if you stay here." She tugged his hand again and stood.

He grumbled, but crawled out of the water to collapse on the blanket she'd laid near the water's edge. Bree retrieved a mesh bag from the river where she'd left it to keep the soda cool. She popped the top and handed one to him, then retrieved one for herself before lying beside him. He extended his arm, and she rested her head on his biceps, his thumb making lazy circles on her arm. Bree's skin pricked as water evaporated from it. Sunlight reflected off the water as it burbled through the bend. Birds gossiped overhead, and in the distance, the mountains stood guard over all. She wished they could stay like this, forever.

She knew Max wasn't asleep when he took a sip from the can. Rolling on her side, she propped her head on her hand. "Okay, are you ready to talk about it?" He shot her a look out of the corner of his eye. "Please, Max, tell me what's happened. Even if I can't help, it may make you feel better to get it out in the open."

He sighed heavily. "I found something in the old trunk that came out of your room. A note."

"And?"

"From Wyatt's mother to my dad. A 'Dear John' note,

I guess you'd call it." He snorted. "Why the hell he didn't burn it, I'll never know."

"What did it say?"

He frowned at the canopy of branches above them. "Wyatt isn't my dad's son."

She didn't know what she'd expected him to say, but this certainly wasn't it. "Huh?"

"The note was short, but very clear." As he turned his head to her, the hurt in his eyes stabbed her. "Wyatt isn't my brother."

Implications bounced like pinballs though her brain.

"I've got to tell him. He deserves the truth." He rolled onto his back. "But how do I begin *that* conversation?"

Her heart ached for him. And Wyatt. She laid a hand on his arm. "Oh, Max."

"Yeah. It seems Ben Franklin was wrong."

All she could do was look at him.

"Three may keep a secret, if two of them are dead."

They were quiet on the ride home, absorbed in their thoughts. Even Trouble was subdued, walking alongside Smooth. Bree reached over now and then to stroke Max's arm, or touch his leg, just to remind him he wasn't alone. He caught her hand, twining his fingers in hers.

"We've got to get you a proper bed." He flashed a mischievous smile. "That board you're sleeping on is going to cripple me before long." He tugged at her fingers. "Better yet, why don't you stay at the house, Bree? I've got a huge bed."

"Oh no, you don't. I've already gotten one lecture from Tia Nita. If you want me to come to you, you've got to clear it with her first."

He looked like a landed fish, his mouth opening and

closing. "I'm not going to ask Tia's permission to have you in my bed. Are you out of your mind?" He squared his shoulders. "I'm a grown man, for chrissake."

She dropped his hand, smiling. "Hey, tell Tia that. I'm not getting busted, sneaking into your bed." She nudged Smooth and he broke into a trot, leaving Max grumbling to himself.

It's called the Little Blue Dummy," Total Bull's new trainer said, placing a rectangular metal box on the mess hall table. Metal wings jutted from either side, attached to a wide leather strap. Armando had returned that afternoon and spent dinner regaling them with tales from his trip.

"JB says it helps train a young bull. You strap it on a two- or three-year-old, and it's enough weight that he tries to buck it off." He pointed to a red button on a small remote. "When he's had enough"—he pushed it and the dummy popped off the strap—"the little guy thinks he bucked it off and feels like he's won."

Sitting next to Miguel, Bree eyed the contraption. "I guarantee you, a woman invented that."

Wyatt frowned from across the table. "Why do you say that?"

Bee shrugged. "Women have been pumping up men's egos for centuries." She tilted her head and batted her eyelashes at him. "Works like a charm."

Max clapped Armando on the shoulder. "Well, let's

hope that thing works. We'll bring the young bulls in from the pasture tomorrow and give you a chance to test it."

He glanced to the end of the table at Miguel and Jesus. "How'd you two like to handle our rolling stock?"

"What's rolling stock?" Miguel asked.

"Well, we've entered Fire Ant in six Challenger Tour events over the next two months. Local venues: Boulder, Fort Collins, Rifle. He's going to need a ride." He gave them a stern look. "Are you two responsible enough to handle this?"

The young men looked at each other, then at Max. "Hell, yeah, boss," Jesus said.

"Beats stringing bob-wire any day." Miguel high-fived his roping buddy.

Bree had mixed feelings about sending the hands. She'd wanted the job, but Wyatt and Max both overrode her vote. The cowboys could bed down in the cattle trailer, where she'd have to pay for a hotel room for safety's sake. Still, the brothers' overprotective attitude rankled.

On the other hand, she was glad not to go on the road. Not right now at least. The image of Max walking out of the river popped into her mind. The water sparkling in his hair, his thigh muscles bunching . . . She let her mind's eye roam up and fanned herself with her hat.

Later, as they left the mess hall, the men followed Armando to the bunkhouse to hear more stories of his trip. Bree let the screen door slap behind her and paused on the porch. Their lack of an invitation and sidelong glances told Bree they were stories she didn't want to hear, probably starring loose women and lots of beer.

The sun hunkered on the horizon, a huge orange ball. She donned her straw hat, and seeing Trouble in the pasture, strolled to the fence. A less flashy horse would have blended with the landscape.

Max's deep voice came from behind her. "I'd trim his hooves before I go to bed, if I could catch the devil."

"You'd better get your nippers, then." Bree put two fingers in her mouth and let out a shrill whistle. Trouble threw his head up. When she whistled again, he cantered toward the fence. She turned to Max and smiled. "Close your mouth; you're gonna catch a bug."

Trouble slowed at the fence, then stopped and stretched his head over. As Bree reached up to scratch under his forelock, he lipped her collar.

Max pushed his hat back. "How did you do that? I've known this nag since he was a colt, and he's *never* done that for me."

She chuckled. "I wish I could tell you that I'm some kind of horse whisperer, but I'd be lying. I have a secret weapon." Reaching into her back pocket, she pulled out a plastic Baggie and opened it. Trouble nudged her elbow as she pulled out long white wedges.

"What are you feeding my horse?"

"Jicama." She laid the spears on the flat of her hand and the horse took them, smearing drool on her palm.

"What is that, some kind of apple?"

She dried her hands on the seat of her jeans. "Nope, a vegetable. It's a root, like a yam."

Max grabbed Trouble's halter before he got the idea to take off. "What is wrong with you? Guys do *not* come running for vegetables."

Bree caressed the soft black-and-white braided rope bridle in the Elk River Farm and Feed. *How great would that look on a paint?* She flipped the dangling price tag and gulped. This gift was beyond her deflated finances.

"Pretty as a pup, isn't it?"

She turned to find Trey Colburn standing behind her. Too close. She nodded, dropped the price tag, and stepped away.

"Hello again." He took off his hat. "Bree, right? I may forget a name now and again, but I'd never forget a face that pretty." Colburn's little boy smile was deadly. Turning his hat in his hands, he inhaled. "Don't you love the smell of a tack store? Makes you want to take out your wallet, doesn't it?"

Bree had to return the smile. "Yes, that's exactly how it makes me feel."

"I saw you at the rodeo on the Fourth. How do you like our part of the country?"

"It feels like home already." She glanced out the plate-glass window next to her. The store afforded a breathtaking view. "I can't imagine being somewhere that mountains don't ring the horizon like a necklace."

"Very well said." He gazed out at the vista, his face serious. "You couldn't drag me out of Colorado for love or money."

He seemed sincere. If she ignored Max's opinion of the man and went only on her own impressions . . . An idea flashed. Max would be pissed, but what if it worked? She didn't see a downside. "Buy you a cup of coffee?" she asked. "I'd like to discuss something with you."

A half hour later, Bree sat across from Trey at a wrought-iron table outside the coffee shop. It hadn't taken much to get him started. He seemed more than happy to talk about himself. Sipping her coffee, she listened for clues to the man in his small talk.

"So, we put in a pool last spring. It makes a great place to entertain. Just last week we had the Chamber of Commerce out for a mixer."

He certainly didn't strike her as the evil man that Max had painted. He had a bit of "little man syndrome" maybe, and from what Max told her, he'd made a few bad moral choices.

I'm hardly one to be throwing rocks when it comes to poor moral choices.

He seemed more like a man who'd never found his place. He wore his life like a cheap suit: binding under the arms, the pants too tight in the seat.

"Trey, do you mind my asking you a personal question?"

"Fire away, sugar."

"Did you ever ask yourself what you'd do if other people's opinions didn't matter?" He threw her a startled glance. "I ask because my life changed when I did that." She watched the cars whizz by a few yards from them as she gathered her thoughts.

"You see people that seem to have it all together: money, prestige, glitter. They look so happy." She remembered the lights of Hollywood at night. "It's *so* seductive, that dream. Like a whirlpool, it's easy to get sucked into it, and by the time you figure out that it's just a dream, it's too late. You've got too much invested to go back."

She shook her head. "One night at a party, I looked around and realized everyone else was chasing the same dream. They all knew it was bull, but they couldn't admit it. There we all were, laughing and posing, trying to convince everyone we lived this perfect life, so no one would know what a huge mistake we'd made." She frowned. "I paid the price for my mistakes, but I feel bad for people who were pulled into that lifestyle by watching me."

Trey's face revealed no glimpse of his thoughts. "What are you trying to say, sugar?"

"I'm asking you to call off the dogs, Trey. Please stop lobbying Denver to close the BLM lands." She put down her cup and leaned forward. "I know you're not doing this for the money. The dream you're following will do damage to a lot of good people." She nodded her head toward the mountains. "And it will hurt this place you love so much."

Trey's eyes glinted dangerously before he ducked his head to put on his immaculate felt cowboy hat. "You presume quite a bit, little lady."

Her stomach dropped. *Max is going to kill me.*

He stood, reached in his pocket, and dropped a five on the table, then leaned in close. "You tell your boyfriend out at the Heather to come see me if he wants to cry uncle. I'm surprised that he'd send a woman to do a man's job."

Bree shot to her feet, anger pounding in the veins of her neck. "You don't really believe he sent me. What, I sulked around the tack store until you happened by?"

Trey's face reminded her of a boy's from high school when she refused to put out in the front seat of his car. Pained, angry, entitled. He turned on his heel and walked away.

Two days later, Max paced in front of the great room fireplace, untouched Rolling Rock in hand. Wyatt sat on the leather couch facing him.

"Max, either spit it out or let me get to work. If you're conducting a carpet wear test, you don't need me."

Max picked at the edge of the bottle's label, feeling

like a naked man climbing a barbed-wire fence. He set the beer on the end table and reached into the back pocket of his jeans. "I found this in that old trunk from the office." He handed over the stiff ivory card, grimy and broken from being in his pocket since the night he'd found it. Wyatt opened it, and in the silence, Max heard his heart pounding in his ears.

As Wyatt read, the color drained from his face. Max put out a hand but then let it fall to his side. "I've been torn up over this, Wyatt. Didn't know if I should tell you or not." He shoved his hands in his pockets and gazed out the window, wishing he were anywhere but here. "Why the hell didn't Dad burn that damn thing?" He turned. "Say something, Wyatt."

Wyatt pointed to the fancy writing. "Your dad." His eyes burned, but beneath it, Max glimpsed pain. "You mean, why didn't *your* dad burn it. Give me a minute, will you?" He reread the note, holding it by one crumpled corner as if it were coated in anthrax.

Max resumed pacing. Why did things always have to change? First, the problems with the ranch, then his father's death, and now this. He'd been forced to accept he didn't have control of many things, but goddammit. He wasn't losing Wyatt.

Wyatt stared out the window. "I never tried to find my mother. I figured if she didn't care enough to take me with her, I didn't owe her." His soft, shaky voice sent a bolt of worry through Max. "How screwed up is it that she may be my only living relative?" A sardonic smile lifted a corner of his mouth. "And even knowing this"—he tossed the card on the coffee table—"I don't know or care if she's still alive."

Max's gut twisted. Except for him, Wyatt would be alone in the world. He remembered the photo of the Hispanic man on Wyatt's dresser. *Yeah, but that's not family.* And family was everything. "You know, something just occurred to me, Wyatt. Maybe Dad's attitude had nothing to do with you at all." He turned to study his brother's face. "I've seen photos of your mother. You look a lot like her. What if Dad's . . . ?" He searched for a politically correct term. "Maybe his distaste wasn't for who you are but who he saw when he looked at you. Hell, for all we know, he had no clue that you were gay."

Wyatt put his hands on his knees and pushed to his feet, as an old man would. "You mean you and he never talked about any of this? All those years?"

Max snorted. "Get real. You know Dad. I couldn't ask him if he knew you were—well, batting for the other team."

"Good point, but are you saying my name never came up? Not even in general terms?"

Max felt his face go red. "Of course your name came up."

"Just not often.

The pain in Wyatt's look hit him like a punch. Max snatched up his beer and took a long pull. "Come on, Wyatt. You grew up in this house. You know what it was like. Dad talked about the weather, the price of beef, and gave orders. Period." He rolled his eyes. "Can you see Angus Jameson talking about his feelings?" Wyatt snorted. A good sign. "Besides, I stayed in touch with you. You know I did."

Wyatt thought a moment. "Yes, I heard from you on Christmas. And on my birthday, some years."

"Can I ask you a question?"

Wyatt shrugged. "What the hell. Go ahead."

"Did you hate women because of your mom? The way she left you?"

Wyatt burst out laughing. Max watched, shocked, as Wyatt nearly doubled over. "You think I'm gay because of my mother?" He wheezed. "Max, you slay me. You really do."

"Well, hell, Wyatt."

"You think I'd condemn an entire gender for the actions of one shallow, self-centered woman?" He sobered, shaking his head. "Being gay isn't about damage, or what happened to you when you were a kid. It's about sexual attraction."

Max inspected the scarred leather of his work boots.

"Sorry if this subject bothers you, but you asked." Wyatt threw his hands up. "Dammit, Max, not everyone gets to hide from reality in their little self-imposed cocoon."

"Hey, I'm just the one standing in front of you, bud. I'm not the one you're mad at."

"Maybe, but you'll do for the moment. I'm so sick of this place, with its attitudes and ignorance. You can't imagine what it's like."

"You're right, I can't." He stepped in front of Wyatt and stared him in the eye. "But I'm trying, brother. I'm trying."

Wyatt's shoulders slumped as the anger seemed to drain out of him. Max understood. The emotions of this afternoon had scoured his insides, leaving them raw.

Wyatt glanced around the room as if he'd never seen it before. "This isn't my home."

"Bullshit," Max growled. "No matter what the old man

wasn't, you've gotta give him credit. He raised you like you were his son. I didn't get anything in the will that you didn't get half of. That's proof that he cared, even if he couldn't show it."

Wyatt glanced to the top of the hill, at the fresh grave beside the older, weathered marker. "I guess we'll never know what the old man thought. Not for sure. The only part that's going to hurt, long-term, is that you and I aren't brothers."

Max's closed his fingers on Wyatt's arm, pulling him around. "You'd better get this straight, Wyatt. You and I *are* brothers. We've always *been* brothers, and no shitty 'Dear John' letter is going to change that." Max blinked away something that felt like moisture and cleared his throat. He pulled his brother into an awkward embrace, Wyatt's arms trapped at his sides. "The only way you're getting out of this family is in a box, and you danged well better get used to it."

Max stepped back, sure his face must be beet red. "And you can just deal with *that*, too." Max turned and stomped out of the room.

CHAPTER 22

A week later, Bree's feet dragged as she walked into the cool shade of High Heather's barn. She'd driven all day, delivering a horse to his new home in Estes Park. Dulcet's owner had bought a chalet in the trendy ski town, telling Bree that Steamboat was "So yesterday."

Tooling through the mountains with the top down on the Jeep was a Sunday drive compared to hauling a loaded horse trailer on the sheer rock-wall-hugging, traffic-clogged roads.

She rubbed eyes that felt like hard-boiled eggs, then reached to massage the knotted muscle in her neck. It had been worth it. They could use the money she'd earned on the trip. Luckily, they now had a waiting list for open stalls, so there wouldn't be any lost revenue. Wondering who'd been talking up High Heather's stable, Bree unlocked the door to her room.

A shower and a cup of coffee, that's all I want. Maybe both at the same time.

She pushed open the door to her room and paused

midstride, staring. Beneath the window, where her narrow bed used to be, a spanking-new queen-sized bed now dominated the space. Her familiar Navajo blanket lay folded at the bottom.

She let out a bray of laughter. She *knew* Max wouldn't broach the subject with Tia of Bree sharing his bed. She was grateful for his old-fashioned modesty. She'd have missed her independence and the refuge this room afforded.

Her heart skipped as she crossed the few steps to the bed and picked up a small bouquet of lavender alpine primrose, held together with twine, from the pillow. As she raised the flowers to her nose, a bubble of happiness broke in her chest. She imagined her tough cowboy bending in the pasture to pick the delicate flowers with his huge hands. *What girl wouldn't fall into this bed with a guy like that?* Grinning like a fool, she turned to the wardrobe to retrieve some clean clothes for after her shower.

Reaching for a blouse, she sobered. *Yeah, but will he still be in my bed when he knows my past?* The drive had given her time to think. She'd made up her mind. Tonight, at the first official board meeting of Total Bull, she was going to tell her partners everything: her former job, prison, and her conversation with Trey. All of it. Her stomach did a nosedive off a cliff, but beneath that, she felt bedrock of *rightness*. It was time.

In the house, Wyatt paced the boards of his bedroom floor. "Juan, do you have a minute?"

"Oh, that sounds ominous. Hang on a second, just let me shut my door."

Wyatt rubbed his forehead. He hadn't called until now, because he didn't know how to voice what he was feeling.

He still didn't, but he felt so lost, he needed the touchstone of his and Juan's relationship to anchor him to the present.

The past that he'd buried so long ago had risen like a zombie in a teen movie and was feasting on his brains.

"I'm here, Wyatt. What's up?" Juan's calm voice flowed over him like a balm.

"I don't belong here."

"Well, no shit, Wyatt. Now can you come home?"

"No, I found out I don't belong here—literally. See, I'm not related to any of these people."

"Wyatt, you're not making any sense. Stop, and take a deep breath."

"No, see—"

"Stop." Juan's all-business voice was the dash of cold water he needed.

He took a deep breath.

"Okay, now, tell me."

"Max found a letter. From my mother to my—Angus." He took another breath. "I'm not his son." His own high-pitched laugh frightened him a bit. "My mother, the only person who I am related to by blood, apparently got around a bit. The only reason she married Angus was to have a safe haven. But when the haven turned out not to her liking, she bailed."

"You're saying she left you with a guy you weren't even a blood relation to?"

"Yeah, that's pretty much it." He stopped pacing and dropped onto the bed. "And of course, that means that Max and I aren't related either."

Wyatt heard Juan's sharp inhale. "Oh man, that blows."

"Like a blue norther off the mountains."

"One thing though, Wyatt. Although it may not make

you feel better right now, you can choose your own family. Blood isn't all that important. Look at all our friends. Could we be closer if we were blood related?"

"You're right, and I know it. But I can't explain the feeling—it's like you grew up knowing the world was flat, and one day, someone gives you undeniable proof that it's triangular. Where do you fit in a world like that?"

"Okay, so if there's good news here, it's that you can come home now and leave all that behind. You don't owe Colorado anything, and it has no holds on you." Wyatt heard computer keys tapping. "I'm checking the airline schedules now."

"I can't leave yet, Juan. My fath—Angus still left me half the ranch and it's still in trouble. Max and I may not be related by blood, but he hugged me the other day and told me that I'm his brother, no matter what a 'Dear John' letter said." He sniffed. "He *wants* me as a brother."

There was silence on the line for so long he was afraid they'd lost connection. "Juan?"

"Well, maybe there's hope for his black heart yet."

There was a smile in Juan's voice that warmed Wyatt's freezer-burned soul.

"If I came out, three would probably be a crowd, huh?"

"I'm working on that. I promise. But, Juan?"

"Yeah?"

"It's so good to talk to you. I need you on the other end of the phone."

"I'm right here, Wyatt. Always."

That night, in lieu of cooking, the board of Total Bull paid a premium to have pizza delivered this far out of town.

Wyatt inhaled. "Is there any better smell on earth than a hot, greasy pizza?"

When Bree leaned over Max's shoulder to pour the Chianti, he made a production of sniffing her. "Oh, I don't know. I'd say there's nothing better than lemon soap and a sweet-smelling woman."

Wyatt laughed as Bree blushed and walked to the opposite side of the formal dining table to fill her own glass.

"I appreciate the sentiment, but right now, my stomach agrees with Wyatt." Bree sat sipping wine while the guys dug in. They pulled slices out of the box, long strings of melted cheese stretching to their plates. She eyed the choices, but the concave discs of pepperoni each held a little puddle of grease. Her stomach rolled. *Not a good choice.* The mushroom and black olive slice she reached for looked better, but when she bit in, the grease coated the inside of her mouth and she swallowed with effort.

Deciding she'd eat something later, she quickly washed it down with more wine. She noticed a tremor in her fingers as she reached for her glass. *I just want to get this over with.*

Max tasted the wine and smacked his lips.

"You like it?" Wyatt asked, swirling the almost purple Chianti before sipping.

"I can choke it down," Max said, picking up another slice. "Goes good with the pizza." He took a bite and added, "Not as good as beer, though."

"We'll turn you into a wine snob yet, Maxie."

Too soon, the boxes held nothing but grease stains and the table was littered with discarded napkins and tomato-smeared plates. Wyatt gathered the mess and pushed it to the unoccupied end of the table.

Bree replaced her plate of cold pizza with her laptop and waited for it to boot. "Okay. The first board meeting of Total Bull is officially called to order." She pulled up a spreadsheet.

Max cleared his throat. "I have something to say first, Bree." His glance skittered away. "I've given it some thought, and I'm now in favor of selling some common stock to Juan if—it's okay with you, that is."

Wyatt's beaming smile brought a cautious one from Max.

Obviously the brothers had been talking. Max slouched in his chair, seeming more relaxed around Wyatt. Funny, they seemed closer since they'd found out they weren't related. This was good for the business, but even better for the two men. She beamed across the table at them. "I'll work out a price per share."

"Sounds good to me. I'll let Juan know," Wyatt said.

She scanned the spreadsheet on the screen before her. "I don't know how much he has in mind to invest, but combined with the money from selling the stock that didn't buck and the fact that we're going into the winter with a smaller herd, we should be in okay shape come spring."

She bounced a leg under the table. It was now or never. *Come on, Madison. Ten minutes to spill your guts and then you can get on with the rest of your life.* "Okay, that's settled." She picked up an income statement, then dropped it. "I could go over the numbers, but you've both seen them. I do have something else to talk to you about."

Wyatt froze. His eyes cut to Max, then nodded almost imperceptibly at Bree.

Her leg bounced faster. "I ran into Trey Colburn in town the other day. I asked him to stop lobbying Denver to close the BLM lands."

Max jumped to his feet, "You did what?" he roared. "You had no right!"

She jerked as his fist hit the table. It might as well have slammed into her gut. "Why don't you just put my cojones on a stump and hand him a hammer?" He sputtered to a stop, clearly so angry he couldn't speak.

Wyatt's voice was calmer. "I think what Max is trying to say is that wasn't the wisest move, Bree. It makes Max look like a wimp." He frowned, looking almost as peeved as his brother. He'd obviously expected her to divulge a different secret.

She took a gulp of wine to avoid their eyes before setting her glass aside and squaring her shoulders. "I really don't think he's the villain you paint him to be, Max. He's just kind of lost and—"

"Your little lost boy punched Max out at the fireworks," Wyatt said.

"He did what?"

Max spat out, "Horse crap. I put that weasel's dick in the dirt!"

As Max thundered on, Bree tuned out his words. Her partners were obviously together on this. Even Wyatt thought she was an idiot. Max's eyes were so cold.

Maybe they were right. Maybe she was still the oblivious fool, bumbling into trouble, too naive to know better. Her heart sank. Hadn't prison taught her not to trust her own judgment?

Max turned on her. "You had no right to talk to that sonofabitch. The Heather isn't part of Total Bull. The land is none of your business."

Wyatt said, "That's enough, Max. I'm sure she was only trying to—"

"No, Wyatt. This is about loyalty." He glared at Bree. "You've got to admit, we've got more to lose here than you do."

More to lose? What about her heart? Didn't Max know that he owned that, too? She imagined packing her few belongings in the Jeep and leaving. Her blood pounded as adrenaline and hot rage coursed into her bloodstream. *How can you lose more than everything?*

Max went on. "After all, we still know nothing of your past." He didn't look down his nose. He didn't use a condescending tone. He just sat back, crossed his legs, and tapped his fingers on the table, which was really the same thing.

She jumped to her feet. "Oh, yes. I'm *so* eager to spill my guts in such a warm, accepting environment!" Acid bit deep in her stomach. "Shame on me for wanting to help. I didn't see a downside. The worst the man could do was say no." She glared at them both. "Of course, it might have helped if I'd known that you two went at it on the Fourth."

Max jutted his chin. "That's man business."

"Well, screw you both and your puffed-up male egos. I am so sick of caveman attitudes." Her jaw locked so tight, the roots of her teeth ached. She was pissed that she had to fight tears, and even more pissed because she couldn't stop them. Bolts of emotions cracked like lightning in her mind: anger, guilt, failure. Disappointment. Another lost opportunity.

"I didn't do it for me." Her damn voice cracked. "Or for Total Bull. Or the money." She stabbed a finger at Max. "I did it for *you*. You sure wouldn't do it." She pointed at Wyatt. "And neither would you." She raked a sleeve across her running nose.

"You belong on this land, and if you lost it because

of dumb pride..." Her shoulders slumped. The hole kept getting bigger, so she stopped digging. "Oh, fuck it."

She took a shaky breath. "Congratulations, boys. You made me cry in a business meeting." Her voice broke as a sob escaped. "Even Vic never managed that." She stood and pushed her chair back.

Max stared at the swinging door, then turned to Wyatt. "Who's Vic?"

Wyatt shrugged.

Bree turned, slammed the heels of her hands against the kitchen door and barreled through. She didn't slow until she was safely behind her locked door. Leaning against it, she took a ragged breath. She'd had every intention of throwing herself on the bed for a good cry. But the new bed taunted her, bringing Max into the room so strongly that it almost choked her.

Whirling, she jerked the door open. Snatching a hackamore from a peg on her way through the tack room, she jogged to Smooth's stall. She put it on him, led him to the aisle, and vaulted onto his back. Sensing her emotion, he threw his head up, and when she dug her heels in, he was off like a shot. As they cleared the barn door, she reined him right and they galloped out of the lighted yard, into the comforting arms of the dark.

Once Max and Wyatt got over their shock, they tore out after her. In the light of the spotlight on the barn, they saw Bree streak past like a wraith, riding bareback, her hair flying and her feet drumming the gelding's sides.

Max jumped from the porch, but Wyatt grabbed his arm.

Max tried to shrug him off. "What're you doing? I've got to go after her."

Wyatt dug his fingers in and hung on.

"Ouch! Let go, dammit."

"She needs some time, Max. Leave her alone."

"Yeah, but we can't leave a woman out there alone!" Max couldn't think through the panic. He'd only reacted like any red-blooded male would have. He didn't need his woman running around, trying to fix things for him. But seeing it through her eyes, he was touched. Misguided though her attempt was, no one had ever cared enough, or risked his wrath, by trying.

Seeing the light die in her eyes made something die inside him. *What kind of man could do that to a person only trying to help?*

He turned to Wyatt. "Don't you see? I think I ruined—"

Wyatt lowered his voice and spoke calmly, as one would to a spooked horse. "She's full grown, she knows the land, and she's a good horsewoman." Max tugged, until Wyatt dug his nails in the soft underside of his arm. That got his attention. "We were just chastised for that exact attitude. Let's make an effort to evolve a bit, shall we?"

Everything in Max screamed for him to go after her.

And say what, exactly? There's no undoing that kind of damage.

Maybe Wyatt was right.

CHAPTER 23

Max leaned on the paddock fence and pretended to watch Fire Ant doze in the midday sun. Inside, he flogged himself. Two days gone, and they still hadn't spoken. He missed her like crazy.

A movement caught his eye and he noticed Janet leading her gray gelding out of the barn. He slapped a smile on his face and meandered over. "Hello, Janet. Are we taking good care of Peanut?"

Janet glanced at her charge's gleaming coat and lustrous tack. "I can't complain."

High praise, considering. "I've been meaning to thank you."

She raised the skirt of the English saddle to check the girth. "Thank me for what?"

"I'm assuming you're the one who's been talking up the High Heather. We've gotten quite a few new boarders, and one of them mentioned that she was a friend of yours."

Janet lifted her perfect nose. "My friends and I have better things to talk about than your stable."

Fire Ant bawled in the paddock, gazing with longing at the heifers in the pasture.

Janet looked over and let out a delicate snort. "I believe that is the ugliest little bull I've ever seen. Surely you're not planning on breeding him."

Max tipped his hat back. "Are you kidding? That's arguably the most valuable piece of cowhide on the ranch."

A wicked smile lifted the corners of her mouth. "No wonder this place is going downhill."

Max laughed. "Looks don't count on the pro bull-riding circuit."

"So that's what you all are doing out here." She narrowed her eyes. "Harrison was telling me the other day of an article in the *Wall Street Journal* about the PBR. Lots of businessmen are investing. Tell me more."

"Well, it was Bree's idea. We've even incorporated."

"Really?" Janet pulled a business card out of her jodhpurs. "Maybe Harrison can help you. He's a CPA, you know."

Max held up a hand. "No, thanks. Bree's got that covered."

Janet's sable eyebrows lifted, "Your groom is your accountant?"

"As well as our partner." Max stared her down. "And a damned fine one, too. She's working out a stock offering for us now."

"Wow. That's some groom you hired."

"You don't know the half of it, lady." He tipped his hat and walked away, wishing he could kick his own ass.

Bree wheeled the Jeep into the Walmart Saturday-morning crush and trolled for a parking spot. Tia rode shotgun.

"Quick, take that one there." Tia waved at a space four cars away. Bree eyed the white pickup bearing down on her and shot into the space. When the driver blatted his horn, she only shrugged. She'd arrived first by at least two feet. As she shut off the engine, out of the corner of her eye, she saw Tia button her cardigan and was glad she'd put the top up. Alone, she'd have braved the precursor nip of fall, but Tia was precious cargo.

When Tia didn't move, Bree turned to see bright black sparrow eyes watching as if she were a crust of bread.

"You're not sleeping again, *mija*. Why?"

"I guess my new bed isn't as comfortable as the old one." *Mostly because I'm the only one in it.*

Wyatt had come to apologize the day following the disastrous business meeting. She'd mumbled one as well, then found something urgent that needed doing elsewhere. She'd hardly seen Max. He was gone before dawn and was taking his meals at the big house. *The mule-headed jerk.*

Bree reached in her woven Navajo purse, but stopped with her hand on the bottle of Tagamet. If Tia saw it, she'd get a real lecture. Instead, she resigned herself to the burn in her gut, slipped the strap on her shoulder, and opened the car door.

"He's afraid of you, you know."

"Who?" Bree closed the door and shifted to face her friend.

"Maxie. He's afraid."

"*Max?* Afraid of *me*?" Tia didn't look delusional, but would Bree recognize a break from reality when she saw one?

Tia's wrinkles collapsed into a grin. "About time, I

say." She settled against the door for a chat. "Max always looked up to Angus—wanted to be like him. Angus was a good man, but being alone on the land so long made him hard, cold, quiet. That's not my Maxie." She looked out the windshield, her face fallen to somber lines. "After that girl threw him over for that Colburn fella, it got worse. I watched him dig a hole inside himself where he'd go to brood. He was more like his father every day. I was afraid my Maxie was gone." Her voice trailed to a whisper.

She turned her head, and Bree felt her watchfulness. It made her want to run.

"You scare him like the red hawk scares a rabbit."

Bree cracked the door once more. She was tired. Tired of beating herself up. Tired of trying only to end up on the outside again, looking in. And more than anything, tired of feeling sorry for herself. "Okay, Tia, if you say so."

Tia poked her arm. "You don't want Maxie in that big bed of yours?"

Bree's head whipped around. She should have known. Not much got past Tia.

"*Hombres* don't like change," The older woman chuckled. "*You* are change." Tia sobered, watching a shopper wend her way between the cars in the next aisle. "He expected to marry a country girl. That's what he knows." Tia looked at Bree's trendy yoga pants. "You are a city girl. One that knows more than him about a lot of things. That scares him too." She sighed. "But he is stuck. He is crazy in love with you. He's like a dog with a piano. He's not sure what to do."

"Well, Tia, from what I've seen, dogs and pianos don't much run in the same circles." Bree reached once more for the door handle.

Tia crossed her pudgy arms over her chest. "Why don't you tell him your secrets?"

Bree's neck cracked as she whipped her head to Tia.

"You want him to trust. Why?" She threw up her hands. "Because he likes your bed?"

"Tia!" Bree's ears burned. Living among men, she wasn't easily shocked these days, but Tia had managed it twice in as many minutes.

"Men don't trust like that. *Sí*, they come running, but the next morning, they grab their *zapatos* from under the bed and go. They do not stay with a woman they don't trust." She gathered her massive purse from the floorboard, then reached for the door handle. "Especially Maxie."

The next day Bree was no closer to making the long walk to find Max. She had chewed over her conversation with Tia a hundred times. She poured oats from the bucket into Charlie's manger, then strolled to the next stall. *Darn it, I am a good person. So why can't I just spit it out?*

Bree knew Tia was right. If she loved Max, she needed to trust him. But look what happened last time. She'd ignored her gut and told Max of her talk with Trey and watched the top of his head nearly lift off. And that was a firecracker compared to the nuclear bomb of her prison stint.

Still, he deserved the truth. She poured the last wisps of grain into Peanut's trough, gave him a pat on the rear as she left, sliding the stall door shut behind her. *This isn't going away. I've got to make a decision.*

Wood creaked. Bree dropped the bucket and whirled.

As if her thoughts had conjured him, Max stood leaning against the stall opposite Peanut's. She put a hand to her pounding heart. "Jesus. You could give a girl some warning, Max." She bent to retrieve the bucket, watching him from under her lashes. His thumbs-in-pockets slouch didn't fool her; he was nervous. His finger-mussed hair and tapping foot gave him away. At least she wasn't the only one.

Max missed nothing as he drank her in. His heart clenched at the haunted look and dark circles around her eyes. *She's not sleeping.* He'd bet anything she was hitting the antacids again. Her fingers worried the bucket handle as she shifted her weight from foot to foot, reminiscent of the high-strung filly that had minced her way along this very aisle this spring. *God, you're a shit.* "I got a phone call this morning."

"So did I. Who was yours from?"

"Our esteemed congressman. Seems that after a review of the BLM proposal, the committee decided not to close the land to open grazing."

The worry lines on either side of her mouth dissolved into a delighted grin, and she looked once more like his fresh-faced girl next door. "Max, that's great news!"

The force of her megawatt smile stunned him and he stood pole-axed, like the hayseed he was. He pushed away from the stall, straightened his spine, and forced his eyes to meet hers. "Just thought you'd want to know."

She stepped closer. "Maybe Trey came through, after all."

He hoped she wasn't getting into the hands' poker games. She'd lose all her money with an open face like that. "I'd guess not. The vulture I talked to went on about soul-searching and constituent interviews. The upshot is they decided the best use of the land is for cattle, not ski bunnies. Maybe there's hope for this state yet."

She held the bucket in front of her like a shield. "I'm so pleased for you. And for High Heather."

"Bree, I'm sorry I yelled at you."

Her eyes skittered away. "No, you were right. I didn't think how it would make you look to Trey. It was a dumb thing to do."

He crossed the aisle to take her hands, noticing their tremor. "Maybe it was." Her head came up, sparks in her eyes. *This* was his Bree, not the haunted woman he'd caught glimpses of this past week. "But you took a chance, and I know you did it for me." She tried to pull her hands away, but he tightened his grip. "I made you cry. I've been ashamed of myself ever since. I'm miserable without you and yet I was afraid to come to you. I was a coward not to make things right before now. I'm sorry, Bree—sorry for it all."

She studied her feet. "You didn't make me cry. It was the wine. I didn't eat much, and I know better than to drink at a business meeting."

He stopped her mumbled excuses with his lips. Lightly at first, asking permission—forgiveness. She opened slowly, as if unsure of her reception. His chest swelled, and he tightened his arms around her.

God, I've missed her. His life had faded to black and white the night she'd galloped out of it. He tried to tell her all this with his kiss as he drank her in, like a man who'd found a seep in the desert. They were both breathless when he remembered. He lifted his head to ask, "What did you want to tell me, Bree?"

She twitched and a bolt of guilt flashed across her face. "Max, I..."

Maybe she was ready to finally tell him the secrets that had stood between them from the very first day. "You mentioned a phone call?"

She hesitated a moment, then smiled. "I got *the* phone call. From Glenn Martin, the stock contractor of the PBR. He said he'd heard good things about Fire Ant and invited us to bring him to the Built Ford Tough event in Denver this weekend!" She bounced on her toes. "Isn't that amazing?"

"*This* weekend? That isn't a lot of notice, is it?"

"Well, they probably had another bull pull out at the last minute. This is our chance. Don't you just feel it?"

As she looked up at him, hope shining on her sweet face, he felt something all right, but her little pissant bull had nothing to do with it. He pulled her into a hug, just to have his hands on her. She hugged him back, but let him go too soon.

"Come on, bucko. We've got work to do." She handed him the empty bucket. "Would you mind finishing this for me? I've got to figure out how to give Fire Ant a bath. He can't go to his debut a smelly mess. Then, I've got to wash the trailer and get our logo put on the truck doors." Max enjoyed the view of her cute butt as she strode away, talking to herself. "Jeez, what should I wear? I mean, I *am* an owner..."

He addressed her retreating back. "Just put the Ant in the squeeze chute and turn the hose on him. He won't be happy about it, but it should get the worst of the dirt off."

He looked down at the bucket, then up at Peanut, who tossed his head and stomped a hoof. "Dang, demanding cuss, aren't you?" he grumbled as he walked to the grain bin. "You've been hanging around your owner too long."

CHAPTER 24

Bree tossed the black halter bra in the vinyl tote on the bed and dug for the matching underwear in the suitcase beneath it. She'd blown another opportunity to tell Max. She recalled the warm acceptance in his brown eyes. There was hope for the future in them.

Home. His kiss made her feel like she'd found home. She might be damned for a coward, but she couldn't make herself say the words to reveal her past. It'd be like stepping in front of a car on purpose. Your mind won't allow you to do it, even if you need to.

Bree considered the little black dress hanging in the armoire. Surely that was too fancy to take to a bull bucking. *But maybe we'll have something to celebrate.* She chose a pastel silk scarf from her considerable collection and tied it on the hanger. *Never hurts to be prepared.* Bending, she retrieved her black stilettos from the very back and wiped the dust off. As long as she was dreaming, might as well go all the way. If Fire Ant somehow managed to go unridden at a televised Built Ford Tough event, the publicity would help to launch him as a sire. And that's where the real money was.

Tucking the dress into a hanging bag, she picked up her tote and walked out to the truck.

Bree checked the sky. Today had dawned fine, but a front was moving in. The eastern horizon looked like it had been bludgeoned. Purple-bottomed clouds spread like an angry bruise, their tops boiling upward. Fire Ant was already loaded in the enclosed trailer, and the cowboys stood by the truck door, grinning and pointing. Max didn't look happy. *One more cloud on the horizon.* She squelched a smile and walked across the yard to face the music.

"What the heck is this?" Max pointed at the magnetic sign she'd put on the door of the truck. She'd created the company's logo: TOTAL bold, black and masculine. *Bull* in fanciful script, and tied to the tail of the last "L," a pink bow.

TOTAL BULL ❧

Her grin stretched wide. He was *really* going to hate the idea she had planned for the event itself. Opening the jump seat door of the truck, she hopped in. "Marketing."

Max looked aghast. "You've got to be kidding me. We're gonna get laughed out of Denver!"

She stuck her head out the window. "Max, the logo makes us different. It takes advantage of the fact that you have a female partner in a masculine sport. Don't you get it? We'll be the talk of the event."

"If you think I'm driving into a parking lot full of good-ol'-boys with *that*"—he pointed to the offending sign—"you're nuts. We'll be the talk of the event, all right. I'll get my butt kicked all over the arena."

Wyatt opened the driver's side door. "Then I'll drive."

"That's not what I meant."

Wyatt pushed Max's back. "Get your butt in the truck, Max. Bree's right. This is a good idea."

"I shoulda known you'd side with her." Wyatt leveled him a chilly stare. Glancing over, Max saw Bree's frown. "Oh, all right." He climbed into the truck and scooted to the passenger side. "But I will never live this down."

"I'm not telling you your business, sweetie, but this is important." Bree addressed her bull, where he stood in the small pole enclosure, chewing cud. She'd worried that the indoor arena, all the people, and the proximity of other bulls would make Fire Ant nervous, but she needn't have bothered. He'd strutted off the truck and settled in to his favorite pastime—eating. "The third ranked rider has drawn you," she continued. "He's not going to be as easy to buck off. I'm not even going to tell you his name. It'd make you too nervous." She paced in front of the fence.

"You've got to change it up. If spinning one way doesn't do it, you'll have to switch direction or lunge forward." As she demonstrated possible movements, Fire Ant turned his back and wandered to the hay manger. "Okay, okay, I know you know this stuff. I don't mean to offend you." After all, the pep talk was more for her anyway.

Bree leaned away from the gate and smiled at the sight of the pink bow tied to it. It matched the shade of her long-sleeved shirt. Their logo had created quite a stir, so she'd decided to carry on the theme. Max wasn't quite as enthused. The few times she'd seen him since they pulled in, he was darting looks around and mumbling under his breath.

She gave Fire Ant one last glance, then wandered through the labyrinth of hallways to the concourse. A broad hall circled the arena itself, packed with concession stands and souvenir shops, all dark this early. Turning in at an entrance to the stands, she looked past the tiers of seats to the dirt-covered arena floor. Butterflies took flight in her stomach.

The "Shark Cage" was set up in the center, a squat, round structure that would house the television cameramen tonight, the platform on top a safe haven from charging bulls. Cables snaked everywhere as workers swarmed to get set up. There were six bucking chutes—three on either side of a wide exit gate, with a catwalk above for riders and bull handlers. Sponsor logos hung from every available surface, to take full advantage of camera time. A huge electronic scoreboard hanging from the ceiling flashed "WELCOME TO THE PBR—THE TOUGHEST SPORT ON EARTH."

Bree slid sweaty hands in her pockets. In forty-eight hours Total Bull would either be recognized as an up-and-coming contractor, or a wannabe outfit.

Anticipation shivered up her spine. The real-life stakes were higher than that. While she had a captive audience in the truck on the way home, she was going to tell her partners of her past. Afterward, one way or another, she could get on with her life.

"Hey, pretty girl." Max hailed her from two tiers of seats above. She watched as he strode the stairs to her, fluid as a cat. Long legs in tight slim-cut jeans, sharp creases faded to white from repeated ironing. A starched red Western shirt tucked in at his waist, showing off his bronzed face and huge shoulders. *How could any girl not fall for a cowboy?* She lingered on his dear, craggy face, and best of all, the warm promise in those dark chocolate eyes. They spoke to her of possession. Though the concept would have seemed barbaric to her in the past, she liked the idea of being possessed by this man.

She felt poised on the blade of time. One side held this man and the fulfillment of the promise in his eyes. A home, a career, maybe even a family. The other side... *I'm not even going there. Not now.*

Max reached her step. "Where've you been? We have to find a hotel room, get cleaned up, and be back here by three." He bent to give her a quick kiss. Well, it started that way, anyway. She put her hands on his shoulders, felt for the riser with her heel and stepped up, so her face was almost even with his. Wrapping her arms around his neck, she poured everything she had into that kiss, wanting to burn herself into his mind like a brand. To make him so indelibly hers that he couldn't make her leave. As he tugged her snug against his hard body, his hat fell off. Not that either of them noticed.

"Jesus, after all this time, you two still haven't found a room?" Janet stood above them at the entrance to the concourse in designer jeans, an electric-blue silk blouse, and lots of bling.

Bree shook her head to disperse the passion fog. "Janet?" *Is there some kind of cosmic law that if I'm making out in public, she has to show up?*

Max bent to retrieve his hat. "You're the last person I expected to see in Denver, Janet. Did you come for the event tonight?"

"Hardly. I'm in town for Fashion Week Denver." She fluffed her hair. "Living in the mountains may be trendy, but it's hell on one's wardrobe."

Bree grinned. "So you just happened to wander across town to the coliseum?" She took the steps two at a time until she stood close enough to be engulfed in the woman's exotic perfume. "You don't fool me, Janet. You want to see how Fire Ant bucks!"

"Don't be silly. Max talked up the PBR, and I told Harrison. He *may* be interested in making an investment, so I'm scouting it out for him."

Bree only smiled.

"Therefore, I will be at the event tonight." With that, she turned on the heel of her shiny Manolos and strutted away.

Max's eyes in the rearview mirror were the color of smoke as he watched Bree. She teased him, wetting her lips and unbuttoning the top button of her blouse. She felt the truck surge beneath her.

"Slow down, Max." Wyatt glanced up from the map in his lap. "Relax, we're not that late. You're going to get a ticket." He pointed. "Turn left at High Street. The motel's next to the park."

Ten minutes later, Max jogged back to the truck, room keys jingling in his hand. "I've got something to discuss with Bree, Wyatt. Why don't you jump in the shower first? I'll be right behind you." Taking the carryall from Bree, he grasped her elbow, hustling her to the room number printed in flaking gold on the green plastic key chain.

When he opened the door, the room looked familiar to Bree from her cross-country trip—small, cheap, generic. She hung the dress in the empty closet behind the door. "I've got to get ready." Max snatched her against him as he kicked the door closed with his heel. She raked her fingers through his hair. "We really don't have time for this."

He growled and captured her lips. His hands slid to the small of her back and down, tilting her hips against him. His iron erection rolled against her through snug jeans. She realized that with the mating dance in the truck, she'd been teasing herself as well. She wanted him. *Now.*

She whimpered, tugging at his buttons. He released her lips to rip the shirt over her head. "I'm gonna help you get undressed so you can hop in the shower." He sucked the tender spot just behind her earlobe. A shudder of passion shot straight to her crotch. He knew all her sexual buttons and seemed hell-bent on pushing every one.

He thumbed the catch to her bra and her freed breasts spilled into his hands. Tossing the bra away, he bent to suckle her. Bree gasped as lust surged into her brain, wiping out all coherent thought. Ignoring his shirt, she tugged at the buttons of his Wranglers. Separating for only a moment, they toed off boots and skinned out of jeans, laughing at their own haste. Max tossed his hat on the bed, not bothering with his shirt. He reached for his jeans pocket, retrieved a condom, and unrolled it on his length. As he turned to her, the want in his eyes made her bold, made her wish *she* could take *him*.

Need screamed under her skin as she reached for him, but he was quicker. As he lifted her, she wrapped her legs around his waist, her mouth taking his. She hardly noticed her back slamming into the wall, because he was there. The tip of him poised at her molten, pulsing center. He went still, except for a fine tremor she felt running through his arms, and his torso, under her thighs. Only their ragged breathing disturbed the room's hush. She opened her eyes. The hard planes of his weathered face and his searing focus would have frightened her before. Before she pushed through the wall of anger to find the caring, conflicted man that lived behind it. His gaze targeted her lips. He waited.

"*Now,* Max."

He thrust, moaning as he filled her. But it wasn't enough. She tightened her embrace, wanting to fuse to him as her greedy body strained for more. When she bit his shoulder, he groaned and thrust deep. This is what she wanted. What she needed. Max. Hard, brutal, fast. She threw her head back as he pumped his hips. His teeth raked her neck, sending shocks coursing to the only part of her that existed—the part connected to him. He grunted, speeding up, as she clung, the raging storm inside wiping out everything.

Her voice was husky in her own ears. "I'm here. Take me."

Their slick bodies slid, his fingers digging in the soft skin of her butt as he bucked against her, harder, faster. "Yes." She panted. "Oh, yes." Her muscles clenched around him, straining to pull him closer, even as she splintered apart.

Suddenly, it was too much. Terrified she'd lose herself and not be able to find her way back, she clung to him, head buried in his neck as the orgasm went on and on. With a deep growl in her ear, he strained as he emptied himself into her.

"I love you." It slipped out on her labored breath. On the heels of surprise, an amazing joy burst in her chest. In wonder, she whispered it again, just to test the words. "I love you."

Bree dragged in several deep breaths and slowly, reluctantly, unwound herself, sliding down the wall and out of his arms.

He missed her arm on the way by. "Bree, wait."

Shy, and afraid of his response, she gathered his clothes, filling his arms with them. "Hurry, Max, we're late."

He stood, chest heaving. "Bree, we have to talk."

She kissed her fingers and touched them to his lips. "What we have to do is grab a shower. We are really late." She hurried to the bathroom, leaving him naked but for his shirt and a confused expression.

Closing the door, she leaned against it, her heart trying to pound out of her chest. Lord, she'd done it now.

Hearing the outer door open and close, she was grateful that he was old-fashioned, insisting he and Wyatt room together. She needed some time. Telling him she loved him before divulging her past hadn't been in the plan. Strangely, she didn't feel the least bit sorry. She wouldn't take back the words for anything.

But. She touched her throat as the happy bubble in her chest popped and icy doubts trickled in. The spigot opened on the acid bath in her gut. *I still have to tell him.*

Would he think she'd said it to soften the sledgehammer blow of her past? Or worse, to manipulate him? She reached to turn on the shower. Surely he knew her well enough to know the truth when he heard it? And who knew? Maybe knowing she loved him would tip the scales when the weight hit the other side of the scale.

The remainder of the day stood before her like a mountain on the horizon back home. She knew that today would always stand out on the landscape of her life.

As either a triumph or her greatest failure.

CHAPTER
25

They checked in at the coliseum and were issued laminated exhibitor badges to hang on lanyards around their necks. Max and Wyatt headed for the bull enclosures to check on Fire Ant. Since they'd been too rushed to eat lunch, Bree volunteered to buy hot dogs. There was no way her burning stomach could handle food, but she wasn't ready for questions from Max.

Someone jostled her in passing, intruding on her thoughts. Bree glanced around, becoming aware of the changes in the concourse. The place was mobbed. People of all shapes and sizes crowded the opposing traffic lanes. Wranglers and cowboy hats were the order of the day, and light glinted off more than one massive silver belt buckle. In her jeans, boots, cowgirl hat, and hot-pink Western shirt, she fit right in. Bree smiled down at a towheaded toddler in Western garb, authentic right down to the neckerchief and tiny red cowboy boots.

The worst bottleneck formed around the beer vendor, and as the crowd moved her closer, Bree saw why. Young girls hired as booth bait were dressed in outfits reminiscent of the Dallas Cowboy cheerleaders. Only smaller—their largest item of clothing being their ten-gallon hats. The noise of the crowd echoed off the high ceiling, amplifying it to a roar. A rollicking country song blared from the speakers, and the smell of hot dogs, popcorn, nachos, and beer mingled to produce the signature aroma of any sporting event.

Bree eyed the food concessions in passing. Their lines snaked into the hallway traffic, forcing an eddy in the flow as people dodged around them. It would take a good fifteen minutes to get to the counter. Pulling her cell phone from her pocket, she checked the time. The boys were going to have to wait to eat. She fell out of the crowd at the end of the concourse and took the stairs two at a time.

She trotted to the bull enclosures, noting that Fire Ant seemed more alert than usual as he paced the fence. Bulls bawled and owners hustled, getting ready.

Max straightened from where he leaned on the fence, Wyatt at his side. "Good, you're back. I've got to get the flank rope from the truck."

She cocked her head. "I've got it, Max. Why don't you guys find your seats? And don't even think of getting something to eat. It's a mob scene up there."

"You mean to flank the bull?" Max frowned. "It's dangerous. No place for a—"

He glanced to Wyatt's frown. "Oh, all right. I'm evolving. I'm evolving."

Wyatt addressed the bull. "Break a leg, buddy." He gave Bree a quick hug, then threw an arm over his brother's shoulders. "Come on, Maxie. Let's let this lady get to work."

The announcer's voice blared from the loudspeakers, welcoming everyone to the PBR. The rodeo clown warmed up the crowd, dashing into the stands and dancing with members of the audience.

Bree listened with half an ear as she tugged her surprise from a carryall. The soft flank rope was hot pink. A young man carrying a clipboard wandered up and introduced himself as a "color man." It was his job to get information on the riders and the bulls for the announcer to use. A copy would be given to the TV announcers as well.

He eyed the gaudy rope in her hand. "Hey, you must be the outfit with the pink sign on the truck. What's the deal?" She explained, and he scribbled furiously.

When a bull handler opened the gate to Fire Ant's enclosure and prodded him into the maze of alleyways that led to the bucking chutes, Bree excused herself. She wasn't worried about her bull. The handlers she'd met were professional and gentle. Fire Ant would be put in a queue in the order he'd perform. She'd told them he bucked better from a right-hand delivery, so he'd be in one of the three chutes on the right. Bulls were like people that way, and Fire Ant was right-handed.

The mood of the tight area behind the chutes crackled with subdued excitement and testosterone. Riders in chaps and spurs spread stickum on their ropes, stretched, meditated with iPods, or joked with their buddies. Here were all the riders Bree had watched on TV every week at the ranch. God, they looked even younger in person! Thirty was grandpa status for a bull rider, and some of these kids couldn't be more than eighteen, struggling to grow a soul patch on their pimply chins. Young they might be, but Bree was in awe of the courage it took to straddle a one-ton animal that wanted nothing more than to gore you and then stomp your guts out.

She got more than one sidelong glance, being the only woman. Or maybe it was the hot-pink rope. Bree sidled up to a group of bull owners. They tipped their hats and conversation died midsentence. Okay, so she didn't fit in here either.

Spying Fire Ant in the alley, she walked over. Might as well get him ready. Picking up a bent metal hook, she climbed the pole fence beside him. Shaking out the flank rope, she laid it across his back to dangle, then reached under his belly with the hook to catch the eye in the end of the rope and lifted it. Centering the rope just in front of his hips, she tied it in a loose half hitch and jumped down. The pink showed off well against his dark spots.

"You look maaavelous, darling." The bull studiously ignored her. Bree stepped back, comparing him with the others in line. He was a dwarf among giants, and his cock-eyed horns gave him an air of confusion. Add the pink rope, and even she had to admit he looked downright comical. "That's okay, baby. It's not the size of the dog in the fight. You hold your head up and show them what a Colorado bull can do."

The line moved up, signaling that they'd loaded the first bulls in the chutes. She gave Fire Ant a pat on the hip and walked to the edge of the stands to watch.

The lights were doused and the crowd went quiet in anticipation. A roadie touched a torch to the fuel oil on the ground in front of the bucking chutes. A soft blue flame advanced, spelling out "PBR."

A fountain of fireworks shot almost to the roof as the announcer's voice boomed in the dark arena, introducing

the attending past champion riders one by one. The spot-
lights hit them where they posed on platforms, high above
the chutes. Each raised his hat in salute, and the capacity
crowd went wild.

Bree smiled at the Hollywood dramatics, but her body
reacted anyway. Anticipation fizzed like champagne in her
veins and spread to the entire building. She was swept up
and carried along on a wave of gut-tightening excitement.

As the lights came up, the safety roper galloped into
the arena on a flashy Appaloosa. Like the bullfighters
who ran in the arena after him, he'd be there to help protect the downed riders.

After a prayer and the national anthem, the announcer
called the crowd's attention to the first chute on the left,
where a tiny cowboy straddled the chute, his head dwarfed
by his hat. He settled on a tall, rangy, slab-sided bull with
a wicked twist to his long horns. Bree leaned against the
rail, heart in her throat. How could the kid's mother stand
to watch this?

The little cowboy nodded, and they swung the gate open.
The bull lunged into the arena, kicking almost vertically.
The rider was thrown immediately, and the bull stopped
bucking when he spied the vulnerable target scrabbling on
the dirt, trying to get away. Bree stopped breathing as the
bull put his head down and charged. One of the bullfighters
"shot the gap," running between the bull and the downed
rider, offering a better target. It worked. The bull charged
after the bullfighter instead, who scooted to the edge of the
arena and jumped to safety on the fence.

Dirt that flew from the bull's hooves pattered the front
of her shirt as he galloped by. When the clown threw his hat
at the bull from the safety of the shark's cage, the laughter

of the crowd broke the tension. The safety roper cantered into position behind the runaway and herded him to the exit gate.

A guillotine-style gate lifted and a huge red bull squeezed into the chute next to Bree. She looked across the arena to see Fire Ant trot into the last chute.

It was time. In fifteen minutes Total Bull would go from dream to reality.

Or dream to nightmare.

She crossed the back of the chutes, half wanting to run to the nearest exit.

A fat man with a clipboard barred the steps to the catwalk. "Sorry, missy. This is for owners and riders only."

She lifted the laminated badge from her chest. "I'm flanking my bull." The man squinted at her badge, then reluctantly stepped aside, disapproval apparent on his pudgy face.

"I may have happened upon the last pocket of pre-historic men on earth," she grumbled, wending her way through the riders and TV cameramen.

The rider directly above Fire Ant's chute bounced on the balls of his feet, pulling at his gloves, blowing deep breaths. Bree took her position at the bull's hips. Surprise dawned on the young man's face, but he reached to shake her hand. "Thanks for the opportunity, ma'am."

She flushed, a bit in awe to be meeting the number-three bull rider in the world. "Good luck, cowboy."

The cameraman took it all in. Bree leaned over the bars to snug up the flank rope, measuring fit by sliding the width of her hand under the rope. Just right.

Her ears perked, hearing her name. The announcer broadcast, "The next bull is new to the Built Ford Tough Series. The Total Bull outfit has made a stir this weekend with their female owner and pink logo. Let's see what the little guy can do."

The cowboy straddled the fence and lowered himself onto Fire Ant's back. Several riders offered advice and encouragement as he jerked his hand along the rope to warm the stickum. A cowboy on the arena side of the chute pulled the rope taut, then passed it to the rider, to wrap his hand in the rigging.

"This is going to be a piece of cake, little dude like this," one of his friends said.

"You get bucked off by a bull this small, you owe me dinner," said another.

Bree's voice sounded loud in the sudden silence. "You kick butt, Fire Ant!" The cowboys sniggered. She didn't care. She kissed her fingers and patted her bull's flank. "You show 'em, baby."

Time seemed to slow as Bree studied the young man's profile. A muscle worked in his jaw, his face hard and focused. He bore down, then nodded.

As the gate opened, Fire Ant exploded, leaping high out of the chute and landing with his signature bone-jarring thump. He started his usual fast spin to the right. The rider was caught a bit behind at first, but shifted his hips in a brilliant move to catch up and negate the strength of the spin. Bree held her breath and glanced quickly up at the clock: 3.45. The numbers whizzed by. If something didn't happen soon, the rider was going to make the eight-second buzzer.

Fire Ant stopped dead, hesitated and spun the opposite way. The rider wasn't ready; he lost his balance first, then the grip with his spurs. Centrifugal force caught and cartwheeled him into the dirt. The bullfighters moved in, but they needn't have bothered.

The minute the rider was off, Fire Ant stopped bucking. He stopped still, looking as if he were posing for the cameras. Everyone scrambled out of the way as Fire Ant strutted slowly to the exit, head held high, as if to say, "Don't waste my time."

Bree finally remembered to breathe, taking in a huge lungful of air as the announcer came on. "The judges score the bull 46.25 out of a possible 50." The crowd cheered. "People might not want to laugh at that little guy's pink flank rope. I think it ticks him off."

Bree bounced on the balls of her feet and looked to the stands. Her partners were both standing. Wyatt tugged on his neighbor's arm, pointing at the arena and jumping up and down. Max pumped his fist in the air and sent a smile for her alone. Bree put her hand on her mouth and giggled. "He did it!" She turned to the cowboys. "Did you see that? Is that bull amazing or what?"

She jogged down the stairs, darted under the girders holding up the catwalk, bent over, and tried not to throw up.

Max and Wyatt got to the bull enclosure first. Fire Ant paced the small area, looking ready to take all comers.

Bree trotted up. Wyatt lifted and spun her in a circle, laughing. He put her down and backed away, frowning. "Are you feeling okay? You look a little green."

"How could I not be fine after that?" She turned to Max. "Are you mad about the pink flank rope?"

Max was so proud of the bull he could kiss him. He settled instead for kissing Bree. "Honey, you can dress him up in a tutu if it'll make him buck like that."

He watched as Wyatt and Bree chattered, reliving every

movement of the ride. In her pink cowgirl getup, you couldn't tell her from a country girl.

Maybe she's earned the right to be called a country girl. She'd certainly taken to the duties. Maybe her attitude wasn't traditional, but he was learning to live with that. Bree's admission this afternoon had brought him up short. He'd been so busy enjoying her the past month or so, he hadn't thought about where it would lead. He should have realized she would.

He smiled. She may be a liberated businesswoman, but she'd be wanting to build a nest and settle down soon. It was how women were made.

Well, that was fine with him. Traditional or no, he loved this feisty woman. He'd let her make the arrangements, but he was looking forward to a long winter, snuggling with her in his bed as the storms howled outside.

He broke into their babble. "We're going out to celebrate tonight, at the fanciest steak restaurant this town's got." He rolled the hideous pink flank rope and returned it to the carryall. "You put on that pretty dress, honey, and Total Bull will show Denver what a party looks like."

"We can dress up, but we don't need to spend a lot of money." Bree frowned. "I saw a Denny's on the way in."

Wyatt's mouth dropped in horror. "*Denny's?* That will not do. I'll choose the restaurant, and it's on me. I've got more than Total Bull's success to celebrate tonight. On this trip, I've found my way back to my brother." He nodded to Max. "So no arguments." He put his arm around Bree. "Besides, I want to see you in those stilettos."

Leaning over the bathroom sink in her underwear, Bree brushed on mascara. She'd decided not to put her hair up. Instead she caught the sides in matching tortoise-shell combs and left the rest to tumble to her shoulders. Not sophisticated, but the style more fit her new life. She adjusted the black lace halter bra and turned to check her butt in the matching high-rise underwear—sexy, but she hoped she wouldn't be tugging them out of her crack all night. They were a bit skimpy.

She grabbed the pastel silk scarf for her neck. She looped it over her head, but then hesitated, taking a close look in the mirror. The scar seemed less red than earlier in the summer.

Could I?

Going without a scarf would feel like strutting through Walmart in her underwear. Tilting her head, she studied her neck from different angles. A thrill of daring shivered through her. In twenty-four hours, Max would know how she'd gotten it anyway.

Maybe it's time to accept that this is who I am now. On her way by the bed, she let the bit of silk slip from her fingers.

No more hiding. Starting tomorrow, what you see is what you get with Bree Tanner—I mean Madison. No. Tanner.

She realized she didn't want to be Aubrey Madison any longer. She was leaving that name behind along with the memories of who she used to be.

Feeling lighter, she pulled the silky black dress over her head and stepped into the tall heels. The mirror reflected the Bree she used to know, sophisticated, competent, self-assured. *They say looks can deceive. They sure convinced me.* She gave herself a mental shake. She wasn't going there. Not tonight. Something told her it was going to be special. Joy fizzed in her chest and potential whispered in the swish of her silk dress.

Except for the freckles, her shoulders were pretty in the backless halter dress, and the full skirt made her legs look even longer. And those shoes. She pointed a toe, admiring. They were worth the chunk of OCT paycheck she'd spent on them. It seemed so many years ago.

A knock interrupted as she'd snapped the cap back on her lipstick. Picking up her black clutch and diaphanous gold wrap from the desk, she opened the door to her escorts.

Wyatt's slicked-back blond hair set off his angelic looks, and the black suit showed off his newly acquired tan. Bree put a hand to her chest. "Wyatt, you take my breath away." She stepped out of the room and the door closed behind her.

Saving the best for last, she turned to Max. She'd pictured him looking awkward in a suit. He didn't. From the crown of the black Resistol hat to the tips of his shiny black boots, he was the epitome of gentleman rancher. If possible, the double-peak yoke of his black Western jacket made his shoulders even wider. He'd opted for a simple onyx stone bolo tie set in silver, a matching onyx buckle at his trim waist. "And *you* take everything else."

His teeth flashed white against his bronze skin, and the heat in those dark eyes made her aware of her nakedness under the silk dress. Somehow the trappings of society made him appear more savage by comparison. She curled her fingers to keep from reaching for him. Dampness touched the scrap of silk between her legs as her body remembered his strength and the thrilling wildness this afternoon.

When his searing gaze followed her every move, she knew they were sharing the same memory. His gaze strayed to her neck, and her hand flew to the scar. Self-conscious heat filled her face. She spun to the door, fumbling for her key in the tiny clutch. "I forgot my scarf."

Max's hand caught her elbow. His other slid lightly across her back. She shivered when he leaned to whisper in her ear, "You look in the mirror and you don't like what you see? Don't believe it. Look into my eyes; I'm the only mirror you'll ever need."

She did. Something in them filled a part of her she hadn't known was empty. He didn't have to speak the words. Bree drank in the love that radiated from his look. His touch.

Wyatt cleared his throat and checked his watch. "Pardon me, but we do have reservations."

Laughing as she stepped onto the sidewalk, Bree inhaled the freshness of the oncoming dusk and the sweet scent of the roses planted next to her door. She felt like this was the prom night she'd never had.

They walked the few steps to the truck, and Wyatt slid into the backseat. She eyed the long step up, but suddenly, Max's arms were there, lifting her onto the seat as if she weighed nothing. Watching him as he jogged around the front of the truck, she shivered with anticipation. *This could be a night I remember for the rest of my life—a night to tell my daughter about someday.*

CHAPTER
26

Max felt the slight pause in the room when they walked in. He noted the wolf-hungry looks on the men's faces they passed. It wasn't that Bree was the most beautiful woman in the room full of surgery-enhanced, pampered female skin, even though she was. He glanced to her freckles and red hair, tamed for once with combs and hair spray. What drew every male eye tonight was her vitality, the sheer femininity that sparked from her like a low-level electric current.

His chest swelled. *Eat your hearts out. She's mine.*

The waiter escorted them to the best table in the place. He had to remember to thank Wyatt later. The panoramic picture window displayed the perfect rolling emerald lawn of the golf course. Not that he'd given it more than a cursory glance. He could hardly look away from the woman beside him and the radiance of soft light the sunset left on her skin.

"Can you believe Fire Ant had the highest score of the round today?" Bree laid a pristine linen napkin in her lap. "He bucked fair, too. No cheap moves. If he keeps this up,

the riders will want him when he gets to be a final round."
She turned to Wyatt. "I forgot to tell you, I got Juan's check
in the mail before we left. Will you thank him for me?"

Wyatt said, "You can thank him yourself. He's flying
in for Thanksgiving."

She hesitated, absorbing surprise. "Oh, Wyatt, I'm so
pleased." She shot a glance at Max. "I can't wait to meet him."

"Man has a right to see his investment." Max cleared
his throat. "Besides, he might as well see the family he's
gotten himself into." He ducked his head.

"I talked to Armando before we left. He says we'll
have four or five promising youngsters next year to take
to Challenger Tour events. If we're hauling a full trailer,
we'll start making some real money."

Wyatt sipped from a crystal glass of ice water. "And
next spring, we'll have calves on the ground from the
semen we bought this year. In a couple of years, we'll see
Bree's dream come to fruition."

Max took his elbows off the table. "We're maybe getting a bit ahead of ourselves here."

"Don't be a killjoy, Maxie. Dreaming is free."

"And dreaming is about all we can afford right now."
Bree eyed the magnum of champagne the waiter proffered for Wyatt's approval. At his nod, the waiter popped
the cork, poured, and set the bottle in a free standing ice
bucket beside the table.

Wyatt raised his glass. "I've taken a page from Max's
book of quotes for the occasion." He paused, waiting for
the partners to lift their glasses. "Success usually comes
to those who are too busy to be looking for it." He took a
sip. "Thoreau." He raised an eyebrow at Max.

"Ah, a challenge. Let me think..." Max raised his

glass. "Success is getting what you want. Happiness is wanting what you get." They all sipped. "Dale Carnegie."

"No fair. I didn't get the memo." Bree chewed her lower lip. "I know!" Smiling, she raised her glass. "We came, we saw, we kicked its ass! Bill Murray." She laughed, and the crystal rang as they touched glasses.

Bree wanted to stop time. She tuned out of the men's conversation and absorbed the luxurious details around her, wanting to burn them into her memory: The stiff linen table-cloth, subdued light glinting on the silver, and the delicious sliding of cool air on her bare skin. With a jolt, she realized that for the first time in her life, she didn't feel like a dressed-up imposter in plush surroundings. As if she'd some-how slipped into her own skin, she suddenly *belonged*. The lights came on outside, bright circles of green on the grass. She sighed, wallowing in the comforting sense of having finally arrived. She glanced at Max. *How did I get so lucky?*

Max halted midsentence, feeling a looming presence at his elbow. A young man in a slouched jacket with spiky bleached hair and two diamond studs in one ear stood at the edge of their table. The jailbait draped on his arm wasn't much better. The shiny pink baby-doll dress hit her upper thigh, and the clunky heels made her feet look like canapés on the ends of toothpicks—tattooed toothpicks.

The man stared across at Bree and said in a California-hip voice, "Well. Aubrey Madison."

Bree's jaw dropped open as if someone had cut the muscles.

"Babe, you're the *last* person I expected to see. You're in town for Fashion Week, right? Who are you working for now, and when did you get out of prison?"

What the hell? Max saw the life drain from Bree's face. Her eyes went dead. He didn't know what was going on, but nobody was talking to her like that. He balled his napkin, threw it on the table, and shot to his feet.

The man addressed the canapé girl. "Aubrey was the controller when I worked at Other Coast Trends until they hauled her away in handcuffs." He looked down his nose at Bree. "Not that she ever fit in there, anyway. Vic must have felt sorry for her. I mean, look at her. Where did you get that hideous scar?"

Max didn't think—he grabbed a fistful of jacket and jerked the twerp up on his toes. "How about you and me have a discussion?" Nose to nose, he saw fear in the bastard's eye. "Outside."

The waiter pulled at his sleeve. "Sir! This is not a saloon! Please!"

Max let the dude go, to stumble backward. "Listen up, asshole. You need to learn how to behave around a lady." He snorted. "And you shouldn't go poking at something meaner'n you." He shot his cuffs as the waiter hustled the couple away.

Max looked across the table at Bree.

He expected angry denials, sputtering outrage, righteous indignation. Bree just sat there. Anyone else would see a beautiful, composed young woman. Until they looked closer, at her eyes; it looked as though her soul had left her body.

A frantic animal fear climbed out of his belly, digging cold-tipped claws into his heart. He wanted to stop time. To roll it back to when he didn't know what his mind was about to comprehend. Bree's secret. Revealed.

The last sign of life was in her eyes, where a spark

burned hot. His brain scrambled for a misunderstanding. A mistake. An excuse.

When the spark flickered out, his hope died.

"I was going to tell you," she almost whispered. "I was going to tell you on the way home."

Alarm ran through Max, quick as a shiver. He narrowed his eyes. "There's nothing to what that SOB said."

Her hand reached up to cover the scar, and like a penitent, she bent her head.

His legs went out from under him. He plopped into his seat.

Wyatt leaned over to touch her forearm. "Oh, Bree." His words trailed off, as if he'd run out of breath. Wyatt sounded sorry.

"You were in prison?"

Wyatt glanced around. "Shhh, Max."

When she looked up, her eyes begged him to wait—to listen. But he also saw the truth that swam with tears in her reddened eyes.

"I tried to tell you," she almost whispered. "The night of the board meeting."

"Bullshit!" Nearby heads swiveled, and he lowered his voice. "You said you loved me." He jumped to his feet, shoving his chair back. "And now I find out I don't even know your real *name*?" His gut threatened to rebel against the champagne, but he waited, desperate to hear some viable explanation.

The frozen horror on her tear-streaked face was his answer. Reaching for his wallet, he addressed Wyatt. "I'll take care of the bill. I'll see you at the motel." He glanced at Bree, almost hoping she'd stop him.

She didn't.

"Oh and, Wyatt? Don't wait up."

He spun on his heel and got the hell out.

Bree watched Max's broad back until it disappeared through the doorway. She couldn't think past the panic as thoughts swirled like a blizzard in her brain. As she'd grab for one, it would melt like a snowflake, leaving nothing of substance behind. She knew she had to do *something*. But what?

Wyatt sighed and folded his napkin on the table. "Come on, Bree. We'll pick him up on the way home."

She jolted upright. "No!"

The tired lines in Wyatt's face creased as he raised an eyebrow.

"You go to him, Wyatt. He needs you." She reached for her purse.

"I'm not leaving you here alone."

Irritation flared at his solicitous tone. And it felt good. Anything felt better than the Novocain numbness of shame.

"Wyatt Jameson. I lived in LA for five years. Alone." She took the tissue he offered and tried to get a grip. "I survived prison. I think I can manage a taxi on my own." She glanced to the empty doorway, then into his eyes. "Please?"

"I don't like it." He searched her face. "But if that's what you want." As Wyatt stood, the pity in his voice cut more than the accusing look. "You were supposed to tell him a long time ago. What were you *thinking*, Bree?"

Max had walked only a quarter mile with his suit jacket slung over his shoulder when he heard the truck engine slowing behind him. As Wyatt pulled alongside, he kept walking.

His thoughts whirred in his head so fast that he caught

only pieces: Bree, jumping Smooth over the creek; her sitting in Tia's sitting room, knitting; her face in the crack of the tack room door before she opened it to him. Opened herself to him.

Those soft thoughts washed away before a flood of new visions—Bree in LA, a flashy businesswoman. Bree in handcuffs. Bree behind bars.

How could both visions be real? He thought he knew what betrayal felt like after Jo left. He realized now that he hadn't had a clue until tonight, when the truth in Bree's eyes opened the earth under his feet.

Wyatt lowered the window. "Max, get in the truck."

"Go back to the motel, Wyatt." He kept walking.

Wyatt kept pace with him, keeping a wary eye on the rearview mirror. "Quit being a baby. Get in the truck."

Max stopped, and his head snapped up. "Watch yourself, little brother. I don't need your shit right now." Wyatt should be grateful there was a door between them.

Wyatt leaned across the seat and opened the door. "Get in. I'll drop you at the bar." Max swung into the cab. "Although I should have more sense."

They rode in silence until Max pointed to a national chain hotel about a mile from their motel. "Pull in here. These places always have a bar."

Wyatt cut the wheel to the left and found a parking space out front.

Colorado had passed an interior smoking ban way back, but this place still carried an undertone of vintage stale smoke. Max glanced around the dim interior. The bar was one step above seedy but a step below tacky. Not that he cared, as long as they had booze. He made a beeline for the backlit bar. Several couples sat in overstuffed vinyl booths at small tables. The low light was designed to hide the dirt or disguise the patrons. Or maybe both. He'd bet his hat most of them were married—but not to their drinking companions.

Wyatt took in a delicate sniff. "Excellent choice, Max."

Max stepped up to the bar and signaled the bartender. "Johnnie Walker. A double." Wyatt slid onto the stool next to him.

"Now, Max—"

Max held up a hand and watched the drink being poured. When the glass touched down in front of him, he tossed it back and signaled for another. Then he sat.

Wyatt ordered a maça martini. "Max, you cannot kill enough brain cells to forget what just happened. You might as well talk about it."

"What the hell is a maça martini?" Max's lip curled. "Why can't you order a beer like a normal person?"

The bartender set the yellow-orange concoction in front of Wyatt. "Picking a fight with me isn't going to make you forget either." He picked up the skewered orange slice and chewed it.

"Don't start on me. Why aren't you off comforting her?" God, he sounded whiny.

Wyatt sipped his girly drink.

"There's no way you can put a good spin on this, Wyatt. Here I am sticking up for her in front of that asshole, and it turns out *he's* telling the truth." He threw back the Walker and looked around for the bartender. "I've been a fool, trotting after her all summer, my dick on a leash."

Wyatt took a sip from the oversized martini glass. "Hey, I'm on your side. The woman lied to you all this time, keeping quiet about being an ex-con."

Max narrowed his eyes and studied his brother's profile. "You agree with me?"

"Of course. Who'd have guessed she'd been in prison for—how long?"

"I don't know."

"Oh. So, anyway, we've got a convicted felon working for us. No, worse yet, she's our partner! What were we thinking?" He rested a chin on one palm and stared at his brother. "What was she convicted of again?"

"I don't know." Max tossed back the drink that appeared before him. "But that's not the point, and you know it."

"Yeah, you're right. A lie is a lie." Wyatt swirled his drink with the red plastic toothpick. "She did straighten out that tax mess that Dad left, though."

"Quit with the stirring. You look stupid."

Wyatt frowned into his drink, watching the vortex as he continued to stir. "And she did come up with the idea for Total Bull."

"Right. An idea that has made us exactly zero dollars so far. The only thing that's made any money is the bull that *she* owns." He reached out to cover Wyatt's busy hand. "Will you stop that? You're embarrassing me."

Wyatt shot him a hurt look. "Sorry. Am I breaking some man law?" He set the toothpick down next to his drink. "She should have told us, Max, no doubt. Except for what happened before we met her, what has she done that is so bad?"

"Goddammit, that's not the point." He *knew* Wyatt would take her side.

Wyatt swiveled to face him. "So what *is* the point, Maxie? Do you really think that Bree is dangerous?" He leaned in, leering, waving his fingers. "Murdered her little old grandma perhaps?" His tone sharpened. "Or is this about your wounded male ego, an antiquated belief system, and Colorado pigheadedness?"

"Don't push me, Wyatt. I'm not in the mood." When the bartender poured him a refill, Max grabbed his wrist. "Save yourself the walk. Just leave the bottle." He waved a hand at his brother. "And, you. Go away."

"It wasn't even her fault. But you don't care about that." Wyatt snorted. "You kill me, Max. You're willing to throw away the best thing that ever happened to you without knowing all the facts." Wyatt cocked his head. "I can't figure out if you never loved her at all, or if you're just the shallowest person I've ever met."

Not her fault? The booze fog thinned, exposing the stark truth. Molten outrage flowed from his brain to pool in his chest, then coursed through the rest of his body, scorching everything it touched. "You knew. All this time—"

Wyatt looked down the delicate nose he'd inherited from his mother. "Do you think I was going to let you go into business, much less fall in love, with someone who obviously had something to hide?"

"You arrogant little sonofa—" Max took a swing. Wyatt jerked back, and his fist whizzed past his brother's chin. The traitorous bar stool swiveled and the momentum spun him off, to land on his hands and knees on the sticky floor. His head whirled, his stomach lurched.

Wyatt looked down on him. "You can walk back to the hotel. Hopefully the cold air will bring you some clarity." He *tsk*ed in disgust. "I'm going to call Juan and book a flight home. I've had all the ignorant I can stand."

CHAPTER 27

Bree paced the floor in front of the window in her hotel room. The Heather truck hadn't been in the parking lot when the cab dropped her off. She glanced to the clock on the nightstand. Two hours ago.

Not that she knew what would happen when they did return. She took an angry swipe at escapee tendrils of ponytail crawling at her neck. She'd changed into jeans as soon the door closed, and the silk dress lay in a heap on the closet floor. She didn't need a reminder of this evening hanging in her face.

Chewing her lip, she took the four steps to the opposite wall. While traversing miles of carpet, she'd dug to the bottom of the sludge pit of guilt she'd covered up with busy the past months.

At OCT, I ignored Vic's illegal activities, because whistle-blowing would have disrupted my comfortable life. She winced, paced four more steps, and turned. *When I got out of Club Fed, I ran—to make the same mistake again.*

Telling the brothers her past, up front, would have

been the right thing to do. The moral thing. Instead, she ignored the elephant, hoping it would go away. How could she not have seen that she was sabotaging her new life?

The answer popped into her mind, as if her subconscious had been waiting for the question. "Home."

Her elusive dream of childhood. She'd watched her classmates, families screaming in the stands at high school sports and parents gathering around them at graduation. The father-daughter dinner she didn't attend her senior year. Mom had done her best, but had been so busy keeping food on the table there wasn't time for much else. Bree had always longed for the closeness, the sense of belonging others took for granted.

Apparently wanted it bad enough to give up my self-respect.

She straightened her spine. The first time, the government took her freedom before she could make it right. This time, she had a choice. An odd coal of pride glowed in her chest, spreading a balm of heat to her frozen extremities.

Grabbing the jean jacket from the bed, she slipped her arm in the sleeve. *I'll explain everything. Then I'll move on, if that's what he wants. They can buy me out when they've got the money.* Jacket half on, she hesitated.

What about her love? Max could hardly pay equity on her broken heart. The motel bed squeaked as she plopped onto it, the coal of pride smothered by a tidal surge of loss.

The price for her first mistake had been prison. The cost this time was steeper. The fantasy life she'd made up had evaporated like the dream it was. She'd have to figure out a way to survive on what remained. Somehow.

Snippets from life on the Heather flashed in her mind: cooking dinner in a warm kitchen with Tia, brushing the cow ponies in the cold hours before dawn, watching the PBR with the men, them teasing her for rooting for the bulls. She massaged her burning stomach. Max in the field beside the road that day, the look in his eyes telling her she was home and he was glad of it.

That was gone now. The lethargy of hopelessness pulled at her. All she wanted was to crawl under the covers and escape in sleep for the next forty-eight hours.

She shook herself. *You've started over before. You can do it again.* Living without Max might leave her an empty shell, but she wasn't going out a coward.

Headlights washed across the facade of the building. Bree shot to her feet. As she reached for the door, the mirror showcased the angry scar, all the more jarring without a scarf. She tore open the top button of her blouse. *Nothing left to hide.*

Pulling a deep breath, she jerked the door open and stepped into the cold night.

The Jamesons' truck pulled into the parking space in front of her room. Raising her hand to block the headlights' glare, she saw only one occupant. She walked to the driver's door. "Wyatt, where the heck have you been?"

"Driving."

"Where's Max?" He turned off the ignition, and in the silence, she heard him sigh. He looked flat tuckered. "Where is he, Wyatt?"

He pulled the keys from the ignition. "At a bar down the road."

"Can I have the keys?"

He eased out of the cab. "When I left him, he was in a surly mood. I doubt that an hour with a bottle of Johnnie Walker has improved his disposition." He regarded her with a frown. "Are you sure this shouldn't wait until morning?"

"Nope. It's waited too long already." Her voice sounded strong. Good. She raised her hand to pat the side of his face. "Go to bed, Wyatt. I'll explain everything to you in the morning. I promise."

He pulled her into a hug. "You don't owe me any explanation, sweetie." He backed up, holding her upper arms. "I know who you are."

"Thanks." She blinked. "As it turns out, so do I." She held her hand out for the keys. "Rest well, Wyatt. I'll see you at the finals tomorrow."

Too soon, a garish neon sign told her she'd found the bar. Her traitorous mind thought up excuses to keep going. Good excuses. She forced herself to hit the turn signal, then parked, got out, and slammed the door. If she slowed, she'd lose her nerve.

Max sat at the deserted bar, relaxed but not slouched. Taking that as a good sign, she stepped next to him. He glanced up. His eyes weren't bleary. In fact they were sharp—so sharp they cut into her stomach, her resolve, her heart.

"I'm going to talk to you, Max." Her voice sounded firmer than her legs felt. "And you are going to listen."

He looked at the drink in his hand.

"When I'm done, you can send me away if you want. But I will have my say." He made no acknowledgment of her presence, so she settled on the stool next to him and waved off the bartender who approached with a raised eyebrow.

She sucked in a deep breath. "It seems like another lifetime, but it started only three years ago. I was living in LA, working as a controller for a trendy accessory importer. You know, sunglasses, iPod cases, stuff like that. I was fresh out of school, gung ho, and naive."

She grabbed a cocktail napkin and tore tiny pieces off the edges, for something to do with her hands. "I had big dreams of moving up, of being somebody." She shook her head. "After a year or so, I started finding discrepancies in the books. Inconsistencies that Vic, the owner, didn't deny."

Max ignored her, but something in the tilt of his head told her he was listening. "I had the proof. I should have told the authorities. I didn't." She forced the words past her clenched jaw. "I liked my designer clothes, my chic condo, my upwardly mobile friends. So I partied on, and kept my mouth shut."

She looked down at the pile of shredded napkin, small, but growing. "A customer called about a shipment of expensive gaming boards he'd gotten by mistake. I traced it and discovered that Vic had them listed on eBay under the seller name 'Madison Avenue Sales.'" She glanced at Max, who now watched her carefully. "My name is Aubrey Madison. Tanner is my deadbeat father's name."

She looked back to her shredding. "Anyway, Vic had it all rigged. He imported the illegal boards, but the customs papers listed a much cheaper board to avoid the high import duty. He brought them into the warehouse, opened an offshore account in Belize, set up the eBay account, then watched the money roll in. I'd stumbled upon his little gold mine.

"The next day, I resigned. I gave two weeks' notice, not wanting Vic wondering about my motives for quitting; I didn't trust him. Two days later, the Feds walked in and arrested me.

"I didn't have a clue where he was hiding the money, or how he was getting it back into the country. And there wasn't much I could do about it in jail. The Feds figured I was lying. So to put the pressure on, they chose a special cell mate for me." She couldn't help the shiver that coursed through her. "The girlfriend of the leader of the Mexican Mafia.

"When I refused to be a go-between in a drug deal, she sent her gang to teach me a lesson." She touched the scar. "In the shower one night, they cut me and left me on the floor to bleed to death."

Max reared back and unbalanced the stool. She put out a hand, but he pulled back as if her touch would burn him. Her gut twisted, but she pushed on, almost whispering. "When I got out of the prison hospital, I was convicted and sent to Soledad to serve four years for fraud.

"I'd still be there if it weren't for Vic's brother-in-law being a cheap SOB." She smiled. It didn't feel right, but she hoped it looked right. "He owned a small trucking firm, importing vegetables from Mexico and Central America. One day, after crossing the border, the driver had a flat. See, they'd packed the tires with cash. The blowout left shredded bills all over the freeway." She chuckled. "The idiot had put cheap Mexican retreads on to save a few bucks.

"I'd have given a lot to have seen Vic's face when they came for him. A ten-dollar retread cost him his freedom!" Her laugh sounded weird, so she made herself stop. "Oh God, that's funny." She rubbed her eyes. "Anyway, my conviction was overturned and I was released.

"They gave me money, a 'victim's stipend.'" She snorted. "I think the DA didn't want a lawsuit. I didn't want their blood money, though. I just wanted to leave the whole sordid mess behind and start over. To do something that was clean, simple, and good." She spread her raised hands.

"That's the money I put up for Total Bull."

Max looked at her, his face unreadable.

"You want to know why I didn't tell you." She sighed, and reached for her purse. "If you'd asked a month ago, I'd have told you it was because I was afraid you'd fire me. You aren't known for your forgiving nature. I thought you'd react pretty much as you have."

She turned from the fluffy pile of napkins to look him in the eye. "The one thing I never lied about, Max, was my feelings. I love Colorado. I love the Heather: Tia, the hands, the horses, all of it. Wyatt feels like the brother I always wished I had."

She raised a hand to touch his arm, but remembered, and dropped it in her lap. "But what made High Heather my home is you. I love you, Max. I grew up without a father around, so I never saw real love between a man and woman; it took me some time to recognize it.

"I thought that if a man like you could trust me, I could believe your opinion and learn to trust myself." She rubbed her eyes with the heel of her hands, then sat straighter. "I know now that love doesn't work that way. You have to be worthy of it—by being an honorable person.

"I didn't understand that until tonight." She slid off the stool and pulled the purse strap over her shoulder. "I'm not telling you this to change your mind. I'm telling you because I owe you the truth." She stood, shoulders squared, chin raised. "And I'm done hiding from it."

Max's face was blank. He stared into his drink once more.

"Do you want a ride back to the hotel?"

He shook his head.

Well, I've got my answer. As she trudged to the door, her stomach calmed a bit. Her life was a bombed-out shell, but maybe she could build a future from the wreckage. At least the hardest part was over. She thought about leaving him.

Well, maybe not the hardest.

Max watched Bree's back as she marched to the door. He ached for simpler days. The days spent with his dad, riding through the mountain passes, gathering cattle to drive to the ranch for the winter. Sweating in the hot sun, digging postholes, dreaming of nothing more than a cool shower and Tia's enchiladas for supper. No gray. Right and wrong were absolutes back then.

He drained the last drops from his glass. He hadn't been drunk in twenty years, but tonight he could see drunk from where he sat. His sigh stirred the bits of paper piled beside him. That was so like her. Always in motion, never able to sit and relax. Before she came, they were barely managing to keep the horses fed and stalls mucked out, much less clean tack and straighten up. Now he'd put his stable up against a professional show barn, and the income from the new boarders more than paid her salary.

She'd worked her ass off for room, board, and a couple of bucks. She'd lightened Tia's load too, worming her way past the old woman's stubborn pride to help out with meals. Those two laughed like little girls in the kitchen. She'd dreamed up Total Bull to put the Heather back in the black. Even the dumb move she made with that snake Trey Colburn had been her trying to help.

He signaled the bartender, pulled out his wallet, and tossed a credit card on the bar.

He reached over and wadded the shredded paper pile in his fist.

Shit, who was he kidding? Those were just flies circling the cow patty. The big issue was that he'd fallen for her, and though he now knew her name, he still didn't know who she was. Aubrey Madison, hip, yuppie controller? Or his groom, Bree Tanner. *His* Bree.

Anger zinged once more along already crispy nerves. And his brother. Wyatt had known about her past and kept quiet, like Max was some hick who couldn't handle the truth.

Betrayals come in many forms.

He stood and signed the bar tab. The ranch used to be a quiet, peaceful place, but everything had changed in the last six months. Wyatt had filled the house with camaraderie and laughter. Bree filled the rest: his barn, his bed, his heart. He lumbered across the room, tossing the wadded paper into the trash as he shouldered the heavy door open.

The parking lot was all but empty, as was the road beyond. A chorus of crickets began a night song, and as he lingered, Max recognized frigid air against his hot skin. He shrugged into his suit coat and glanced up at the stars, like diamonds scattered on black velvet. He'd taken the night sky for granted until Bree had talked about it, the night he'd courted her with candles and wine.

He settled his hat on his head and started walking.

Hell, Bree wasn't a bad person. He tried to picture what prison would be like to a naive young woman like her. He shuddered. She'd made a dumb mistake and almost paid for it with her life. It had taken a ton of guts for her to start over.

His head hurt. All he wanted was to be sure of the things around him and for the ground to settle under his feet. He was so tired of making concessions. First Wyatt and his lover, now Bree and her secrets. He was a simple man, unused to all the angst, and it worried at his nerves. The sound of a freight train rumble drifted on the empty wind, and he buttoned the coat against the cold.

Soon Wyatt would return to Boston. Bree would go... wherever. No more noisy, communal meals. He'd go back to eating by himself at the main house like he used to. He'd ride out mornings and spend the day working with the hands, the land, and the cattle. The scenario didn't have the allure it used to. In fact, it sounded downright boring.

Where the hell is that hotel?

He wouldn't even have his father's taciturn presence to fill the evenings. He thought about the long winter months ahead, when he'd be housebound. *Jesus.*

He could drive them all away. It'd be easy. Looking back at his recent actions, it seemed he'd tried to do just that. Reality hit him like a two-by-four upside his head.

I could keep the ranch, and my way of life, but still lose everything.

CHAPTER
28

Bree hit the red button on the remote and the farm report shrank to a tiny dot on the TV. Hog futures just weren't holding her attention. Rolling over, she kicked off the covers and plumped the pillow, but within minutes her eyes popped open. She stared through the crack in the insulated curtains to the false daylight of the sodium-lit parking lot.

If only she could go back and change the past. To any one of the hundreds of chances she'd had to tell Max. In bed that first time. At the initial board meeting of Total Bull. That day at the bend in the river, when he'd spilled his father's secret.

This is a waste of time. No matter how much she wished to, she couldn't go back and make it right. Neither the first mistake that blew up her life, nor the second. Sitting up, Bree looked at the radio alarm. The red numerals read four thirty. *Might as well take a bath.* If she drew it out long enough, by the time she finished, the coliseum would be open to the bull owners. Her stomach growled, protesting the lack of dinner. She padded to the bathroom to run the tub, reminding herself to choke down something to put out the fire in her belly.

An hour later, dressed and packed, Bree looked around to be sure she hadn't left anything. The finals began at ten, and there was work to do to ready the trailer to go home. *Home.* Her stomach fluttered, but beneath the simmering acid of nerves, she felt solid for the first time in—ever. Tossing in bed last night, she'd decided on a new goal. To find a place she fit in. No more building her life like a house of cards, with either a yuppie lifestyle or a lie to hide behind. She deserved a home and happiness, and by God, she was going to find it.

"If you're going through hell, keep going." The empty room smothered her words with silence. She swallowed and tightened her fingers around the carryall handle.

Yeah, but go where?

Time to get started. Again.

The jangling phone cleaved Max's skull. A jackhammer fired up in the crevasse, pulverizing his brain. Over the din in his head, he heard Wyatt pick up the phone. He cracked an eyelid. Light from an opening in the blackout curtains lasered his optic nerve. He slammed his eye shut and groaned.

He heard Wyatt hang up the phone. "Come on, Maxie. Daylight's burnin'."

He ran a sandpaper tongue over his lips. "Who was the message from?"

"Bree. She'll see us at the finals." He leaned over and stripped the covers off Max. "Come on. We've got time for breakfast if we hurry. We didn't eat dinner last night, and I'm starving."

Max threw his arm over his eyes. "Do you have to yell?" Damn, he'd just fallen into his first dreamless sleep of the night.

Wyatt's face loomed over him. "You look like shit, Max." He straightened as he shrugged into a wrinkled T-shirt. "And you deserve every bit of it."

Max sat up and put his pulsing head in his hands. "Don't I know it." How could booze taste so good going down yet leave such a vile aftertaste the next morning? "You'll be glad to hear that I pulled my head out of my butt last night."

A smug grin spread across Wyatt's face. "I heard a loud pop, but I assumed it was someone next door, opening a bottle of champagne."

"Shut up. I'm trying to apologize. Look, I know that I can come across as opinionated—" He lifted his head. "Please don't go back to Boston, Wyatt."

"Save your apology, Maxie. I forgive you. But only because you're my brother. You'd better save the really good stuff for Bree." He walked to the end of the bed, but stopped and frowned over his shoulder. "You do mean to mend fences there, don't you?"

Max scratched his chest. "Of course I do. I may be a Cro-Magnon, but I'm not a fool. And I hope you've got my back. Otherwise, it'll be a long, quiet drive home."

Wyatt sauntered into the bathroom, his voice echoing off the tile walls. "If I were you, I'd be more worried about a long, quiet future."

Max threw his legs over the side of the bed and hung on to the edge as the room spun. "I am, brother. I am."

A half hour later, they stood outside a crazy-busy IHOP, waiting to be called to a table. Max bounced his foot and ran a hand through his hair. "Wyatt, we're going to be late."

"Relax, Max. I just checked. We're next." Wyatt leaned against the building, legs crossed at the ankle, hands in his pockets.

"How can you think of your stomach at a time like this?"

Wyatt took off his sunglasses and rubbed them on his alligator shirt. "Hey, my love isn't pissed at me." He held the lenses up and squinted, checking for smears. "Of course, he's currently two thousand miles away, but—"

"And I'm sorry for that, too, Wyatt." The surprise on his brother's face hit Max in his already churning gut. "I should have told you from the beginning to bring him with you. I was so wrapped up in my own drama, I never spent a second thinking about how hard this has been on you."

"Well, thanks for that, Maxie. It means a lot."

Max looked down at his feet, but realization forced his gaze up to his brother's. "Wyatt, why don't you and Juan move out here?"

"Are you out of your mind?" Wyatt scoffed. "It's one thing for the locals to listen to my techie advice. It's a whole 'nother thing for me to bring my lover here to live. And you know it."

A speaker overhead blared "Jameson. Please come to the desk to be seated."

Max slapped hands over his ears, but it was too late—the sound jackhammered into his already throbbing skull. "Screw that. I took care of them once. I can do it again."

Wyatt pushed away from the wall, his eyes sad. "We're not kids anymore, remember. You can't fix prejudice with your fists." He held up a hand when Max would have protested. "We love Boston, Max. We have a life there. A good life."

Max stood, and they followed a waitress to a tiny table. "Well then, maybe we could visit each other. You guys could come out for a couple of months in the summer." He sat and rested his hat on the back of the booth. "And you know how miserable February is here. Maybe I could—"

"We've got a spare bedroom and a bed big enough for two, you know." Wyatt picked up a menu and perused it.

"Well, it's just gonna be me, if we don't get to the damned arena on time."

But the restaurant was packed, the service slow, and the taxi even slower.

Max scrambled out of the taxi before it stopped in the back lot of the coliseum. At a muffled roar from the crowd inside, his muscles jerked taut to run. He threw some bills at the driver. "Jesus, Wyatt. I told you we didn't have time to eat. That danged restaurant took forever, and now we're late, for chrissake."

"Oh, this is not good, Max."

He trotted to where his brother stood, staring at the door to their truck. "Wyatt, come on. We're gonna miss Fire Ant's go." He glanced at their logo under the truck window. The pink ribbon on the trailing end had been torn off. He jogged to the passenger door to see that logo missing there, as well. They looked at each other across the hood of the truck, then bolted for the door of the arena.

Fire Ant trotted into the bucking chute. Bree kept her eyes down to keep from scanning the packed stands one more time. Shutting out the bustle around her, she bent over the top bar of the chute to work the flank rope.

She'd been floored when the PBR's stock contractor told her Fire Ant had been chosen as the 'Ride with the Best' bull in today's contest. The winning cowboy from yesterday's round would be pitted against her bull. If he rode, he'd win ten thousand dollars. If he got bucked off, the money went to the bull owner. This was a real coup for a debut bull, and if Fire Ant won, the money would pay her way to Wyoming.

Bree was so proud of the little guy. She was proud of herself, too, for buying him, even though everyone who saw the cock-horned little bull told her she was nuts. She'd miss him.

It looked like her idea for Total Bull was a good one, too. She'd leave, knowing that it had at least a chance of being a success. Maybe it would help wipe out her karma from LA.

The announcer's voice boomed overhead. "Next up is the little bull with a fashion statement who's earned some respect here this weekend. Now let's see if he can earn some money for his owner."

As the rider lowered himself onto her bull's back and got settled, Bree tightened her slip knot, kissed her fingers, and patted Fire Ant's mottled back. "You kick butt, baby."

This time, no one sniggered.

The rider was all business as he wrapped his hand in the rigging. His buddies worked as spotters to keep him from being hurt in case Fire Ant got fractious in the chute. Gripping the top pole of the fence, Bree threw a quick prayer skyward.

The cowboy shoved his hat down, and the muscles of his forearm bulged when he pulled himself tight against the rigging. He nodded his head.

The gate opened. Fire Ant launched. With a violent leap, he kicked his heels over his head, standing almost vertically on his front hooves. Bree didn't even have time to cheer him on; the ride was over before he'd cleared the chute. The rider, a surprised look on his face, landed on his pockets in the dirt just outside the gate.

Grinning like a fool, she watched Fire Ant strut from the arena.

"Here, ma'am, let me help you down." The fallen rider had dusted the rear of his jeans and offered his hand.

The cowboy next to her saw her confused look and said, "You have to go into the arena to collect your check."

"Oh." *Holy smokes, there are cameras out there!* She wished for her neckerchief, but then remembered her vow. Shaking in her boots, she took the rider's hand and hopped off the fence.

The rodeo clown stood before the bucking chutes, a two-by-three-foot placard check in his hands, waving her over. Gritting her teeth in what she hoped resembled a smile, she stood for photos, then fled to the gate.

Several stock contractors stopped her on her way back to the pens with congratulations. *Where the heck are the guys?* If they were still mad at her, that was fine, but this was business.

Fire Ant had arrived by the time Bree got back to the enclosure. She stood by the gate and blew him a kiss. "You're my hero, little man."

Smiling sadly, she unwound the huge pink ribbon from the pole fence. She was leaving them Fire Ant, but she was keeping that bow.

The bull threw his head up, and she turned at the sound of running boots. The Jameson brothers skidded to a stop in front of her. Wyatt put his hands on his knees and tried to catch his breath.

Max's gaze searched her face. "Did we miss it? Tell me we didn't miss it."

Wow, he looked bad. A day's stubble darkened his gaunt cheeks, his eyes so red-rimmed and bloodshot it hurt to look at them. "You missed it."

"Damn, I *knew* it. How'd he do?"

She straightened and pulled the real paper check from her back pocket. "He won." She managed a wobbly smile. She looked down at the check. It was made out to Total Bull. Which meant it wasn't hers.

Wyatt beamed. "Not bad for a little pissant bull, huh?"

She handed the check to Wyatt. *I can stop somewhere and do an odd job or two if I run low on money.*

Max barked a cough into his hand. "Looks like you were right about him all along, Bree. Good job." He watched her, his face giving no hint to what went on behind it. "Let's get packed up. I want to get on the road."

After a last lingering look at her bull, she said, "Now that you two are here, I'll be going. I'm catching a ride back with Janet." She forced her feet in the opposite direction and kept moving.

"Wait, Bree." At Max's deep voice, she felt something tear in her chest.

And still, she kept going.

Getting out of the coliseum took a lot longer than getting in. First, they had to check out and handle wads of paperwork. Then they waited in a long line of cattle haulers until Fire Ant was finally ushered down the loading ramp and into the trailer. Max jerked a fresh toothpick from his stash in the ashtray and chewed furiously as he waited for Wyatt to lock the tailgate.

"Scoot over. I'm driving." Wyatt opened the driver's side door and grabbed the steering wheel. "You've got a massive hangover. Besides, you look like you just got your guts stomped out." He gave Max a shove. "Get your ass over."

It wasn't worth arguing. He slid to the passenger's side. Wyatt put the truck in gear, checked the mirrors, and pulled out. Max grabbed a gimme cap hanging on the rifle rack, pulled it over his eyes, crossed his arms, and leaned back, planning on catching up on a few Z's. But all he saw on the back of his eyelids was Janet's Mercedes, Bree riding shotgun, getting farther down the road.

He mumbled out of the corner of his mouth, "Is this as fast as you can go?"

"She's leaving." Wyatt spoke his thoughts. "You know she's leaving, don't you?"

Max ignored him, settling into a more comfortable slouch.

"I'm amazed how she's able to resist your guileless country charm."

He gave up pretending to sleep and tugged the cap brim up. "Shut up, Wyatt. I'm trying to come up with a strategy here."

Wyatt shot him a look and snorted. "That's like putting Pee-wee Herman in charge of a battle plan."

"Goddammit, Romeo, stop poking at me and start throwing out some ideas."

"Well, actually doing something might be a good start. Why did you let her walk away? You should have gone after her and made her listen. You should have thrown her over your shoulder if you had to."

"Oh, look who's the caveman now." Max watched the scenery roll by his window, glad to see the buildings spread out as they quit the city. Denver had lost all its glitter after last night. His world had somehow tilted wrong on its axis the past couple of days. He must be in some alternate universe—sitting here getting lovelorn advice from a guy who'd never been with a woman in his life. Max shook his head.

But Wyatt had steered him right before. That date behind the barn led to his first night with Bree. He remembered her, her head thrown back and eyes closed, a look of taut anticipation on her face, like she trusted him to take her where they both wanted to go.

Shit. What am I doing, sitting here licking wounds while she gets away?

He sat bolt upright and scrabbled for his phone. He hit speed dial. "Tia? It's Max. I need your help. Bree is on her way there with Janet." He listened. "Well, she's a bit upset with me, and—" He winced, pulling the phone from his ear. "I'll explain it all later, and you can yell at me then, *Mamacita.* In the meantime, I need you to keep her from leaving until we get home. Can you do that for me?"

Janet kept one hand on the wheel as she rummaged in her purse. "You look like a dirt road after a monsoon, Tanner. What the hell is going on?" She handed Bree a crumpled tissue smelling faintly of Chanel. She winced as Bree honked into it.

"I'm okay. At least, I will be. Slow down, will you? You're going to get a ticket."

"Harrison will handle it if I do." Janet hit a button on the burled wood dash and the sunroof rolled back. "And don't give me that 'me against the world' crap. Spill your guts, woman. You know you want to, and I don't have all day."

Janet was right. She did want to.

It came out in a rush, the whole sordid story: her former life in LA, OCT, prison, her falling for Max. Eight tissues and an hour later, after describing the debacle at dinner last night, Bree finally ran out of words.

Janet whistled through painted lips. "That's some story, sister. What are you going to do now?"

"When I get back to the ranch, I'll pack my stuff and hit the road before they get back." The confession had wrung the last ounce of tension from her, and she fell back into the contoured leather seat, liquid and boneless. "I'm going to start over. Again. And this time, I'm going to do it right."

Janet raised a plucked, perfect eyebrow and tapped a carmine nail on the wheel. "You don't learn very fast, do you?" She speared Bree with a look. "Do you have some kind of mental defect you haven't told me about?"

She should have known Janet would kick her when she was down. "Listen, I'm sorry I brought it up. Just drop me off, and you can go on with your *important life*."

"Jesus, why do I bother?" Janet threw both hands in the air. The car veered to the right. "Poor judgment is what got you into trouble in So Cal, and it's clear that you've learned nothing from the experience.

"If you walk away now, you're going to lose more than Max, your partnership, and High Heather. You're going to lose your self-esteem."

"Max—"

"Oh, screw that!" At Janet's long-suffering glare she sat up straight. "This isn't about Max. If he's stupid enough to let you go, what the heck would you want with him?"

"But you said I should—"

Janet's dramatic sigh almost fogged the windshield. "You need to stand up to him for *you*, chickie. Not to grovel or try to convince him. It's time you stood up for yourself. Let him know what he's losing. That way, if he lets you go, you'll at least walk away with some self-respect."

Janet floored it, pulling into the oncoming traffic lane. Ignoring the car that hurtled toward them, she passed the beer truck and tucked back into the lane with at least fifteen feet to spare.

Before Bree could catch her breath, or pull her nails

out of the armrest, Janet looked her in the eye. "Men come and go. The only thing a woman has that no one can take away is her opinion of herself."

Max's fingers tapped a frantic drum cadence against his thigh. "Can't you push this rig faster, Wyatt?" The closer they got to the ranch, the faster the ants on his skin crawled.

It might have settled him to have a plan, but he'd racked his brain and hadn't come up with anything close. His foot jounced on the floorboard. *Wouldn't you know, the one time I need speed, we're hauling a loaded cattle trailer.*

By the time Wyatt finally pulled into the Heather's long drive, Max was close to jumping out of his skin. As they pulled up to the corrals, he noticed Bree's Jeep parked alongside the mess hall, facing the road, driver's seat empty.

Thank you, Tia. Not that he was above chasing Bree down on the open road, if it came to that. Max had his door open before the truck braked to a stop. He shot a look over his shoulder.

"You go. I'll handle Fire Ant." Wyatt's encouraging smile did nothing to quell Max's quivering guts. He was very aware that the next few minutes would decide his future.

He jumped from the truck and jogged to the Jeep. Bree's battered suitcase and laptop took up the space behind the seat. Neatly folded on the passenger's seat sat the Navajo blanket from her bed, topped by a familiar huge pink bow. He glanced up to the mess hall. The windows spilled warm light and an old song by Garth, bragging about friends in low places.

Chest tight, nerves strung like a loaded crossbow, Max

took the three porch steps in one bound and yanked the screen door open so hard it slammed against the wall. The music snapped off. The cowboys seated at the table glanced up and froze. Time seemed to stop. Janet sat next to Bree, and Tia stood alongside, having just set a cupcake topped by a lit candle in front of Bree.

"What is this, a going-away party?" he growled.

Bree's lips opened—to blow out the candle—or out of shock, he didn't know. "Not your problem, cowboy."

The blades in her words didn't cut. He knew they were thrown in self-defense. "You're afraid. Afraid that Vic was right, that you have no backbone. That's why you ran when you got out of prison." He tipped his chin, at the Jeep through the window. "That's why you're running now." She flinched. Her lightning-quick glance around the table told him he'd hit home.

"That's why you still feel guilty." He walked to her. "That's why you kept your past a secret. Not because of what we'd think—but because of what you thought."

She shifted on the seat, still holding his gaze.

Maybe there's hope yet. The others had to hear the pile-driver hammer of his heart in the silent room.

"You're afraid you're going to find out something that proves Vic was right." He didn't know where this stuff was coming from, but at least he had her attention.

He heard Wyatt's light step behind him and the soft *shush* of the screen door closing. Bree looked down at her cupcake. The flame guttered in a small pool of wax. She stood.

"Bree." He waited. Her shoulders squared and she lifted her head. "You made mistakes. But the biggest mistake you made was to believe Vic.

"I *know* who you are. From the first time I met you, you've done nothing but give: your honest labor, your knowledge. Your heart."

Her mouth twisted. "Oh yeah, and not whistle-blowing takes *so* much backbone."

"I can relate to denial." Max looked up at the bare beam rafters, trying to imagine the room empty, save her. "I've hunkered down here for years with my hard, silent Dad. I held on tight, trying to keep things from changing." He looked down at his bloodless fists. "I said I did it for the ranch, for the family legacy." He opened his fingers and forced his gaze to meet hers. "But that's a lie. I did it because I was afraid. Afraid to be wrong. Afraid to admit... I didn't know what the hell I was doing." He couldn't seem to stop spilling his guts, but it didn't matter. Because she still listened.

"I drove away anybody who tried to get close." He shot a glance to Wyatt. "I turned away from someone who cared about me, just because he didn't fit into that black-and-white world."

He looked back. Bree's tight face gave no hints. Only her intent focus let him know she hadn't made up her mind. "Then you showed up, so full of color that it bled into everything around you, and I realized how boring black and white is."

He walked around the table to her side. He took off his hat, and his fingers worried the brim. "Lady, your name doesn't matter. I know *you*."

A flick of pain crossed her face, and her lips twitched. "Thanks for that, Max." She raised her chin. "Admit it. We both know I don't belong here." She spun on her heel and hustled for the door.

He stood frozen as the screen door slapped behind her.

"What the hell are you waiting for?" Wyatt said in a hissed whisper.

"Yeah, boss. You're not going to let her get away, are you?" Armando said. The rest of the hands nodded like idiot bobbleheads.

He jogged to the porch, his own personal peanut gallery shuffling after him.

She was halfway to the Jeep. He raised his voice. "You don't have to wear a power suit to be a businesswoman, Bree. And you don't have to be born here to be a part of the land."

She kept walking.

"*Dammit* woman, I'm trying to tell you that I love you!" She stopped dead, but didn't turn.

His peanut gallery pulled in a collective breath and held it.

He planted a hand on the rail and vaulted it, jogging over to block her way. He reached and clasped her upper arms, feeling a tremble that ran through them like a live wire. He whispered, "I've loved you since I first saw you in those drugstore cowgirl clothes, looking at me like I held the future.

"But if you don't know all this about yourself, it doesn't matter what I think." He shut his mouth, closed his eyes, and grabbed for all the guts he had.

He let her go. His hands fell to his sides. It was her choice. In this, he had no control.

Head down, her curtain of hair covering her face, she brushed by him.

"Know one thing." He didn't turn to see that she stopped, only heard the gravel stop clicking and skittering.

"I'll be here. Waiting. For as long as it takes."As she turned, Max held his breath. Her gaze raked over the peanut gallery, then him.

Come on, baby, one more step. He willed her forward. *Just one more.*

Her face broke into a beatific smile that made her look like an angel come to earth. She ran the steps between them and launched herself into his arms, sobbing and giggling at the same time.

He bent to catch her lips, tasting her laughter. The kiss turned deadly serious, and he tightened his arms. He told her with his kiss of his relief, his love, his need. He wasn't letting go. Ever.

She pulled back before he wanted her to. "I was only going to visit my mom, to give you time to smarten up and miss me." She smiled up into his eyes. "You're not getting rid of me that easy, cowboy."

Their audience burst into applause. Fire Ant, still locked in the trailer, bawled his displeasure.

"Thank God." Janet frowned, hand on hip. "Now maybe you two will settle down and I won't have to run into you making out every time I round a corner."

Max set Bree back on her feet but kept his hand on her waist, not trusting to let go. "I wouldn't count on that anytime soon, Janet. I'd say about twenty years or so." He threw a stern glare to the peanut gallery. "The entertainment is over. Give us a hand unloading the truck."

Home. Bree felt that her feet didn't quite touch the ground as Max led her to the Jeep, her hand tucked into his huge one. He reached in to retrieve the huge pink bow and then tugged her toward the truck. As they passed the driver's door, he asked, "You can have new signs made for the truck, right?"

She felt her cheeks flush. "I have another set. I wasn't sure if you'd rip the first ones off the minute you laid eyes on them."

Max stopped in front of the truck and stooped to fasten the garish bow to the grill with a few twists of the wire. "Just so you don't get any ideas," He lifted a pinch of material from the sleeve of his Christmas-red Western shirt. "This is as close as I'm going to get to the company colors." He straightened and tipped his hat back.

She *tsk*ed, smiling up at him. "Don't you know, Max? *Real* men wear pink."

"Well, then, I guess I fall into whatever category's left."

Wyatt walked by carrying a cooler, a shit-eating grin on his face. "Welcome to the fringe, bro."

Max cuffed the back of his brother's head, then pulled Bree into his arms.

Look for the next book in
Laura Drake's

Sweet on a Cowboy series!

Please see the next page
for a preview of

Sweet on You.

CHAPTER 1

Another night of blood and adrenaline.

Katya pulled her shower-wet hair into a bun. The weight of exhaustion tugged at her, but the fine hum of tension running just under her skin warned her that she wouldn't sleep.

Beneath that, resting close to her heart, was a firm pillow of satiety. They'd saved two soldiers' lives last night.

Finding herself alone in the small, fake wood–paneled room of the B Hut was a rare occurrence, given that her three roommates were medical personnel. They must be working a shift. The army was so desperate for medics that Katya had been transferred from physical therapy to become a triage medic two years ago.

She took the few steps to the American flag–draped wall and the small chalkboard underneath it, almost covered in chalk lines. Neat bundles of five, representing men that they'd saved from the enemy. She picked up the chalk to add her night's conquests, but hesitated. Keeping score against the bad guys only made sense if you were clear that there *was* a bad guy.

That's not right. The enemy they fought in the ER wasn't the Afghani insurgents.

It was death.

She brought the chalk down on the board so hard that it broke. She made two marks, one crossing four others—another neat bundle.

Beep beep! The bleat of a Jeep through the thin walls got her moving. Shouldering her rifle and pack, she opened the door and slammed into the dry blast of Kandahar heat. By the time she had the door locked, her shower had worn off.

Murphy grinned from the seat of the Jeep he'd commandeered—best not to ask where. Last night in the ER, when he'd invited her on a trip to town, she couldn't resist. Most soldiers longed for a taste of home. They cheered when fast-food franchises opened on base. Not Katya. She loved exotic spices and unfamiliar local dishes. She'd even tried the boiled sheep's head a street vendor once offered, finding the flavor of the facial meat fabulous once she got past the staring white eye and the grinning exposed teeth.

She tossed her pack in the Jeep and climbed in, cradling the rifle in her lap. "I don't remember it being this hot last May." She put her hand to her cloth-covered helmet, shifting it to blot the sweat tickle that made her scalp feel as if it were crawling with bugs.

Murphy's cool green eyes watched her with appreciation. "It's probably just my proximity, ma'am. I have that effect on women."

She knew she shouldn't encourage him, but couldn't help smiling at the combat medic. He looked like a pencil wearing a helmet—all long bones and knobby joints. His helmet covered buzz-cut red hair, but even if she hadn't known his surname, the flushed, freckled skin declared him a Celt.

He gunned the engine but drove at a sedate pace to keep the dust down until they cleared the security check at the entrance of the base.

She would have loved to be alone for a while, but knew that was impossible. Kandahar was not safe—especially for a solitary female. Even a female second lieutenant.

The wind swirling behind the windshield cooled as well as a fan in hell. Katya looked out at the receding puddles and rapidly parching grass at the side of the road, thanking God for the road the Corps of Engineers had built last year. Spring rain in the desert was beautiful, but it was hell on goat-track roads that morphed from sliding mud pits to foot-deep cement-like ruts overnight.

Eyes on the road, Murphy yelled over the wind, "We could swing by the airport on the way back and watch the planes do touch-and-go's. Not very romantic by normal standards, but it's the finest that this corner of Afghanistan has to offer."

Like everyone, she enjoyed the Nebraskan's down-home, upbeat sense of humor that had lit up the ER since he'd transferred in a month ago. But comments like these made her wonder if the E-4 had a bit of a crush. "Did you miss the lecture about not fraternizing with officers in boot camp, Corporal?"

"I think that must've been the day that the general's daughter and I were—uh, indisposed. ma'am."

She smiled. *Incorrigible.*

He slowed as they rolled into town. The two-story stucco buildings might have been handsome before the bombing. They passed one with a missing front wall, exposing jagged rooms like broken teeth. Between the damage and the dust, the town looked tired, weary of all it had seen. Murphy parked, and they got out. Katya shouldered her pack and rifle, wondering when it had stopped feeling odd to carry armaments on a shopping trip.

Tourists were an extinct species in a war zone. The shops were shuttered, but people still needed to eat. Intrepid vendors had set up tables in the narrow band between the buildings and the street. Vegetables mostly, sold by men with light, loose clothing and disrespectful eyes. The bright blush of pomegranate skin and green grapes looked incongruous in the sepia scene.

Dusty muslin awnings extended from the buildings, blocking the sun, but didn't help much in the torpid air. She and Murphy joined the shoppers, keeping their rifles slung but remaining alert. Instinctively, when Murphy bent to examine something on a table, Katya's eyes scanned the crowd.

An hour later, the cloth bag on Katya's shoulder held her treasure—local figs. She found their dusky sweetness cleared her palate after a mess hall dinner. "I'm ready to head back if you are, Murphy."

She glanced at her sweat-slicked companion, looking as if his M16 would overbalance him. He carried a palm-sized, hand-sewn stuffed rabbit.

"You know, you may want to tuck that under your pillow at night, or your roommates are going to give you hell."

He lifted the toy to his lips, kissed it, and dropped it into the pocket of his damp shirt. "It's for my new niece. I haven't met her yet, but I'll show you photos when we get back."

They headed for the Jeep. The next block was unpopulated, its bombed-out buildings long abandoned. The

light seemed harder here, as if showcasing the damage—
throwing it in the onlooker's face. In contrast, the inky
black of the narrow alley on her left made Katya shiver,
conjuring pictures of scorpions and snipers. Katya's skin
pricked, but it wasn't from sweat. She moved quickly past.

A boy stepped around the corner, a few buildings ahead.
He held his forearm, and blood dripped between his fingers
into the dust. He was nine or so, wearing a traditional long
shirt and loose pants, a round pakol cap on his head. He
shuffled toward them, tears streaking his dusty face.

Kayta's heart rate shot up, kicking into triage mode.
Quickening her pace, scanning the boy for other injuries,
she reached into her bag for her ever-present first aid kit.

Then she hesitated. The boy's eyes darted, his movements jerky with fear.

The gun was in her sweaty hands almost before she
knew she'd unslung it. Sound ceased. She tried to remember when a vehicle last passed.

Murphy rushed past her, his still-slung rifle bouncing, as
he reached for his first aid kit. Alarm sirens of panic echoed
through her head. Something was wrong. She snatched at
Murphy's arm, but missed. "No. Murphy, wait!"

He reached the boy and leaned over him, blocking her
view. Katya took two running steps forward.

The harsh light exploded in a starburst of yellow and
red. A giant fist of percussion punched her, followed by a
roaring wall of sound.

Then blessed blackness.

Katya listened. The hushed conversation and echo
of hurried squeaky shoes sounded familiar. So was the
smell—dust, antiseptic, and the metallic undertone of

blood. She shifted her arms, her legs. All there, thank God, but her slight movement woke a hot poker stab in her side and a throbbing in the fingers of her right hand.

She lay still in the dark, afraid to open her eyes. Afraid to assume the responsibility, because she sensed, deep in her mind, something lurked that she did not want to know. Opening her eyes would force her—

"Welcome back, soldier." The deep voice was familiar too.

Katya pulled her eyes open. Major Samuel Thibodaux, her superior officer and lead surgeon at Role 3, leaned over her. She turned her head, disoriented to see her work environs from a reclined angle. Beds in rows, most filled with wounded—white skin, brown skin, no skin.

The major peeled back her eyelid and flashed a penlight in her eye. The light seared to the back of her brain. She flinched.

"Headache?"

She closed her eyes and nodded.

"Nauseous?"

A brush of air as the sheet was pulled to her hips. He gently prodded her side.

She winced and shook her head, frowning. It was coming. A hulking memory lumbered down the pathways of her brain, moving fast.

"You were downtown. A bomb—"

The rest was drowned out by the sound of a wailing moan. She realized after a beat that it had come from her. The heat, the sound, the *light*. "Murphy." She opened her eyes.

The major's jaw tightened, pulling his lips to a thin line. She realized she hadn't stated it as a question. Her stomach muscles pulled taut, to protect her solar plexus from the blow. A memory came forward, burned into her brain. Murphy bringing the toy to his lips to kiss it. "No. Oh no." Her legs writhed, trying to find an outlet for the pain—the horror.

The major pressed the plunger on a morphine drip. "We took shrapnel from your side, along with your spleen and a chunk of your liver. You lost the fingernails on your right hand, but you're going to be okay."

A face swam to the surface of her mind. Wispy black hair, huge, dark eyes full of liquid fear. "The boy." Her voice came out as a thready whisper, fading.

He shook his head. "Suicide bomber."

She rushed to meet the sweet blackness that rose to swallow her.

Cam Cahill coughed up dust. The sun branded his skin through his shirt. He kicked his borrowed gelding to a canter, chasing down another steer, wild from months on the winter slopes.

How could it be this hot and dry in Texas in April? He tugged the bandana off his nose, where it was doing nothing to block the dust, and settled it around his neck. It would at least keep sweat from rolling down his back.

Another billow of dust rolled over him as Len Robertson reined up alongside. The old man's hair might be gray, his face tanned and creased as a burlap sack, but he sat relaxed in the saddle even after ten hours. "You know what Phil Sheridan said about Texas, don'tcha?"

"Go east, young man?"

"Close." Len smiled, showing the gap between his front teeth. "He said, 'If I owned Texas and hell, I would rent out Texas and live in hell.' " The old coot cackled and rode on ahead, his horse kicking up more dust.

He actually enjoys this. Cam spit mud and reached for his canteen. *Five more miles till the home corrals.* He uncapped the bottle and took a long drink of the hot, metallic-tasting water.

And more of the same tomorrow. Cam hadn't expected a stock contractor's life to be glamorous, but the past five days convinced him he could cross this off his short list of careers.

Which left . . . exactly nothing.

His last season as a rider on the pro bull riding circuit was half over, and his future resembled a black hole in space, sucking light, gravity, and all his peace. He capped the water jug and hung the loop over his saddle horn. He should be content—it had been a great career. The first rider to win back-to-back titles and he had the belt buckles to prove it. He reined left, to try to stay upwind of the small herd.

What if the past fifteen years had been the best of his life? Thirty-two was too young to give up and do nothing, even if he had enough money to live on the rest of his life. The drive that pushed him to the top hadn't lessened with the years, even if his reaction times had.

He shifted in the saddle to ease his sore hip. His body was about done.

He'd planned to have a wife and kids by now. He'd planned to settle on his own ranch in Banderas and live out the rest of his days in peace. But he no longer had a wife, much less kids, and after years of traveling, the thought of holing up in his run-down cabin all alone wasn't a happy one.

What good were gold buckles and bull-riding stories, when you didn't have a life?

THE DISH

Where Authors Give You the Inside Scoop

♥ ♥ ♥ ♥ ♥ ♥ ♥ ♥ ♥ ♥ ♥ ♥ ♥ ♥ ♥

From the desk of Jaime Rush

Dear Reader,

Enemies to lovers is a concept I've always loved. Yes, it's a challenge, and maybe that's what I like most. It's a given that the couple is going to have instant chemistry—it is a romance, after all! But they're going to fight it harder because they have history and a good reason. Each person believes they're in the right.

That's how Kade Kavanaugh feels. Being a member of the Guard, my supernatural world's police force, he has had plenty of run-ins with Violet Castanega's family. They live in the Fringe, a wild and uncivilized community of Dragon shifters who think they are on the fringe of the law as well. And mostly they are, except when their illegal activities threaten to catch the attention of the Muds, the Mundane human police. Because Rule Number One is simple: Never reveal the existence of the Hidden community that has existed amid the glitter and glamour of Miami for over three hundred years. Mundanes would panic if they knew that Crescents—humans who hold the essence of Dragons, sorcerers (like Kade), and fallen angels—lived among them.

Violet is fiercely loyal to her Dragon clan, even if it does sometimes flout the law. But when one of her brothers is murdered by a Dragon bent on firing up the clan wars, she has no choice but to go to the Guard for help. There she encounters Kade, whom she attacked the last time he tried to arrest her brother.

My job as a writer is to throw these two unsuspecting people together in ways that will test their loyalties and their integrity. And definitely test their resolve to resist getting involved with not only a member of another class of Crescent, but a sworn enemy to boot. Juicy conflict, hot passion, and supernatural action—a combination that truly tested my hero and heroine. But their biggest lesson is never to judge someone by their name, their heritage, or their actions. I think that's a good lesson for all of us.

We all have magic in our imaginations. Mine has always contained murder, mayhem, and romance. Feel free to wander through the madness of my mind any time. A good place to start is my website www.jaimerush.com, or that of my romantic suspense alter-ego, www.tinawainscott.com.

Jaime Rush

❤ ❤ ❤ ❤ ❤ ❤ ❤ ❤ ❤ ❤ ❤ ❤ ❤ ❤ ❤

From the desk of Kristen Ashley

Dear Reader,

While writing MOTORCYCLE MAN I was in a very dark time of my life. An *extended* dark time, which is very rare. Indeed, it's only ever happened that once.

In fact, I wrote nearly an entirely different book for my hero, Tack. He had a different heroine. And it had a different plot. Completely. But it didn't work for me and it has never seen the light of day. I abandoned it totally (something I've never done), gave it time, and started anew.

I had thought it was rubbish. Of course, on going back and reading it later, I realize it wasn't. I actually think it's great. It just wasn't Tack. And the heroine was not right for him. But never fear, I like it enough; when I have time (whenever that is in this decade), I intend to rework it and release it, because that hero and heroine's story really should be told.

Nevertheless, when I finally found the dream woman who would belong to Kane "Tack" Allen in MOTOR-CYCLE MAN, I was still questioning my work because things in life weren't going so great.

You see, sometimes I battle my characters. Sometimes they urge me to take risks I feel I'm not ready to take. Sometimes they encourage me to glide along an edge that's a little scary even as it is thrilling. And when life is also scary, your confidence gets shaken in a way it's tough to bounce back from.

But Kane "Tack" Allen is an edgy, risky guy, so he was pretty adamant (as he can be) that he wanted me to just let go and ride it with him. Not only that, but lift up my hands and enjoy the hell out of that ride.

But as I was writing it, I still fought him. Particularly the scene in Tyra's office early on in the book, where they have a misunderstanding and Tack decides to make his feelings perfectly clear and in order to do that, he gets Tyra's attention in a way that's utterly unacceptable.

I fretted about this scene, but Tack refused to let me soften it. I even sent it to my girl, a girl who knows me and my writing inside and out. If I remember correctly, her response was that it was indeed shocking, but I should go with it.

Ride it out.

In releasing MOTORCYCLE MAN, I was very afraid that my life had negatively affected my writing and the risks Tack urged me to take would not be well received.

As you can imagine, I was absolutely *elated* when I found I'd done the right thing. When Tack and Tyra swiftly became one of my most popular couples. That Tack had rightly encouraged me to trust in myself, my instincts, my writing, and give myself to my characters to let them be precisely what they were, let them shine, not water them down, and last, give my readers the honesty. They could take it. Because it was genuine. It came from the soul.

It was real.

And because of all this, MOTORCYCLE MAN will always hold a firm place in my heart. Because that novel and Kane "Tack" Allen gave me the freedom I was searching for. The freedom to ride this wave. Ride it wild. Ride it free.

Lift up my hands and ride it being nothing but me.

Kristen Ashley

♥ ♥   ♥   ♥

From the desk of Christie Craig

Dear Reader,

Here are two things about love I took from my own life and used in TEXAS HOLD 'EM:

1. Love can make us stupid.

Sexy PI Austin Brook is a smooth-talking good ol' boy Texan. Where women are concerned, he wings it. Why not? He's got charm to spare. But one glance at Leah Reece and he's a stumbling, bumbling idiot. First he accidentally blows his horn as she's passing in front of his truck, causing her to toss up her arms and drop her groceries. Wanting to help, he snatches up a plastic bag containing a broken bottle of wine and manages to douse Leah with Cabernet from the waist up. And since he likes wine and wet T-shirt contests, it only makes her more appealing and him more nervous.

For myself? On a first date with a good ol' Texan, we were both jittery. I'd dressed up in a short skirt. The guy, thinking he should be a gentleman, pulled my chair out in the crowded restaurant. I had my bottom almost in the seat when he moved it out. *Way out.* *He* might've looked like a gentleman, but there was nothing ladylike about how I went down. All the way to the floor, legs sprawled out, skirt up to my yin-yang. Laughter filled the room. Snickering in spite of his apologetic look, he added, "Nice legs."

Later when he dropped me off at my apartment, I struggled to get the door of his sports car open. Forever the gentlemen—hey, that's Texans for you—he rushed to open my door, and then shut it. Standing close, he heard my moan, and completely misunderstood. He dipped in for a kiss.

I stopped him. "Can you open the car door?"

"Why?" he asked.

I moaned again. "Because my hand's still in the door."

With a bruised butt, and three busted fingernails, I eventually did let him score a kiss. It's amazing I married that man.

2. Love is scary.

Divorced, and a single mother, I wasn't looking for love when I met Mr. Craig. Life had taught me that love can hurt. And I'm not talking about a sore backside or fingernails. I'm talking about the heart.

Neither Austin nor Leah is open to love. Isn't that what makes it so perfect and yet still so dad-blasted frightening? We don't find love; love finds us. And like me, Leah's and Austin's pasts have left them leery.

At age six, Leah realized her daddy had another family, one he obviously loved better because they had his name and he called that home. Oh, when older, she still gave love a shot, got married, expected the happily-ever-after, and instead got a divorce and a credit card bill for all his phone sex. It's not that Leah doesn't believe in love; she just doesn't trust herself to know the real thing.

Austin, abandoned by his mother at age three, passed from one foster home to another, and learned caring about people gave them power to hurt you. His last and final (he swears) heartache happened when his fiancé dumped him after he got convicted of a murder he didn't commit.

As scary as love is, Leah and Austin give it another shot. Not to give away any spoilers, but I think it'll work out fine for them. I know it has for me. I'll soon be celebrating my thirtieth wedding anniversary. So here's to laughter, good books, and getting knocked on your butt by love.

Happy reading!

Christie Craig

♥ ♥ ♥ ♥ ♥ ♥ ♥ ♥ ♥ ♥ ♥ ♥ ♥ ♥ ♥

From the desk of Laura Drake

Dear Reader,

There's just something about the soft side of a hard man that I've never been able to resist—how about you?

Max Jameson looks like a modern-day Marlboro Man. He's a western cattleman, meaning he's stubborn, hard-working, and an eternal optimist. But given his current problems, there's not enough duct tape in all of Colorado to fix them.

To introduce you to the heroine of NOTHING

SWEETER, Aubrey Madison (aka Bree Tanner), I thought I'd share with you her list of life lessons:

1. Nothing is sweeter than freedom.
2. It is impossible to outrun your own conscience.
3. "When you're going through hell, keep going." —Winston Churchill
4. There are more kinds of family than blood kin.
5. A stuck-up socialite can make a pretty good friend when the chips are on the table.
6. Real men (and bulls) wear pink.
7. "To forgive is to set a prisoner free, and discover that the prisoner is you." —Louis B. Smede

I hope you'll enjoy NOTHING SWEETER. Keep your eyes open for a cameo of JB and Charla from *The Sweet Spot*, and watch for them all to turn up in *Sweet on You*, the last book in the series!

♥ ♥ ♥ ♥ ♥ ♥ ♥ ♥ ♥ ♥ ♥ ♥ ♥ ♥ ♥ ♥

From the desk of Rebecca Zanetti

Dear Reader,

I met my husband camping when we were about eight years old, and he taught me how to play Red Rover so he could hold my hand. He was a sweet, chubby, brown-eyed boy. We lost touch, and years later, I walked into a bar (yeah, a bar), and there he was. Except this time, he was six-foot-five, muscled, with dark hair, a tattoo, a leather jacket, and held a motorcycle helmet under one hand. To put it simply, I was intrigued. He's still the sweet guy but has a bit of an edge. Now we're married and have two kids, two dogs, and a crazy cat.

People change…and often we don't know them as well as we think we do. In fact, I've always been fascinated by the idea that we never truly know what's in the minds or even the pasts of the people around us. What if your best friend worked for the CIA years ago? Or the mild-mannered janitor at your child's elementary school is a retired Marine sniper who didn't like retirement and has found a good way to fill his life with joy? What if your baby sister was a criminal informant in college?

What if the calm and always-in-control man you married is one of the deadliest men alive?

And what if you're now being threatened by an outside source? What happens to that calm control now? That was the main premise for FORGOTTEN SINS. Josie Dean, a woman with a lonely past, married Shane Dean in a whirlwind of passion and energy. Then he disappeared two years ago. The story starts with him back in her life, with danger surrounding him, and with the edge he'd always partially hidden finally exposed.

Of course, Shane has amnesia, and in his discovery of finding himself, he reveals himself to the one woman he ever truly loved. He'd always held back, always treated her with kid gloves.

Now, not knowing his deadly training, there's no holding back. The primal, arousing man she'd believed existed has to take the forefront as he protects them from the danger stalking him from his past. Yeah, he'd always been fun and sexy…with hints of dominance in the bedroom. Now the hints disappear to unveil the true Shane Dean—the man Josie hoped she'd married.

I hope you truly enjoy Shane and Josie's story.

Best,

Rebecca Zanetti

RebeccaZanetti.com
Twitter, @RebeccaZanetti
Facebook.com/RebeccaZanetti.Author.FanPage

♥ ♥ ♥ ♥ ♥ ♥ ♥ ♥ ♥ ♥ ♥ ♥ ♥ ♥

From the desk of Kate Meader

Dear Reader,

FEEL THE HEAT is the first in my smokin' Hot in the Kitchen series, about an Italian restaurant–owning family and the sexy, sizzling chefs who love them. And don't we all want a hotter-than-Hades, caring, alpha chef like Jack Kilroy in our lives? A man who cooks, defends his lady, and knows how to treat her right both in the kitchen *and* in the bedroom is worth his weight in focaccia (and the British accent doesn't hurt). But sometimes we've got to work with what the gods have given us. So if you have a husband/boyfriend/sex slave who believes guy cooking = grilling, but outside of the summer months, you won't catch him dead in an apron, read on.

"But he just makes a mess" or "I'm a better cook," I

hear you whine. Who cares? The benefits to encouraging your man to cook are multifold.

1. Guys who cook know how to multitask. If he can watch a couple of bubbling pots, chop those herbs, and pour you a glass of wine, all while *you* put your feet up, it'll eventually translate to other areas. Childcare, taking out the trash, maybe even doing the dishes as he whips up that *coq au vin*.

   Guys who cook know how to get creative. You might ask your man: "Is this made with sour cream, babe?"

   Cue worry crease on guy's brow that looks so adorable. "No, I didn't have any so I used Greek yogurt instead. Does it taste okay?"

   Hold praise for a beat "That's so creative, babe, and less fattening."

   (Positive reinforcement is key during the early training phase.)

2. Guys who cook have a direct correlation to a woman's TBR list. He's brought you that glass of Pinot and he's back in the kitchen where he belongs. Now you can get down to the important stuff—making a dent in your stories about fictional boyfriends who probably cook better than your guy. (In the case of Jack Kilroy, Shane Doyle, and Tad DeLuca, the sexy heroes of the Hot in the Kitchen series, this conclusion is a given.)

3. Guys who cook will evolve into guys who shop for groceries. Nuff said.

4. Guys who cook make better lovers. Chefs have very skillful hands, often callused and scarred from years

of kitchen abuse. Those fast-moving, rough hands are going to take your sexytimes to the next level! As long as your guy is burning himself while he learns, it can only be beneficial to you further down the road.

So get your guy in an apron and let the good times roll. Remember, chefs do it better...

Happy cooking, eating, and reading!

Kate Meader

www.katemeader.com